THE DREAM HUNT

THE DREAM HUNT

THE DREAMSCAPE SERIES BOOK 2

CHRISTINA FARLEY

The Dream Heist

The Immortal Legend

The Immortal Secret

The Immortal Heart

Gilded

Silvern

Brazen

The Princess and the Page

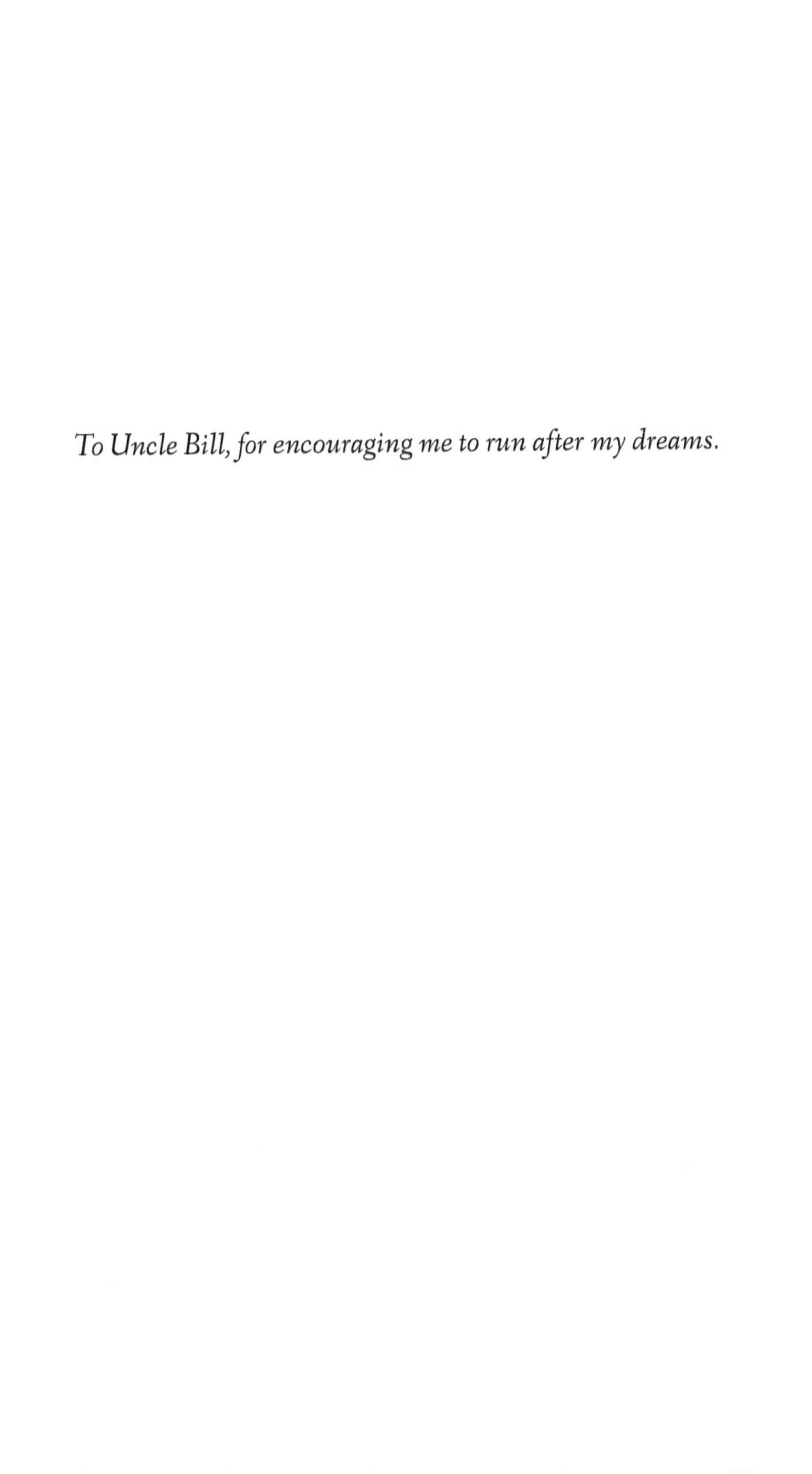

To Uncle Bill, for encouraging me to run after my dreams.

ONE

THE INTERVIEW

New York City, U.S.A.

I HOVER at the edge of the stage, smoothing down my silver dress and wishing I hadn't chosen these strappy high heels. Being interviewed on the Night Show is a big deal. I agreed to it because Dad was hoping it might bring extra funding for MaxLife. But as I watch Troy Mikes from the sidelines lean back in his cream-colored chair like a king sitting on his throne, chatting with my dad in front of a live audience, I'm starting to think curled up on the couch in my flannels would've been a better choice.

Sudden laughter erupts and I jerk straighter, my heart racing. It doesn't take much these days to put me on edge. My therapist says that's to be expected after what I've been through, but sometimes, I miss my old self. The one not that didn't suffer from break-ins, kidnapping, or sleeping all night without worrying I might be murdered in my dreams.

"You okay?" Jake whispers in my ear. He slips his hand into mine and the warmth of his touch instantly relaxes me.

I smile at him. "Thanks for coming."

"It was a tough choice. Sit home all alone and eat my mom's cooking or stand here beside the most beautiful girl in New York City."

I roll my eyes, but his words work their magic on me as they always do. "Your mom's cooking isn't that bad."

"You haven't had her cooking yet. You've only had the take-out she pretended was her cooking."

"Should I tell her you said that?" I giggle as he shakes his head violently, and then sigh. "What would I do without you?"

"I'm going to say your life would completely suck so you should keep me around forever."

Clapping fills the studio and music erupts. Dad shakes Troy's hand as his segment of the interview is finished. This is our cue to walk out onto the stage. Troy is smiling expectantly at us with bright white teeth while an assistant is half-shoving me out onto the stage. I stumble out, dragging Jake alongside me.

I nearly trip on my heels, blinded by the bright lights and overwhelmed by the crowd. Do these people really care about what we're doing at MaxLife or are they just curious about the millions of dollars stolen? My worries are drowned out as the audience leaps to their feet, cheering and clapping. I give a little wave while Jake nods his head, eyes darting to the exit as if he's thinking about bolting.

"Don't even think about escaping, Jake Sutherland," I whisper-yell at him.

His face twists in guilt as we settle into the two chairs opposite Troy. "I'm beginning to think you're a mind-reader rather than a Dreamwalker."

"Ah!" Troy proclaims into his mic on his shirt lapel in his deep, announcer-style voice. "The dynamic duo. Your father told us all about how the two of you and your team of Dreamwalkers managed to save him and recover millions of stolen dollars. How does it feel to be heroes?"

"I don't think either one of us were trying to be heroes," I say. "We were just trying to do the right thing. When I realized that my dad was kidnapped, I knew I would do anything I could to save him."

"How did that feel?" Troy leans in. "Nearly losing your father?"

My chest tightens like someone has their fist wrapped around it. I take a deep breath, but my eyes wander out to the sea of people hanging onto my every word. Right now I don't want to think about how I felt or the desperation I had knowing I needed to enter people's dreams to get answers.

Instead, I try to change the subject and say, "It was

tough. But my dad is with us again and now we can focus on our work trying to save dementia patients' memories."

Thankfully Troy moves to safer ground, asking how things work at MaxLife.

"Dreams are basically a way for the brain to organize and process information," I explain. "They can tap into past memories people normally would've forgotten. That's why what we do is perfect for dementia patients. It allows us to capture those memories and store them for our patients so the memories aren't lost. Hopefully, at some point, we can find ways to recover all of a patient's memories."

"A cure for dementia then?" Troy asks.

"That's the dream," I say.

The audience laughs and my shoulders relax. As long as we can stick to the topic of MaxLife and our work, I think I can handle this.

"So Jake," Troy continues. "How was it possible for these hackers to be able to steal so much money so quickly? I mean we're talking about 81 million dollars here."

The crowd gasps.

"The hackers were smart," Jake says. "They used one of Swift's most vulnerable features—its global aspect. Basically, they planned their attack around time zones where some banks were closed so they couldn't reach each other to confirm or deny issues.

"In fact," he continues. "They were attempting to steal

a whole lot more money. 951 million to be exact. Thankfully, they weren't successful."

The questions continue on until finally, Troy stands up, his black suit somehow remaining perfectly pressed, and addresses us. "Thank you, Aria and Jake for coming to talk to us here on the Night Show. It was utterly riveting. Let's give up a cheer for our budding scientist and her cyber expert."

I go to push myself off the creamy white chair when I spot a slip of paper tucked into the folds of the cushion. I nearly ignore it, except my name is scrawled across it.

Aria Hale

Frowning, I pick it up and flip it over, reading the sentence on the other side.

This isn't over yet.

My heart stills and I look out at the audience once again, but this time, my vision is sharper, and the sound of the audience fades as I scan each person's face, desperate to find the person who wrote this note. I bet anything they are here watching, waiting to see if I got their message.

And that's when I see her.

An Asian woman, her hair tucked into a tight bun, wearing a midnight blue pants suit and sunglasses. A slight smile curves on her mouth as our eyes meet. It's as if she were waiting for me to seek her out. A shark eyeing its prey.

"Zhang Lau," I whisper.

My arch enemy. The woman who was working with

Dr. Reasner and whom I fought against in her dreams. Not only that, she tried to kill me and my friends after Jake and I barely escaped Reasner's twisted-up Dreamscape.

Before I can move or utter a cry of warning, she slips out of her chair and vanishes through the main doors.

TWO
TOURISTS IN LOVE

The audience thunders their applause as I stagger offstage, my brain whirling. I grab Jake's hand and tug him into the corner to avoid the assistant eager to whisk us back to the green room.

"I saw her," I whisper.

Jake's smile drops. "Saw who?"

"Zhang Lau. She left me this note." I pass the slip of paper to him.

His face darkens as he reads it. "Not over? Are you fricking kidding me?"

"Why would she be here in New York City? In the audience."

"Maybe she still wants your dad's Dreamscape. Or maybe she's still pissed we outsmarted her. But you're right. Why go to such an effort to come out in the open and leave you a note?"

"To show she can," I mutter. "She loves to flaunt how powerful she is."

"Excuse me," the assistant interrupts us. "You'll need to leave this area as our next guests are coming in. If you could follow me, I'll return you to your father."

"Yes," I say, eager to find my dad. "And I need to talk to someone from security right away."

The lady's face bunches up in annoyance, but she touches the side of her headphone saying, "Can I have someone from security meet our guests in room eight?"

We trail after the assistant as she clips her way through a side door and down the long corridor. My nerves tighten with each step. I eye each person we pass by, wondering if they're one of Lau's hitmen. My thoughts flit about in my head, trying to understand what Lau is up to. When we step into the room where the three of us prepared for the interview, I practically run over to Dad.

He's relaxing in a large armchair, legs stretched out, and sipping a Coke, watching the Braves play. My steps falter. He looks so relaxed and calm. His peppered-gray hair is slightly disheveled but in an endearing way. I bite my lip, hating I'm about to ruin the peace that we've had since returning from his kidnapping in China.

"Dad." I brace myself and then hold out the slip of paper for him. "This was in my chair during our interview."

His forehead wrinkles. He slips on his reading glasses and sits straighter. "What is the meaning of this?"

"Also," I continue, "I saw Zhang Lau in the crowd. She was there, Dad, waiting for me to see her."

Now he is on his feet, snatching the note from me. He barks to the assistant, "Where's security? We need to talk to them asap."

The assistant's eyes widen at Dad's urgency, and she clears her throat. "They're on their way right now."

The next hour is a nightmare. Security arrives and then the police. It's like the events we thought we'd left behind have been drudged back up to haunt us. I explain what I saw, and then we all review the security footage of the event. But Lau is clever. There isn't a single camera that manages to pick up her face except for one that has a hint of her profile.

"You sure this is Zhang Lau?" the officer asks me, freezing the footage so her profile fills the screen.

"One hundred percent." I stare at her, remembering how we narrowly got away that night in the warehouse in Macau, China.

"I'll need to take that note for evidence," the officer says. "We'll check for prints and do a signature scan. But if she's as smart as she appears, we're not likely to find anything."

"Do you think we're safe?" I ask. "What if they kidnap my dad again?"

"Lau was only after the money," Dad points out. "It was Reasner who was obsessed with the Dreamscape and trying to get me to give him its coding. But since he's safely six feet under, we don't have to worry about him. I don't know what Lau wants, but she obviously could've hurt us by now and chose not to."

"Plus," Jake adds, "the last person Lau wants to anger is Sun's uncle, Ma Yuzhu. She's probably just bitter."

"Just in case, I'll assign you a security detail to stand outside your hotel room," the officer says. "I'd rather be cautious and safe, plus it will give you peace of mind."

By the time Dad, Jake, and I trudge from the taxi in the cold, biting air into the hotel, I'm worn thin between the interview and the investigation. But as much as my body screams to curl up in bed, my stomach is louder.

Jake chuckles. "Was that your stomach?"

"Ha, ha." I shoot him the evil eye. "Don't tell me you're not hungry."

"If I don't get some food soon, my stomach's going to join yours in harmony."

"I vote we grab some food at Tony's Italian." I point to the hotel's one and only restaurant attached to the lobby.

"You two go ahead," Dad says. "I'm ordering room service and heading to bed. Just don't leave the hotel and be careful."

"Where is your trust?" I squeeze Dad's arm. "Don't forget it was us who came to your rescue."

Dad kisses me on the forehead. "Promise you'll be careful."

"I promise."

Jake and I find a quiet table in the corner lit by a single

candle, and since we can't decide what to get, we splurge and order two main courses, each opting to treat our meal like a buffet. Soft music fills the air, mixing with the scent of freshly baked bread. Outside, snow falls softly onto the street, piling up around the streetlamps and benches. It's such a contrast to the weather back home in Florida where it's probably warm enough to wear shorts and flip flops.

Jake takes my hand. "I didn't expect to be going out on a date with you tonight."

"If Lau hadn't ruined the night, it would've been the perfect ending to our trip to New York City."

"What if we don't let her ruin it then? Let's pretend we're just two normal teens who didn't have to go on a rescue mission to save your dad or track down millions of dollars. No talk about Lau and her stupid notes or creepy sunglasses."

"Creepy sunglasses? That's the best you've got?"

He laughs. "Tomorrow, we've got all day before our flight leaves. We could be tourists."

I want to argue and tell him things will never be the same, but his eyes are soft and there's a hint of a smile on his lips. I like it when he smiles.

Besides, he's right. I really need to move on if not for my mental health.

"Okay. I'm in. Tourists, it is. Tourists in love."

"Sold!"

Our food arrives, which is good since I'd been eyeing the sugar packets and salt and pepper shakers to curb my hunger. Steaming lasagna, creamy fettuccine, calzones oozing with cheese, and a bowl of salad piled with plump olives. And when I take a bite of the fettuccine, I realize it tastes better than it looks.

I groan. "This is heaven."

Jake's lips quirk and his green eyes take on a mischievous glint. I pick up an olive and throw it at him. "Get your brain out of the gutter, Batman."

We spend the rest of the dinner talking and laughing. By the time the server arrives with the check, I've almost forgotten about Lau's stupid note and creepy sunglasses.

"I hope you've enjoyed your meal," the server says.

"It was wonderful," I say. "We'll be charging the meal to the room."

He sets the black check holder on the table. "No need. Your meal has been fully paid compliments of a mystery benefactor."

"A benefactor?" Jake pales. "Did they leave a name?"

"No." The server grins as if he's just given us the best news of the year. "That person did leave you a note though."

"A note?" I croak.

All the delicious food sours in my stomach. I flip open the black holder to find a paper folded in half and tucked inside.

Meet me by the pool. Just the two of you.

THREE
ZHANG LAU

"This is a bad idea," Jake mutters as we slip out of the restaurant and cross the lobby. "A few months ago, Lau practically had us killed when she was working with Reasner."

"This a public place," I point out. "What is she going to do? Murder us in front of all the guests?"

"I wouldn't put it past her."

"If that was the case, she would've done it at the interview with a captive audience."

Jake runs his hands through his hair, studying each person in the lobby. His body has lost the relaxed pose he had at the restaurant. His jaw clenches tight and his muscles tense. And I get why. Every person here is a suspect. The busboy lugging a suitcase, the couple walking the poodle across the marble floor, the two ladies laughing on the sofa.

My steps slow. Maybe Jake is right. Maybe walking straight into Lau's clutches is a bad idea. I grab his hand and tug on it, stopping him in his tracks.

I lift up on my tiptoes and brush my lips across his. "You may have a point," I say, and then chuckle when he raises his eyebrows in surprise. "It's stupid to just waltz in there without backup. Let's talk to our assigned officer and show him the note."

"Thank you." Jake takes both my hands in his, and his shoulders loosen in relief. "I think that's a wise decision."

We turn to take the elevator when the lady holding the poodle's leash strolls over to us, blocking our path. She's wearing a white polka-dotted dress that poofs out like it belongs in the fifties. Her red lipstick smile reminds me too much of Lau's style, and her shiny dark hair is tucked neatly in a tight curl at the nape of her neck.

My heart catches slightly because she doesn't even need to open her mouth to tell me that she's a messenger of Lau's. It's evident in her sharp, glittery eyes, which narrow in on me.

"Lau is pleased you got her message," she says. "I'm going to walk Sugars outside for a stroll around the pool. Won't you join me?"

"Think we'll pass," Jake says. He tries to push past her, but Poodle Lady's partner steps in the way.

The tip of the cane the man holds glistens in the chandelier light. He lifts it up and twists it in his gloved hands as if he's sending us a warning message.

"I wouldn't recommend passing," he says. "Not when so much is on the line."

I eye the elevator. The revolving door. The hallway. If we sprint, can we outrun them?

But the reality is I'm wearing heels and a dress. Besides, I can't remember the last time I even went on a jog. Maybe 9th grade gym class.

"Oh, darling," Poodle Lady coos to her partner. "What can we do to convince our new friends to join us for a stroll?"

"We're not going anywhere with you," I snap. "Tell Lau I'm tired of her games and she needs to leave us alone. I have nothing to talk to her about."

"You know," the man says as he pulls out his phone. "You need to tell your mother to not work so hard. She really should take more breaks."

"What?" Worry churns in my stomach. "What does this have to do with my mother?"

The guy holds up his phone to show a video of my mom adding soil to one of her pots. She's wearing her flowered blue gloves and the apron I made her as a Christmas gift when I was twelve. My handprints on the apron have faded pink after six years of use. Her expression is smooth and relaxed, and the way her lips are pressed together, it looks like she's humming. Probably Bach. She thinks the plants love classical music and it helps them grow. I used to always tease her about it, but now the thought threatens tears to my eyes.

I bite my lips, determined to not let these people see that their tactics are working.

A tiny red word blinks LIVE in the top right corner. I dart a look at Poodle lady's partner and he's grinning like this is some joke between the two of us. A cold chill washes over me, and I cling to Jake's arm for support.

"Why do you have a video of my mother?" I demand.

Poodle Lady rolls her long, fake eyelashes and jerks her head to the glass doors that lead out to the pool deck. Jake clutches my hand tighter, and his face is red like it's taking all his concentration to hold in his fury.

"When the authorities catch you," Jake says through gritted teeth. "You'll go to jail for a long time."

"It would be best if you just left and headed back to your room," the guy tells Jake. "You are unnecessary. It is Aria we need to speak to."

"Oh, I'm definitely staying." Jake holds my hand tighter than ever, and knowing he's here, calms me.

"This won't take long," Poodle Lady says. "For your mother's sake, I recommend you join us outside."

I suck in a deep breath and trail after Poodle Lady while her partner strides along at my side, his cane clacking against the tile floor like a death toll. The cold air hits my face with a sharp gust, sucking the air out of me. I shiver, wishing I had my coat. At least I changed into my jeans and sneakers after the interview.

But then I suppose that was all part of Lau's plan. She

wants to put us on the defensive, and I hate that it's working.

The pool is covered up for the winter, but the area is lit up with icy blue spotlights that illuminate the trees and bushes edging the walkways. We're led to a sitting area that's situated just off the side of the pool. A fire snaps and crackles in the center of two couches and a chaise.

Flanked by two security guards completely dressed in black, Zhang Lau lounges across the chaise, bundled in a thick fur coat, smoking from a vape. She's still wearing her sunglasses even though it's dark. I don't blame her. I could very easily be carrying around my NightFlash and put her to sleep just like I did at Reasner's lab in China.

That thought settles my nerves a little. She's just as wary of me as I am of her.

"Nǐ hǎo, Aria," Zhang Lau greets me. She lifts her vape to her lips and blows out a cloud of smoke into the night air.

"Why are you videoing my mother?" I say, not caring that I'm speaking to one of the most powerful and wealthiest women in the world.

"It always behooves me to keep a close eye on my assets," Lau says blandly as if intruding on my family's privacy is no big deal.

"You need to turn that camera off and leave us alone," I say. "What you're doing is illegal."

"Perhaps, but you are still alive, are you not?" Her lips slip into a smile. "If it were not for me, your entire family would be dead, and you would be kidnapped. You think you can walk away with that kind of technology without consequences?"

"Just get to the point," Jake says. "We don't have time for your games."

She hands her vape to a man beside her and rises. "You have captured the attention of some very dangerous people and even governments. Has it ever occurred to you that your dream therapy might be able to recover more than just an Alzheimer patient's memories?"

My breath sucks in the chilled air at her statement. What is she talking about?

"Of course you haven't. You are a college freshman whose head is stuck in the clouds. With your Dreamscape, a government could retrieve top secret information within hours rather than waiting around for interrogations that often are useless."

"We've taken precautions to protect the Dreamscape," I say, but my brain whirls as I try to process what Lau is telling me. The reality is Zhang Lau is too powerful, too big of a player in the black market to be standing here and talking to me, a nobody college student, if she didn't think this was a big deal.

"Your precautions are admirable, but we have an issue. Apparently, someone got a copy of Reasner's Dreamscape before his lab was apprehended. My people have traced the file to Lima, Peru. We believe it is being used on hostages who have sensitive intel."

"That's bad." Jake rubs his forehead. "We get it. But right now, we don't want to be a part of any of this. We just want to go back to Florida, forget about all of this, and focus on the next stage in our lives."

"He's right," I say. "We did our part trying to make things right. If you want to fix that problem, go for it, but don't bring us into it. I'm sure there are plenty of people more qualified for the job you need done. Like you said, we're college students."

"Except we suspect the same people who have this Dreamscape are the ones trying to apprehend you."

My heart sinks as I realize what she's saying. "Because Reasner's Dreamscape doesn't work properly."

"Now you understand." She holds out her hand and her assistant passes back her vape.

"Thanks for the warning," Jake says. "But we're going to head back to our room now."

She smirks and takes a long drag. "Good luck with that." Then she pulls out a card and hands it to me. "My number. You will need it."

I eye it suspiciously. "I'll pass."

"Ah. You are a stubborn one. It could've kept you alive." She tosses the card in the fire. "But it seems as if you prefer death."

FOUR

ATTACKED

"She's a cryptic one," Jake says as we ride up the elevator to our suite of rooms. "You were smart to not trust her."

"Lau always has an agenda." I pull out the room key card. "There's no doubt about that. But this whole situation in Peru concerns me. My dad created the Dreamscape to help people, not to be used as a weapon."

"When there's a way to make money and gain power, corruption is always present."

"With wisdom like that you should open your own advice column," I tease. My muscles loosen the higher we rise and the further we put space between Lau and ourselves.

He chuckles. "I doubt anyone wants to hear the advice of a nineteen-year-old game designer."

"Well, you aren't wrong so maybe people should."

I smile up at him and take his hand as we exit the

elevator and step onto the plush geometric carpet. Calm, lilting music echoes through the corridor, and warm beams of light pool over us from the cam-lit ceiling. A yawn escapes me, and I blink back weariness from the interview and confrontation with Zhang Lau at the pool. More than anything, I'm looking forward to curling up in bed with the covers tucked around me and forgetting about Dreamscape problems and sudden appearances of people I had hoped to never see again.

But when I go to push the key card into the slot of our hotel room's door, I falter. The door is slightly ajar. Frowning, I push it open just as Jake grabs my arm, holding me back.

"Wait," he whispers. "It might not be safe."

"I have to make sure Dad's okay."

"Where is the officer who was assigned to this room?" Jake wonders.

The door swings inward, and I gasp. Drawers have been opened. The couch cushions in the suite's sitting area have been slashed, and clothes litter the floor.

All reason and caution flies out of my mind. I barrel into the room, shouting, "Dad!"

"Aria!" Jake calls after me. "Wait. We should call the cops first."

I ignore him and instead race into Dad's room. When I find it empty, I spin around and search the rest of the suite. My heart pounds against my temples and my thoughts scatter.

"It's not safe here." Jake hurries to my side, his phone pressed to his ear. "I'm calling the cops. They'll take care of it."

"No one is here," I say, breathlessly. The room spins a little as panic lodges in my chest. "Where's my dad? Do you think he was here when they...when they..."

I can't get the words out. Even though it's been eight months, it feels like only yesterday Dad was kidnapped by Reasner. Dread pools up into the pit of my stomach and churns like hot, burning liquid.

I hunch down, covering my head with my hands, and rock back and forth. "This can't be happening again. Tell me this is some horrible dream."

Jake pulls me up and then circles his arms around my body, so I'm cocooned in his warmth. Through the fog in my brain, I hear him talking to the 911 operator.

"Hey," a voice calls out from the doorway. I glance up just as a policeman enters the room. "What are you doing here?"

"Thank God you're here," I say. "We're on a call with 911."

But then to my horror, the officer lifts his arm so that the barrel of a gun is pointed at us.

"Drop that phone," he demands.

Meanwhile, Jake pauses mid-sentence in his talk to the operator. The click of the officer's safety snaps. This guy is going to shoot us!

I shove Jake left and dive alongside him just as the

officer lets off a shot. Bullets rip across the ground where we just stood. My ears thrum from the sound of the gun.

We scramble to our feet and stumble back into Dad's room, slamming the door shut behind us. My hands shake as I lock it while Jake shoves the dresser in front of the door.

"To buy us time," he grunts.

"I take it that guy isn't a police officer," I say. "What do we do? Is 911 on their way now?"

"Don't know. I dropped my phone when you shoved me."

"You mean when I saved your life."

The door shudders, and then the lock shatters as bullets tear through it.

"I wouldn't bet on the saving part." Jake grimaces and scans the room. "Because I don't think we'll be alive by the time the real cops arrive."

I pull out my phone and stab in the number I memorized earlier.

"Who are you calling?" Jake throws back the curtains and unlocks the balcony door only to dive back inside as a pattering sound fills the night, followed by shattering glass.

I scream and throw myself behind the cover of the bed. Jake dives to my side, wrapping his arms around me. My whole body shakes as a voice answers on the other line.

"Hello, Aria," Lau answers smoothly. "So glad you called."

"I changed my mind," I say. "You wouldn't happen to be able to get rid of the sniper on my balcony, would you?"

"Are you saying you're agreeing to my proposition?" Lau asks.

"You never actually proposed anything." I glance over at Jake whose eyes are wide and confused.

"I thought she burned the card with her number on it," Jake whispers, glancing furtively around the side of the bed.

"I've got a good memory."

"Yes or no?" Lau pushes.

The door to the main room shoves harder against the dresser, allowing enough space for a man's leg and the end of his gun to peek around the corner of the doorway to the balcony.

"There's two of them now," Jake says.

Crap

We're going to be shot in seconds. Even Lau is a long shot at this point. The man's body squeezes through the crack, his gun scanning the room.

"Yes," I whisper.

"Excellent." Lau's voice has a smile to it. "I'll send in the extraction team."

The phone line goes dead. Suddenly the guy entering from the balcony grunts and crumbles to the floor. A shot ricochets through the air. His gun tumbles out of his grasp.

"Come on." Jake grabs my hand. "This is our chance."

We race toward the balcony, but before we exit, Jake snatches up the gun.

"Just in case," he explains.

"Do you even know how to use it?"

He tentatively peeks out into the balcony. "I've played a few video games."

"Video games?" I sputter.

Jake steps out onto the balcony, gun raised. I follow only to find the policeman-wanna-be is there, waiting. He points his gun at Jake, and just as he shoots, his body jerks, causing his aim to go off. It's not enough because Jake cries out and holds his arm.

Gunfire consumes my every thought.

"No!" I scream and reach for him. Blood seeps through the shirt's sleeve on his arm. "You've been shot!"

Complete terror sends a cold numbness through my veins. A humming sound fills the air and a helicopter swerves into view. A long rope flies out the open door, snaking down to where we're standing.

"Grab on," a man inside the chopper yells down at us. "Compliments of Lau."

"You agreed to Lau?" Jake scowls.

"It was that or be killed."

"This is a bad idea," Jake mutters, cradling his bleeding arm.

The wanna-be police officer sprawled on the balcony floor grunts and touches his ear. "Send backup," he barks.

The idea that more of these men who obviously want us dead are coming sends my pulse racing.

"I vote we take Lau's offer," I tell Jake and shove the rope into his hands. "We tackle one problem at a time."

"Yeah," he says with a groan. "The idea of backup doesn't sound so appealing anymore."

I grab another section of the rope. Maybe Dad is in the helicopter above or he escaped to safety. Instantly, we're lifted into the air toward the helicopter. I have to believe he's okay.

But more than anything, I can only hope calling Lau didn't just make things worse. As we're pulled in through the helicopter doors, someone in a black mask steps toward me with a syringe.

What have I just agreed to?

FIVE

THE DECISION

I blink back the fuzziness hugging my mind. The room swims before me and I try to process what happened. Vaguely, I recall being hauled into the chopper, feeling the relief of the firm hard flooring against my body. Swinging through the air and dangling on a rope one hundred feet above the ground isn't something I want to repeat.

I thought we were safe until someone in a mask stepped up to me with a needle and stabbed it into my neck. That's the last thing I remember.

Now, as my vision focuses, I realize a person is sitting across from me. A woman with onyx hair sitting in a white leather chair. I can't make out her features yet, but I'm not an idiot. I know exactly who she is.

"Lau," I say, my voice rasping as if not used to being used.

"Nǐ hǎo," Zang Lau says. "It is fortunate that you are still alive. For a brief moment, I was not sure you were going to make it out of your hotel room. You called me just in time."

I lick my dry lips and try to stand up, but I can't seem to move. My heart starts racing as panic fills me. My vision is still a little blurry, but something is strapped across my lap and my hands are strapped to the armrest.

"What's going on?" I ask, fighting against the restraints. "Let me go."

"It is merely precautionary measures," Lau explains serenely. "Sometimes people wake up and feel disorientated. This allows you to gain your bearings in a calm, composed way."

My ears buzz, but my vision finally clears. A quick assessment alerts me that I'm in an airplane, private I'm guessing based on the size and the expensive leather seats. My arms are cuffed to the seat, and it's a seatbelt that's keeping me in place. Lau sits across from me, wearing a sleek white suit and spiked silver heels. Her long, shiny black hair is pulled into a stylish ponytail, and she's leaning back in her chair looking as if she has all the time in the world.

I search the area for Jake, but all I find are two security guards and another person sitting a row behind Lau. And that's when the real panic sets in.

"Where's Jake?" I demand, clenching my fists. "What have you done with him?"

"He was bleeding." Lau clicks her long, silver nails against the armrest. "He's being treated."

My heart dives. "Is he okay? I need to see him right now."

"Relax. Most likely he will live, and you can see him after he has rested. He was shot, and though it was a sheer flesh wound, he still needs to be treated with care."

"Shot?" Yes, that's right, I now remember. On the balcony. I close my eyes and take a deep breath to calm myself. The thought that he's hurt is killing me. "I need to see him."

Lau frowns. "Perhaps later."

"Perhaps? No, I need to see him now. And why am I here? What's going on? Please tell me we're headed back to Florida."

"About that. We are taking a short detour."

I gulp. "What do you mean?"

"You agreed to my proposition, remember?"

Crap. What did I agree to? I don't think she ever told me. But I keep my face neutral and say, "I didn't agree to anything."

"Oh, but you certainly did." She smiles thinly and my head spins, desperately trying to think a way out of this mess. "As I told you at the hotel, Reasner sent a copy of his faulty Dreamscape to someone in Lima, which was transferred to an unknown facility. And I need that copy destroyed.

"You have proven that you are the best," she continues.

"You managed to hunt down the money from one of the greatest cyber heists of all time."

"I don't understand why you need me. I'm just a nineteen-year-old college student. All I want right now is to focus on school and get on with my life. You don't need me, you need experts. People who actually know how to track down this copy for you."

She rubs her temples and presses her lips together as if something is truly bothering her. For the first time, I get a hint that she might actually be human.

"I have hired the experts," she finally says in a lower voice. "I have searched all across Lima and found nothing. I have no leads other than a city of eight million people."

"You must be desperate to come to me."

"Really? Because if I remember correctly, you managed to track me down in China, which is something no one has ever been able to do before."

I bite my lips, thinking about Sun, Tony, and Javier and how we used Dad's Dreamscape to enter the dreams of our enemies to get information. "I had help. I couldn't have done it alone. But that's all in the past. I'm done."

"I am highly motivated to find the facility that Reasner's Dreamscape went to. I will pay you well. Very well. Enough to fund your father's research for life."

"Why?" My eyes narrow, and I lean forward. "I'm not going to risk my life so you can get your hands on that Dreamscape, too. No, thank you."

"Without my doctor's treatment, Jake might not survive the night."

"There it is," I say, glaring at her. "That's the Lau I know and love. The one who resorts to threatening."

She stiffens. "I do what I must to get what I need. If it takes threats, so be it."

"Uncuff me," I demand. "I can't continue to have this conversation locked up. I want to see Jake with my own eyes. If you can't do those two things, I'm not continuing this conversation or considering of your demands."

She studies me carefully and then nods, so slightly that I almost miss it. Instantly, a man strides over and unlocks my restraints. I lift my hands and rub my wrists. They are sore to the touch.

Lau rises from her seat. "Come with me."

I unclip my seatbelt and trail after her down the aisle of the airplane. When she reaches the rear of the plane, she pulls back a curtain to reveal a small area. I step inside to find two bunk beds on either side and a nurse putting away equipment under a counter. Jake is lying on the bottom bunks, strapped down and secured, eyes closed. His shirt is gone, revealing a well-defined, muscular chest, and bandages along his side.

I press my hand over my mouth to stiffle my cry and run to his side. Seeing him lying there so hopelessly cuts deep inside me. This is all my fault. If he hadn't been with me, none of this would've happened. I bend down and clasp his hand in mine, tucking it against my chest.

"So do we have a deal?" Lau asks.

I swallow hard. "What do you want me to do?"

SIX

YOUR MISSION SHOULD YOU
CHOOSE TO ACCEPT

"I have managed to capture an individual who I believe knows the location of the facility that is using the Dreamscape," Lau explains from the doorway of the back of the plane. "Also, my people *might* have borrowed your father's Dreamscape kit. These tools will help you find Reasner's Dreamscape."

I frown, not liking where this conversation is going. "My dad never lets that kit out of his sight." Except, when we went for the interview, Dad put it in the hotel safe because he didn't want to be walking around New York City carrying one-of-a-kind technology.

"You always underestimate me, Aria. I have loyal connections everywhere."

"Loyal as in they are bribed or too dead to stand against you?"

Her lips drip into a frown and her eyes narrow. "Careful. You might find you are not as valuable as you think you are."

"If I'm guessing correctly, you want me to enter the Dreamscape that you stole from my dad and interrogate your prisoner to reveal the location of the facility that has Reasner's Dreamscape. Because as you said, I'm the only one who can do it. Except the real problem you have is I'm not an interrogator so I don't think this is going to work."

She sighs and settles onto the bed across from where Jake is still lying peacefully. She presses her fingers to her lips, but as she studies me, she looks older than she did moments ago. Her thin shoulders sag and dark shadows ring her eyes.

"You are not wrong," she admits. "So far, none of my agents have found success entering your father's Dreamscape. They don't last seconds."

This does not surprise me. Not only are her people untrained, but they're probably not using the equipment correctly. Besides, when I discovered that the Dreamscape was modeled after my brain, I realized I'll always have more control over it than anyone else. Plus, I can outlast any Dreamwalker. But I'm going to keep that information to myself.

"There is someone at this facility who means a great deal to me," Lau continues. "I have to extract that person before—"

She swallows, and for a moment, I think she's going to

choke up. I'm a bit startled. The great, impenetrable Lau has a beating heart? But then she lifts her eyes to bore into mine, and I see that resolve in them, glittering harder than diamonds. Okay, so maybe a heart, but one made of stone.

"You should've told me this was a rescue mission," I say. "That would've convinced me quicker than threats."

She lifts her eyebrows. "Does it?"

"It does because unfortunately my heart is not made of stone. I can't do this mission of yours alone." I gently place Jake's hand back on the bed and smooth his strands of hair into place. He stirs slightly. Whatever drugs they used on him are wearing off. "I always do it with a team. It's too dangerous otherwise."

"Jake cannot work with you?"

"He's injured if you haven't noticed," I say sharply. I cross my arms and stand in front of him. Suddenly, I wish I was some badass taekwondo girl who could kick everyone's butt on the plane and then fly us to safety. Right, I laugh inwardly. Only in the movies. "Besides, the only time Jake entered the Dreamscape was when he was captured and forced into a deep sleep. Subjecting him to that again is not smart."

A man steps into the backroom with us and bows low. "Apologies. The pilot says we have begun our descent into Lima, Peru."

Lau nods tightly and turns to me. "So you need your team members?"

"Peru?" I gasp, realization hitting me that I'm about to

land on a new continent. My mind whirls. I have no money, no passport. I don't even have clothes that aren't bloodied or ragged. I've never been there so I don't even know how to survive. "Seriously? You took us to Peru?"

"Of course. The American border is far too difficult to bring in persons on their watchlist. It was simpler to bring you here. We must return to our seats for landing."

Before leaving Jake, I double-check to make sure he's secure. Then I return to my seat and snap on my seatbelt. I push open the window of the airplane and look out. Toasted brown, desolate mountains rise up, stretching out as far as my eye can see. The plane tilts slightly and soon we're flying over a desert-looking coast with indigo-blue ocean waves crashing onto the shore. It's unlike anything I've ever seen.

Lua snaps her fingers, and I'm jerked back to face her and the reality of my life. Great, my heart sinks. Now I'm one of her minions that runs to the snap of her fingers. She's holding a tablet in her hand, and after touching it once, she shows me the screen.

I suck in a deep breath because it's a picture of everyone on my team who went with me to rescue Dad.

Sun, Javier, Tony.

I clench my jaw. She didn't just show me that.

"Who on your team do you need to make sure you can complete the mission?" she asks.

If I didn't hate Lau before, I really despise her now. Her ruthlessness has no boundaries.

The plane bumps a little, and I grasp the armrest a little tighter. I glance out the window, watching as the plane veers down, barreling toward the runway. I lick my lips, and with a deep breath say, "I don't need anyone. I can do this by myself."

"Excellent," Lau says, and there's a smile in her voice that sends a chill down my spine.

———

I EXIT the plane and step out onto the top of the boarding stairs, looking out onto the runway. A cool breeze washes across my face, and the air smells dusty and dry, so different from our moist Florida air. I've always seen pictures of Peru with places like the Amazon or Machu Picchu, so I had no idea there were parts of the country that were in fact a desert.

I'm tempted to take off running, screaming for someone to help. But other than a few fuel trucks passing by and parked airplanes, there isn't a person in sight except security guards from our flight and the guards flanking the three limos parked below. The only thing keeping me firmly planted at the top of these stairs is knowing that with Jake's injury, there's no way he's fit to run. And there's no way I'm leaving him.

Two guards exit the plane with Jake shuffling between them.

"Jake!" I hug him, careful to not crush the side he was shot. "You're moving."

"Aria, tell me this is a dream." His eyes are still a little unfocused and bloodshot as he takes me in. "Because I really don't want to believe I got shot."

I cringe and rub my hands up and down his chest as if willing him to heal. "I'm so sorry. I wish I could tell you it was." I help him take the stairs, trying to keep myself from panicking. "This is all my fault. If you hadn't been with me, you would be safe in Florida."

"And playing some video game," Jake agrees. "Sounds boring if you ask me."

"Be glad you got shot, otherwise I'd hit you. How are you feeling?"

"Like crap, but the nurse said it was a surface wound. I just need to be careful to not break the stitches."

"That's such a relief."

"You?"

"I'm great," I say, unable to keep the bitterness from my voice. "Just great."

"Yeah, you look amazing." His words slur like he's still loopy from whatever drugs they gave him while they sewed him up. "Did I ever tell you that you're gorgeous?"

I blush and focus on making sure he doesn't trip.

Once we get to the bottom of the stairs, he closes his eyes and pauses as if to catch his breath. I grit my teeth, angry he's in so much pain, but I remind myself that we're both still alive. I'm going to do whatever I can to keep it that way.

Lau clips past the two of us without a single glance and heads toward the three limos, her heels clicking with perfect precision. Two bodyguards I secretly suspect are Kung Fu masters escort her on either side. Poodle Lady and her partner scamper after her.

"Follow me," one of the guards orders Jake and I, and we shuffle after him.

Lau disappears inside the first limo with her scary martial arts warriors while the rest of her entourage climbs into the second car. Meanwhile, our guard leads Jake and me to the last limo. I hesitate for a brief moment, but the guard moves his hand to his hip where I spy a gun holstered.

Fabulous. Just what I needed. Another reminder of how dangerous every second of my life is. I slip inside the limo, and as I settle onto the plush leather seat, I realize we're not alone with our driver. A man with Southern Chinese features is sitting across from us. He's wearing a black suit that looks more expensive than my beat-up car back home.

Suit Guy nods slightly in greeting while Jake grimaces beside me as he straps on his seatbelt. The limo takes off before I even have managed to secure my own safety belt.

"Where are we going?" I ask Suit Guy.

"To the hotel," he says. "We should be there soon."

"But aren't we going through customs?" Jake asks.

"We won't be bothering with those formalities." Suit Guy shrugs. "Besides, you don't have your passports, do you?"

"Can you even do that?" I ask.

"Some people can," he says criptically.

I swallow, suddenly feeling naked without any of our personal effects.

"Rigghhtt," Jake drawls. "Quite thoughtless of us to forget. Too distracted from packing with the dodging of bullets and all."

"Evidently," Suit Guy says, unfazed by Jake's sarcasm. "We had to make other arrangements."

"Great. So we're here in the country illegally." I lean back in the seat and close my eyes. The panic bubbling inside me is ready to explode, but I can't let it. With Jake still out of commission, it's up to me to keep my cool and my mind under control. I need to get as much information out of this guy as possible. I sit straighter and focus on Lau's henchman. "So you work for Lau. What is it that she really wants from Reasner's Dreamscape?"

Suit Guy pushes a button and the privacy divider between us and the driver rolls up. I stiffen, not sure why he did that, but it can't be good.

"I'm a secret operative working for the U.S. government," Suit Guy says abruptly, causing me near whiplash from shock. "You can call me Joe."

"Se-Secret Operative?" I stammer, my head spinning.

"Sure, Joe," Jake says. "And we're super secret spies working for Russia."

"We don't have time for jokes," Joe (who's obviously not really named Joe) says. "We should be arriving at the hotel in fifteen minutes. So I need you to listen to me very carefully."

SEVEN

THE LIMA, PERU ASSIGNMENT

Lima, Peru

I gape at Secret Operative Joe, unsure what to think. "Why should we listen to what you have to say?"

"No, offense, man." Jake rubs his arm that was shot and grimaces. "But we're both not really big on trusting people. We've been burned a few times too many."

"Specifically, bombed, shot, chased, back-stabbed, kidnapped," I add. "And the last ten hours haven't gone great for us either. So yeah, you're going to need some solid proof for us to even continue this conversation with you."

Operative Joe nods and presses a button on his phone, holding it in front of him so we can hear the conversation. It rings once and suddenly my dad's voice comes over the speaker.

"Dr. Hale speaking," Dad says briskly.

My heart slams against my ribcage hearing his voice, and I lean forward. If Joe is fishing, he's picked the perfect bait for me to bite. "Dad?"

"Aria!" Dad's voice twists into panic. "I heard Lau kidnapped you. Thank God, Joe found you. Are you okay? Is Jake there, too?"

"I'm here," Jake assures him. "We're safe...for now."

"Dad," I say. "The hotel room was trashed. We were so worried about you. Are you safe?"

"Thirteen minutes," Joe half-growls, a reminder that we have very little time.

I glance out the window. We're twisting through the streets of Lima. Buildings cram the sides of the roads, and cars fight to maneuver through the heavy traffic.

"I'm fine," Dad says. "Don't worry about me. Did you get my note?"

"What note?" I ask.

"I was pulled to work with the U.S. government on an operation relating directly to what you're dealing with" Dad explains and then sighs. "It happened right after I left you. I should've told you and made sure you were safely on a plane before I agreed to go with the officers."

"Dr. Hale," Operative Joe interrupts. "Sorry to disrupt this family reunion, but we have to get these two briefed before we arrive. Lau wants them to enter the dream of a person she's kidnapped. She believes that individual knows the secret location of the operation where they're holding our people and Lau's husband."

I startle. "Lau's husband?"

Jake groans and leans back in the seat. "This is all starting to make a lot more sense now."

Joe nods grimly. "I need you to ask your daughter to enter the Dreamscape and get the location of the facility for us. Then I'll be sure to extract her from Lima."

"Lima? As in Lima, Peru?" Dad shouts and starts spouting a string of words that I've never heard him say before. He's always been in control and level-headed so hearing him lose it startles me. "Get her out of there Joe. Now. Aria isn't a trained operative. She's a nineteen-year-old who's in college studying neuroscience, not training to be a government operative."

Joe's jaw clenches and his eyes narrow. Apparently, Dad's response wasn't the one he was hoping for.

"I can't do that, Dr. Hale," Joe says. "We've got our own people who are being tortured by their dreams this very second. And if we don't find this facility and destroy our enemy's Dreamscape software, things are only going to get worse."

"There's got to be someone else who can do this job," Jake says.

"Trust me," Joe says. "We've tried. Even Lau has. There isn't anyone who's been successful yet, but we believe Aria and her skills can get the job done."

I lean forward, planting my elbows on my knees and

rubbing my temples. This is too much. Too much pressure, too many demands, too many lives at stake, including my own. I agreed to help Lau but knowing how much Dad is against this changes everything. Can Joe get us out of here without me having to go into the Dreamscape? Will he?

And who is he truly loyal to? The U.S. government or Lau? I groan.

"Eight minutes," Joe growls.

I lift my head and glare at him. "This isn't an easy decision."

"You're a real jerk, you know that Joe?" Jake says.

"Dad's right," I finally say. "I'm not trained. Even in our Dreamscape back at home with my whole team, I would often fail."

"Bring her home, Joe," Dad says. "Or I won't cooperate here. I'm not doing a single thing to work on this situation until she's back home, and I know she's safe."

Joe hangs up on him.

Jake chuckles darkly. "I take that didn't go how you expected it."

Joe pockets his phone and focuses on me. "You know this isn't going to go away. People's lives are at stake, Aria."

Then he pulls out three pictures from inside his jacket. He hands me the images. A man with his arm around a little boy dressed in a baseball uniform. A woman flipping burgers at a grill, laughing with an older couple beside her. And another man wearing a uniform lined with medals.

"Why are you showing me these?" I ask.

"These people are operatives currently being tortured by U.S. enemies using your father's Dreamscape technology," Joe says. I jerk back like he just slapped me. "They all have access to information that could jeopardize the fate of every American. So we're not talking about just saving three people here, it's far bigger than that."

"Thanks, Joe for reminding me how high the stakes are," I say, sarcastically, and take deep breaths, trying to calm myself down.

"Way to dump on the pressure," Jake says. "You know, the more you talk, the more I really don't like you."

He doesn't even glance at Jake. "You're nineteen, Aria. You can do whatever you want."

I stare back out the window. We're zooming along the edge of a barren cliff. The ocean spreads out below us, slipping in and out onto brown, sandy beaches. Everything around us is desert with only a few palms waving in the dusty breeze.

I bite my lip. I don't want to do what he's asking of me. But my eyes drift back to the pictures I'm holding. I hate it, but I know what I have to do.

"Okay, I'll go into the Dreamscape," I say. "But I can't promise I'll find the location. I go in once and whether I get the location or not, I want you to get both of us out of Lau's clutches and home right away."

"This is a bad idea," Jake grumbles. "We don't even know if we can trust him."

"Do we have a choice? I whisper. "I feel like we've been put into an impossible situation."

Jake's eyes fill with concern, but he grabs my hand and squeezes it. It's his way to tell me that he's going to be with me no matter what.

"Excellent." Joe's face is tight as he glances out the window. We're pulling onto a street, and I suspect we're nearly at the hotel. "Go into the dream, get the location of the facility that's holding the hostages. But you're going to tell Lau the location is Trujillo, Peru. If all works to plan, she'll ask me to bring you back to Florida because as of this moment, she still believes I'm working for her. That's when you can tell me the real location."

The limo door swings open before I can respond. We're here. I slip out and step onto the sidewalk. The air is dry and cooler than I expected. Lau and her entourage are striding into the hotel lobby without so much as a glance my way. It's as if I don't exist. As if she didn't fly all the way to New York City herself to ensure my kidnapping went as planned.

"Welcome to the JW Marriott," the valet greets me with a polite smile. "Can I carry in your luggage?"

"No, thanks," I say, and then give Operative Joe a dark look. "I'm not planning on staying long."

Then Jake and I follow Joe, and I'm only too aware that we've gained two additional large guys trailing behind us. The lobby is grand with a sparkling chandelier above, glittering its light across the marble floor and walls. We don't stop at the granite check-in counter but head straight into the elevator. Its walls are glass so when it shoots us up, I get a clear view of a shopping mall below. It's situated at the top of a cliff, overlooking the deep, dark waters of the Pacific Ocean. The sky is hazy and steel gray, but I can make a slight outline of the sun desperately trying to burn its way through the fog.

The elevator feels stifling with all five of us crammed inside. No one speaks a word, but Jack slips his fingers through mine and his touch reassures me. I can do this. I've been in the Dreamscape nearly a hundred times. It's what I've been trained to do.

The elevator door slides open, and we exit. But as we walk the hallway, my heart rate kicks back up. I swallow down the rising panic, except it feels like it's lodged in the back of my throat, keeping me from breathing properly. Joe stops abruptly at room number 856 and knocks twice.

The door swings open, and we step into a large suite. But instead of finding it furnished with couches, chairs, and lamps, those have been replaced by a medical cart, a table holding a MaxLife computer—I'm guessing the one Lau stole from the hotel safe—and on either side of it, are two rollaway beds. One has a man with light brown hair and fair skin lying still as stone on it. His eyes are shut, and he's hooked to wires attached to the laptop and an IV. How long have they kept him in this sleeping state?

Beside him is an empty bed with crisp white paper stretched across it. Seeing this setup sends chills slipping up my spine, and more than anything, I just want to run out of the room. Because I know that stretcher is meant for me. No special sleep pods or state-of-the-art equipment like we have at Dad's facility, MaxLife, to ease the mind into the Dreamscape. Just the bare minimum.

I try to remind myself that's what I did over and over when I was on the hunt across the world to find my dad. I can do it one more time, right? Except, deep down, I know the mind can only handle so much and who knows if these people even know what they are doing. It's not like they went through MaxLife's employee training.

Lau is staring out of a floor-to-ceiling window, her hands clasped behind her back. As we step inside, she turns to face us.

"Hungry?" she asks.

My stomach twists. There's no way I can stomach any food. I think back to MaxLife when after our team would complete a Dream Walk we'd celebrate with doughnuts. Those were fun times, always joking—well, mainly Tony was joking, and Sun was lecturing—but still, it was fun. Besides, we knew what we were doing was for a higher purpose. Finding paths in people's brains to reconnect them to their memories.

I close my eyes and remind myself that I'm saving lives here, too. Sure, the stakes are higher, but the crux of why I'm doing this hasn't changed. At least if I'm to believe Lau and Operative Joe.

"I just want to get this over with," I say. "The sooner I

can get in, get the information, and head back to home, the better."

Lau smiles. "Excellent."

A man wearing a lab coat and scrubs steps forward and waves an invitation at the empty stretcher. "If you would please lie down here, Aria."

I go to follow, but Jake pulls me back. His face is twisted like he wants to tell me to stop what I'm doing right now and say no. My eyes wander to the guards' guns that were hidden while we strolled through the lobby but are very visible now.

"If I don't do this, we're worthless," I whisper to him. "I have to or they will kill us."

"Come back, okay?" He presses my hand to his chest. "Don't get lost in the dream."

He's thinking about his experience in the Dreamscape, and even now, I know those memories still haunt him. He lifts my fingers to his lips and kisses them. Unable to stop myself, I lean into him and kiss him on the lips, soundly and then urgently.

I drink in his taste and smell, desperate to focus on him rather than what I'm about to face. He caresses my cheeks as I wrap my palms around the back of his neck and pull him in closer. At this moment, I ache to be with him, alone and safe. Just the two of us eating ice cream and playing video games. Kissing under the stars at the park. Taking long rides to the beach.

"For good luck," I explain when I finally pull away.

The others in the room shift awkwardly, some clearing their throats. But I don't care. I'm actually surprised I don't get a lecture from Lau, but maybe she just doesn't want to jinx her moment of victory. I let my fingers slide from Jake's and clamber onto the stretcher, cringing at the sound of the crackling white paper lining it. I lie down facing the ceiling. The doctor steps forward and checks my blood pressure and pulse while a nurse comes to my other side and starts hooking me up to a monitor.

"Her pulse is elevated," the doctor tells Lau.

"That's not good is it?" Jake asks. "She shouldn't go in if her body isn't ready."

"Get him out of here," Lau orders her guards. "I can't have him distracting her from getting the job done."

"I'll be okay," I tell Jake as two guards grab his body and haul him out. Seeing him treated roughly sends me sitting back up. "Be careful! He's recovering from being shot!"

"I need you to relax," the doctor tells me, pulling me to lie back down. "Stay calm."

"When I wake up," I tell Lau. "I'm not giving you any information until I see him and make sure he's not hurt."

"Of course," she says serenely, stepping closer to me like a cat hunting its prey.

"What am I supposed to look for?" I ask. "What should I expect? Aren't you going to give me some sort of information on who this guy is before I go in there?"

Lau stands at the foot of my stretcher. "Use whatever

means you have to get the location of the facility from James Locket."

"James Locket," I murmur. "That's his name?"

She nods slowly, her eyes are bright and eager.

The nurse slips a Neuro-Read sleep mask over my eyes and then plugs a set of headphones into my ears.

"Ready?" the doctor asks me. I swallow hard and nod, feeling my heart clattering against my chest. Instantly, the cry of gulls fills my ears, and right away, I know he's enacted the Sound Oasis.

I clench the sides of the stretcher. I know I should relax and stay calm, but the last time I was in the Dreamscape, I thought I was dying. And now here I am, about to do this all over again.

"Counting down into the Dreamscape," the doctor says. "Ten, nine, eight, seve—"

EIGHT
THE RACE THROUGH THE JUNGLE

A wave of nausea washes over me as I push aside the fog in my brain. It's been a long time since I last entered the Dreamscape since I decided to take a break from Dreamwalks for a while, but my training comes back to me like riding a bike. Assess the situation, locate the dreamer, find the Vault.

Except today, I'm not looking for the Vault of Memories. I need to question the dreamer and discover the location of this mythological facility that Lau, and apparently the U.S. government, are looking for.

My vision solidifies. Soft dirt beneath my feet. Vibrant green leaves draping over my shoulders. Trees with trunks as thick as my car, climbing high toward a sharp, blue sky. I push away the branches and step out of the bushes, taking in my situation. I'm in a forest of some sort.

A rainforest?

The dreamer must be close to me because the dream is clear, so clear that if I didn't know better, I'd have believed it was real. This can be a problem for some Dream Walkers. They enter the Dreamscape, and it feels so real that sometimes they lose their sense of time and place. Their sense of themselves.

A muffled sob reaches my ears and I whip my head around to find the source of the sound. That's when I spy the very same man, James Locket, who was lying on the cot beside me in the hotel room. Except he's not peacefully sleeping with his clothes neat and clean. This man is huddled beneath a palm as if he's hoping its fronds are protecting him. Which in fact, might have been true if he had been quiet. Then I might not have seen him at all.

Slowly, Locket rises from his hideout, revealing a flushed, dirt-smeared face with wide eyes. His white dress shirt is shredded, and his black pants are ripped along the side so they flap about. He's barefoot and his hair sticks out as if he hasn't combed it in days.

I hesitate. Do I go up to him with a smile and introduce myself or pounce him and demand he give me the facility's location? The truth is, I've no idea. I'm not trained for this sort of thing. This is what secret agents and trained operatives do. I'm nothing more than a girl who's planning on getting a degree in neurological science. The girl whose head is buried in a book. Yep. I'm the ultimate geek and definitely not cut out for this.

Then I think about the deal I made with Operative

Joe, and all the people depending on me. I suck in a deep breath. Maybe I'm not a super cool agent in real life, but in the Dreamscape, I'm practically invincible.

I straighten and step toward Locket, plastering on my most welcoming, calm smile. "Hello there," I begin.

But I don't get much further because the guy's eyes bug out, and he stares at me like I've got three heads and blood spewing from my eyeballs.

"Please." The guy holds out his hands and backs away. "Don't shoot."

"Shoot? Why would I shoot you?" I lift my palms so he can see.

He glances over his shoulders and frowns. "What do you want? Why are you following me?"

My mind whirls, trying to figure out how I'm going to get the location of this facility without Lau actually finding out. Dad developed the Dreamscape so our technicians at MaxLife can watch the events unfold on the laptop and be ready to assist us at any time. So if the guy tells me the location, Operative Joe isn't going to get the upper hand in this situation.

"I'm a little lost. Where are we exactly?"

"A little lost?" He laughs. "Lost in the middle of the Amazon is what you are."

I perk up at that. Okay, so we're in the Amazon rainforest. Either the facility is close by or it's a mere coincidence that he's dreaming about this place.

"Could you please take me to the nearest facility

where I can find a phone?" I ask, hoping to gain the guy's trust. "I need to make a call."

His eyes dart about furtively. "It's not safe here. You need to leave as soon as possible."

I press my lips together. Lau said she tried to send others in and failed. And now I realize, not only had they failed, they made my job even harder. At least he's talking to me, right? If I can just keep the conversation moving along in the same mentality as the secret facility, it might trigger his mind to show me where it is.

"This is my first real job," I say, making up a story. "I got recruited to work for a highly advanced tech company. But it's all very top secret so I can't tell you about the details."

"Little young, aren't you?"

"I'm an intern, but I figure if I work hard enough, I can work my way up. The problem is I missed my flight, so no one was there to pick me up. Now I'm completely lost, and I'd hate to start off my new job coming to work late. You wouldn't be able to help me, would you?"

Locket rubs the scruff on his chin. His eyes scan the jungle, but he seems to be considering helping me.

"You and I might work for the same company," he finally says.

"Really?" I let out a relieved sigh. "This is great news. Maybe you could show me the way."

He presses his lips together and shakes his head side to side as if debating what to do, but then he reaches into his pocket. He pulls out his phone, but the moment he touches it, bullets ricochet off the tree trunk beside him, splintering the bark like it's confetti. We both dive for the ground.

"This was a trap, wasn't it?" Locket glares at me.

"No! I promise it wasn't."

But I'm too late. Locket scrambles to his feet and takes off into the jungle. Meanwhile, voices and more gunshots echo through the air. Since there were only two cots set up in the hotel room, I can only assume these people shooting at Locket are those he made up in his dream, not other Dream Walkers sent in by Lau.

This is so messed up.

I take off after Locket, determined to not lose track of him. If I let him get too far ahead of me, I'll be kicked out of his dream and wake back up before I've gotten any information. I pump my arms, leaping over fallen logs and darting beneath low branches. I splash through a puddle and slip and slide on the muddy path.

Bullets zing past me, hitting trees and splashing the puddles on my either side. Fear snags at my nerves, and I can't help but worry that I'll get hit by one of the bullets. It's not real, I try to remind myself. This is just a dream. Even still, the dream feels so real that it's hard to tell my brain otherwise.

Locket zigzags down the path like a madman as he tries to duck and avoid the bullets. It takes all my concentration to keep him in my sight.

Suddenly, we break out of the jungle into what looks like some sort of compound, complete with A-framed huts, thatched roofs, and winding paths lined with gardens. My mind struggles to process the contrast.

What is this place?

Could this be where they're holding the hostages?

Except it looks more like a resort than a medical research center. There's no time to wonder because Locket continues to sprint at full speed ahead of me. His pant legs flap in the breeze, and his shirt whips behind him like a sail.

I glance over my shoulder to see three men with blurred faces, wearing suits and holding guns. And yep, they're definitely still chasing us. Locket really must be obsessed with these men to still be dreaming about them.

Which is problematic since how am I supposed to get information from him when we're too busy running for our lives?

Up ahead, I spy a long dock that stretches out into a dark blue river. Meanwhile, Locket is beelining toward a set of three kayaks lying on a wide, grassy bank. Great. Locket is going to jump into one of those and paddle away before I can reach him.

"Locket!" I call out, hoping he'll stop or slow down, but he doesn't. If anything, my words seem to only propel his legs faster.

The dude sure spooks easily, which tells me he's holding more than a few secrets, and he knows how to keep them locked away. No wonder Lau had such a hard time breaking him.

The moment he reaches the first kayak, he grabs it. Somehow, he simultaneously pushes it off the shoreline and leaps into it in one swift movement.

Only in your dreams, Locket, I think in annoyance.

There might be two more kayaks on the shoreline, except I've never kayaked before. I haven't even held a paddle for a canoe. Note to self. Learn how to paddle when I get back home. That is if I ever make it back to Florida.

By the time I stumble to the shoreline, Locket is already paddling away in his kayak, and the Faceless Suits are nearly upon me. My only consolation is when I glance their way, they haven't seemed to notice me yet, instead, they're racing along the dock, shooting at Locket.

I scurry to the first kayak and snatching up a paddle, I shove the boat into the water. I'm not as graceful as Locket so when I climb inside, it tips, causing water to slosh into the hull.

I grit my teeth in frustration, especially when I look down and notice the water along the shoreline is getting fuzzy. The Void is encroaching on me and fast. The forest has disappeared, and I watch in horror as the path I had just run along vanishes as Locket slips further and further from the shoreline.

Frantically, I tip the kayak, dump out the water, and then belly-flop inside. I shimmy myself to sitting. I've no idea how to paddle, so I just start plunging the oar into the water and frantically push the water back, dousing myself with water like a true novice.

Thankfully, my efforts manage to propel me away from the approaching Void. I must have gotten the Faceless Suits attention because I hear them yell, and then the water around me splatters as bullets patter the water around me.

I duck as low as possible and paddle for my life. Somehow I seem to be gaining on Locket. I shove the oar deeper into the lake and grunt, pushing all my muscle power into my actions in hopes I can get within speaking distance of him.

"Locket!" I call. "Where are you going?"

"I'm taking you to safety." He paddles harder. "Just follow me."

My heart lifts. He believed me! I almost feel bad for the guy who dreams he's being chased by Faceless Suits' until I remind myself he helped kidnap and torture three U.S. operatives. Stay focused on the mission, Aria, I remind myself.

Soon I realize there's an island in the middle of the river just ahead of us, and Locket is heading directly for it. Could that island be where the facility is located? But there must be a million islands in the Amazon rainforest. I need more information and something solid to go by.

"We're almost there," Locket says, panting heavily.

"Is this where we work?" I ask, hoping my use of the 'we' word will help him to trust me.

But he isn't given a chance to answer because suddenly Locket looks over his shoulder and his eyes widen. "Uh-oh," he says.

I glance back to see what has gotten Locket so freaked out. That's when I see Faceless Suits pull out an RPG. One guy lifts it up and aims the barrel at us.

Why, oh why do I have to enter a guy who dreams about being blown up by RPGs?

And then a rocket launches out of it, flying directly toward us. I scream.

"Jump!" Locket orders.

Technically, a dream is about mind over matter so theoretically, I could survive the explosion, but the truth is, I really don't want to risk my life testing that theory.

I jump.

My body plunges into the chilling water. I gasp from the shock of the cold as I sink below the surface. My shoes yank me down, but I kick my feet and push my head out of the water. When I emerge, that's when the grenade hits and both of our kayaks explode. Flames burst into the air, and my ears ring from the sound.

"Swim!" Locket tells me. "And fast before the piranhas eat you."

"What?" I gasp. "Piranhas?"

You've got to be freaking kidding.

I really hate your dreams, Locket.

"They bite hard." Locket takes off swimming. "But if you swim fast, you'll reach the island mostly intact."

Right on cue, I feel little bites nipping at my jeans. Fear curdles through me, and I start kicking and swimming as fast as I can. It feels like years that I'm swimming, but no matter how much I swim, the island still looks so far away.

"Locket," I gasp. "What if we don't make it?"

"If I don't make it," he says. "Ask for Mono. Then you'll find your way."

My arms burn and a quick glance tells me that I'm all bitten up from piranhas nibbling away at me like I'm their mid-day snack.

Dizziness washes over me. How long have I been in this dream? It feels long. Longer than usual.

Suddenly, it's like someone yanks a cord around me and jerks it hard. My chest seizes, and I gasp as all the air inside of me is sucked away. My heart seizes in panic. What is happening?

Before I can make any sense of it, the world around me fades. My ears buzz and blackness floods my vision. I open my mouth to scream, but no sound comes out.

NINE
ESCAPE

My eyes blink open. An oxygen mask presses against my mouth. Jake leans over me, his eyes bright and wide with fear.

"Aria, baby," he says in a choking voice. "You're okay. Oh, god. I was so worried."

"Jake?" I ask. Is he in the dream? Or have I left the dream?

No, this is the real world.

Suddenly it's like all my other senses and sounds catch up like a thundering train. People are shouting and there's a pattering sound that reminds me all too much of the bullets in our hotel room back in New York.

I shove the oxygen mask off my face and try to sit up. The room spins and I press my fingers over my eyes to reorientate myself. Meanwhile, I feel Jake frantically ripping off the wires attaching me to the Dreamscape.

"We need to move," Jake whispers in an urgent, tight tone. "Now."

My brain is still trying to refocus, but I nod, trusting Jake. I swing my legs over the edge of the cot while Jake wraps his arms around me to keep me from falling.

"You're not getting out of here alive, Lau," a voice calls from the far side of the room.

"I am not dying anytime soon," Lau replies, her voice cold as ice. "But I cannot say the same of you and your men. Gesner must be given a message and your bodies will be my signature."

I've woken up in a middle of a shoot-off? I do a quick mental reassessment of the situation: Lima. Hotel room. Lau. Operative Joe. Locket.

Locket. I frown. What happened to us in the dream?

My eyes flicker to where Locket is sleeping on the cot next to me. A horrifying, dark splotch pools in the center of his chest. Crimson liquid seeps onto the cot's once crisp white sheet, tainting it like a sheath of death. Drops of blood plink one by one from the edge of the cot to the floor.

I gasp, and a shuddering sound emits from deep within me.

"Shhh," Jake whispers in my ear and drags me to the ground.

My whole body starts shaking. That complete blackness I experienced at the end of the dream was...

Oh, no. No, no, no.

I was in a dead man's dream.

I shiver in horror and another sob pushes out of my chest. Crap. I'm going into shock.

"What was that?" someone says.

"Why not come and find out for yourself." Zhang Lau chuckles.

My vision clears enough to discover she's hiding behind a couch, a silver gun pressed between her palms. Her eyes glitter, and she looks more alive at this moment than I've ever seen her. Two bodyguards crouch on her either side, ready to spring to action at her command.

Jake tucks his arm around me tighter and directs me to start crawling. I don't question him but focus on the hard wooden floor. I move one leg at a time. From the corner of my vision, I spot the doctor's body on the ground, arms sprawled haphazardly. Do not look closer, I warn myself. Otherwise, I know I'll fall apart.

Stay alive. Follow Jake.

I press my lips together to keep my sobs quiet and force my body to move. Somehow, we cross the threshold of the connecting room. Operative Joe is leaning against the wall, gun poised, peering around the edge of the doorway. He's the one who kept me safe this whole time, I realize. It's because of him I'm still alive.

Operative Joe points to the far wall with two fingers and shakes them twice as if telling us to move there and quickly. Once clear of the doorway, I try standing, but my legs buckle beneath me. Quickly, Jake holds me up, grimacing a little, and I realize the gunshot wound must hurt when he's working his body too much. We manage to reach the wall next to an outer door when Joe darts over to join us.

"What's going on?" I ask.

"As you can see," he says, "while you were in the Dreamscape, a team of assassins arrived with the intent to kill any or all here. Even Locket."

"Why would they kill him?" Jake wonders. "Isn't he one of their own?"

Joe shrugs. "Either he's disposable or knows too much."

"What kind of people are these?" I say.

"People like Sadir Gesner," Joe says grimly. "A quick photo scan indicates these assains work for him."

"I take it he's not your favorite guy," Jake mutters.

"Isn't it good to know who we're dealing with?" I ask.

Joe's face darkens. He moves to the door and peeks through the peephole. "Tell me you found out the location of the facility holding our people."

I shake my head. "Nothing specific. Only that maybe it's in the Amazon Forest."

"The Amazon Forest is two and a half million miles of wilderness," Joe snaps. "How am I supposed to work with that?"

Tears creep at the edge of my eyes. I know I must seem like a wimp, but I can't handle this. I just can't.

"Well, considering *you're* the trained investigator, Joe,"

I quip in sharp tones. "I'm sure you'll figure something out."

His face softens and he takes a long breath. "You're right. I'm going to get you two kids out of here. Back to where you belong."

I nod frantically. Yes, *out*. Away from the blood. Away from the dead strewn across this hotel room like a morgue. Joe swallows hard and his body tenses in a way that tells me he's gearing up for something intense.

"I'm going to open this door and step out into the hallway," he explains. "Follow me but turn right and sprint toward the stairwell. Take the stairs and exit the hotel. Get in the first taxi you find and head directly to the U.S. Embassy. Got it?"

We nod. He opens the door and darts outside, gun held out before him. Jake and I scramble into the hall. A quick glance reveals two guys standing outside the door of the main room. They spot us and pull out guns but hesitate to shoot.

Joe yells, "Run!"

We take off toward the EXIT sign at the end of the hall. Jake slams his body against the heavy door, and we barrel into the stairwell. My heart pounds as I race down the stairs, taking them two at a time. At ground level, we're given a choice to enter the lobby or exit the hotel. I shove on the outer door, spitting us out onto the sidewalk of a busy street.

I spin in a circle, terror stretching my nerves taut.

"I don't see any taxis," Jake says breathlessly. He presses one hand to his side where he was shot and grabs my hand with his other. "Come on. Let's get as far away from this hotel as we can."

We bolt down the street and head toward the crowded lawn beside the outdoor mall. Skateboards zip past while a trio of singers, strumming on their guitars entertain a group of couples pausing to listen. The air smells of grilled meat and sea from the crashing waves below the cliffs.

Suddenly, it hits me how bad of a situation we're in.

"Jake," I say, trying to control the panic that's shoving its way up my throat. "We're in a foreign country with no money, passport, or phone. What are we going to do?"

"Yeah." He pauses and rakes a hand through his hair. "We just need to get to the embassy. They can help us."

"But we don't have any money for a taxi," I say.

I glance back at the hotel just as two guys stride out of the lobby with determined purpose. They scan the area as if they're looking for someone. I clutch Jake's hand and nod in their direction.

"Someone is looking for us," I say. "We need to lose ourselves."

My eyes land on a group of tourists trailing after a lady waving a flag. The group is heading toward a large tour bus parked along the edge of the street. I tug him in the direction of the tourists while making sure to not catch the notice of our kidnappers.

I skirt up to the loud tour group, and while a group of

ladies chatters and takes a selfie, I squeeze Jake and myself in behind them. Jake lifts an eyebrow at me.

"I take it we just joined a European tour group," he notes. "Do you think they'll let us off at the embassy?"

"Right now." I climb up the stairs into the bus. "All I care about is getting as far from any of Lau's or Gesner's hitmen as we can."

We shuffle down the bus aisle until we reach the back where the seats look empty. My body nearly collapses into the seat while Jake's face looks pale with a wet sheen across his forehead. How much longer can we keep this up?

I peer out the window as the bus door hisses closed and the engine roars to life. Neither of the guys at the hotel notice us. The bus jerks to life, rumbling down the street. I lean my head on Jake's shoulder in relief.

"We made it out alive," I whisper.

"I didn't know if we would," he says. "If we get to the embassy, we'll be safe."

Except a tickling sensation in the back of my head warns me that's the first place Lau will look to find us.

TEN

THE ACCIDENTAL TOURISTS

My body rocks forward with a jerk, and my eyes fly open. The pounding of my heart sharpens all my senses, and I take in my surroundings. I'm on a bus with a bunch of people I don't know. Tourists, I suddenly remember as my mind refocuses. Right, I let out a sigh of relief, as I realize that I'm safe.

At least for now.

I must have fallen asleep, surprising me after all that has happened. But then the last forty-eight hours haven't been exactly what I'd call a holiday trip. I glance over at Jake beside me. His head is leaning back against the seat of the bus, eyes closed. His face is smooth without the wrinkles of worry bunching up his forehead. I take in his sharp jawline and the way his hair flops over his forehead. Seeing him resting so peacefully, relaxes me.

It's funny how nearly a year ago, we barely knew each

other. Strangers passing through the hallways at school. But now our lives are so intricately woven together that I can't imagine life without him. No one understands me better than him or has gone through these same experiences. I suppose there really is something about people bonding after going through trauma.

But the important thing is we escaped. I take a deep breath and snuggle up against Jake's side, letting his solid body and warmth settle my nerves. Vaguely, I hear the tourists on the bus laughing and chatting. I've no idea what language they're speaking. I hope one of them speaks English because when I get fully awake, I need to ask one of them if they can drop us off at the embassy.

A quick glance out the window tells me we're driving around a circular roundabout somewhere in Lima. Flowers bloom in the center of the circle while gray buildings stretch up on the outer side of the road. Their Spanish influence is obvious with intricate carvings etched in the pillars and designs filling every crevice.

This section of Lima definitely has an older feel to it, and I wonder when these buildings were constructed. They have to be hundreds of years old. My thoughts are interrupted as a man rises from his seat and takes the mic at the front of the bus. He starts speaking and the group cheers.

Beside me, Jake stirs and blinks awake. Instantly, he grips my arm as if he's trying to protect me even in his disorientation.

"What's going on?" he whispers.

"The tour guide is talking to the group." I shrug. "But I've no clue what he's saying. This area must be a place that tourists visit though."

I point out the window to a group of people standing in the center of the roundabout, taking pictures of a statue of a man.

"We need to ask someone here where the embassy is." Jake rubs his eyes and peers out the window.

"I just hope they'll help us. The last thing I want is to be abandoned on the side of the road."

Before I can process how best to approach the tourists, the bus slows down and slips along the edge of the curb, stopping with a hiss. Right away, everyone on the bus leaps to their feet and begins exiting.

"I guess it's now or never," Jake says grimly.

I smooth down my shirt, realizing I haven't showered or changed clothes since after the TV studio interview. The knees of my jeans are torn, and the front of my shirt is smeared with dirt and is that blood? I nearly gag. I suppose it makes sense between the explosions at the hotel in New York, holding Jake when he was bleeding, and crawling on the floor here at the hotel in Lima.

Since we have literally nothing other than the clothes on our backs, it doesn't take us any time to get out of our seats and shuffle along with the tourists down the bus aisle.

"Excuse me." I touch the shoulder of a blonde lady in front of me. "Could you tell me where we are exactly?"

The woman turns around, and her mouth opens in shock. "Ohhh!" she says, and then rattles off a bunch of words I don't understand.

I take it she's just now realized they have two stowaways on the bus that don't belong here. Suddenly, everyone turns to stare at us. It's obvious from their wide eyes and pointing that they're not sure what to think about us.

Finally, everyone exits the bus except for the lady who talks rapidly to the guy who I'm guessing is the tour guide. He nods and frowns as she explains something.

"This man, Dario, help you," she says and pats my arm in a motherly fashion. Then she too steps off the bus, leaving Jake and me alone with the bus driver and tour guide.

"What exactly are you doing on our bus?" the tour guide asks, skeptically, but I find myself relieved because his English is clear and easy to understand

"We need help," I explain. "We were wondering if you could take us to the U.S. Embassy."

He grunts and crosses his arms, clearly not impressed with what we're asking. "We are not a taxi service. Besides, the embassy is far from here and I have a tour group who is waiting for me."

"But we don't have any money or a phone to call for help," Jake explains.

The man's eyebrows shoot up in skepticism. "You American tourists should keep a better eye on your belongings."

"Yes!" I seize what he's implying. It's the perfect explanation. After all, losing our stuff is far simpler and more believable than telling someone that we're running for our lives after being kidnapped and coerced to gather intelligence. "We lost everything. If you can't give us a ride, could we borrow your phone? That would be helpful."

"We'd also like to call our families so they can help, too," Jake adds.

Dario's eyes soften at our words as he takes in our disheveled look. Then he pulls out his phone, saying, "I'll have Jose call the embassy for you and tell them your location. You can use my email account to reach your families since there aren't any international fees connected to it."

"Thank you so much," I say, taking the phone.

Dario tells the bus driver something in Spanish while I quickly shoot off an email to Dad.

> Dad, this is Aria using a tour guide's email. We need help. Things did not go well. We are headed to the embassy.

I look over at Jake. "This seems like a good idea, but what if he doesn't open the email? Or it goes into his spam folder since he doesn't know Dario."

"What about social media?" Jake offers. "Is he on any of those platforms?"

I shake my head. And then a thought hits me. I hate bringing her into all of this, but we're desperate. "Sun," I say. Sun Li might be a co-worker from MaxLife, but after she roped her brother into letting us use his plane and came along with us to hunt down my father's kidnappers, I consider her practically a sister. "She's always on her Instagram account. I can message her. Tell her what's going on."

"Could you please hurry?" the guide asks, shuffling back and forth. "My group needs me. We have a tour set up at the Saint Francis Church that starts in five minutes."

My fingers fly over the keys on the phone as I log into my Instagram account and type up a message to Sun.

> Jake and I have been kidnapped. We escaped but have no phone, money, or passports. We are in Lima, Peru. Trying to get to the embassy. See if you can find someone to help us. Got to go!

The tour guide eagerly takes his phone back and pockets it. The driver tells him something in Spanish, and the guide nods. He says, "Stay here, outside of the Saint Francis Church. The embassy is sending someone over to pick you up, but with traffic, it could be nearly an hour's wait."

"Thank you so much," I say, relief washing through me.

"Next time." The guide wags his finger at us. "Keep a closer eye on your bags, okay?"

"Absolutely," I say, trying to smile. "Nothing ruins a day faster than a lost bag."

"Except for maybe kidnapping or murder," Jake mutters under his breath.

I nudge Jake to behave, and then we stumble off the bus, trailing after Dario through a wrought iron gate and into an open square. The tour group is waiting by a golden fountain and cheers when they spot Dario. He explains something to the group, and they all turn and look at us like we're lost kittens. One lady digs through her purse and pulls out some granola bars for us while a few others give us some cash. My heart aches at how kind these strangers are.

"Thank you," I tell them, tears threatening to spill down my face. After how horribly we've been treated and used, it's reassuring to see that the world has good people in it. "We really appreciate your help."

We wave goodbye to the tour group, and then they turn and face Dario who reverts into his tour leader role.

"I'm not going to lie." Jake lifts the granola bar. "I'm starving. This might not be burgers and a plate of fries, but I'll take what I can get."

"They'll have some food for us at the embassy," I reassure him. "But in the meantime, let's sit down and eat these. I'm feeling shaky."

We stroll across the large slabs of stone that make up

the square in front of the church. The church building is a light yellow that stands out like a flower against the smoke-gray sky. The building is beautiful, designed in the style of Spanish Baroque architecture. Two towers rise up on either side of an ornately carved stone center. A massive wooden door practically two stories high rests in its center.

"The church is gorgeous," I say as we settle on the edge of the steps that lead up to the main doors.

We devour our granola bars in what feels like seconds. A flock of pigeons swoops down, landing only a few feet from us, gazing hungrily at our food. They wait patiently for any spare crumbs, but I shake my head at them.

"We ate every last bit," I say, laughing.

"Sure didn't last long." Jake stares forlornly at his empty wrapper. He counts up the money that the tour group gave us. "Maybe we should go find some food while we wait."

"Dario did say we might have to wait an hour." I scan the vendors set up along the edge of the wrought iron gate that circles the church's courtyard.

And that's when my eyes land on two men wearing suits emerging from a black car. I grip Jake's arm.

"Do those guys look familiar to you?" My voice trembles. "Because if you ask me, they look just like the guys that followed us outside of the hotel."

"But that's impossible," Jake breathes, dropping his granola wrapper.

The birds eagerly swoop down on the wrapper, pecking at it while I take Jake's hand in mine.

"We need to hide," I say. "Before they spot us."

"Slowly. No sudden movements to pull their attention this way. They haven't seen us yet."

We rise to our feet and slip alongside another tour group entering the church. When we reach the gate and discover there's a fee, my chest tightens.

"What do we do?" I ask Jake. "Do we pay the money and hope we don't need it later or use it to get a taxi to the embassy?"

"It's a tough decision." Jake counts the money up and shakes his head. "I don't even know how much a taxi ride is or if we have enough in the first place."

I glance over my shoulder to see where the men are now. I frown. They're looking intently at an iPad. Then their faces lift up, and they scan the courtyard until they stop on me. Our eyes lock and I suck in a breath.

"They just saw us." I clench Jake's hand tighter.

Jake growls in frustration. "They must be tracking us somehow. We need to find a place inside the church and hide until the driver from the embassy arrives."

Jake grimaces but passes over the cash. My stomach sinks knowing we are spending money we might need later for food or transportation. We duck inside the long narrow stone corridor of the monastery. For a brief moment, I'm overwhelmed by the stunning beauty and serenity of the place.

The ceiling is painted with beautiful stories and the walls are filled with brightly decorated tiles. More than anything, I wish I were strolling along these ancient hallways, breathing in the old wood and flowery scents instead of creeping around corners and looking over our shoulders.

We dart down the hall, searching for a place to hide. Soon we find ourselves entering a walkway that surrounds an inner courtyard. Stone arches along the perimeter open up to give picturesque views of the beautiful gardens that span the center of the courtyard. A network of geometric patterned pathways cut through the gardens, around trees, all leading to a large fountain in the center. The air is full of chirping bird sounds that I've never heard before and the sweet scent of flowers.

"This way." Jake glances over his shoulder to make sure no one sees us, and then tugs me through a door and into a dark paneled room, smelling of ancient wood.

Without hesitation, Jake pulls my shirt over my head and starts running his hands over my body and hair. I stiffen in shock.

"What are you doing?" I ask, startled. "Why are you undressing me?"

Sure, we've kissed, but he's never touched me under my shirt before, so this is a whole new level of intimacy. But Jake isn't deterred. His eyes are focused, and yet there's a desperation to them.

"I think Lau put a tracker on us," he explains, hurriedly. "I need to find it."

I nod, suddenly understanding how they've been able to find us and also a little relieved that Jake has a reason just to jump to us hitting this next level in our relationship at a time like this. "Okay, that makes sense. Just next time warn me before you start ripping off my clothes."

He chuckles. "Right. Guess I got a little carried away. But maybe the practice might come in handy for the future?"

I hit him on the arm and roll my eyes. Then I quickly pull off my jeans, checking every seam and pocket, trying to not feel weird standing there in my underwear in front of Jake.

"Wait!" My heart thumps in my chest. "Our shoes!"

When I check the bottom of my sneakers, they look normal, but then when I start digging on the inside, and that's when I feel something small and hard tucked into the flap of my shoe. My heart sinks.

"I think I found it," I say breathlessly. I point to the place that looks like someone sewed up the edge.

Jake's jaw tightens as he rips at the seam. A tiny metal piece smaller than a dime tumbles into his palm.

"You're right." I gasp. "They've been tracking us this whole time."

ELEVEN
THE CATACOMBS

"What do we do?" I ask, inspecting the tracker, my stomach twisting with fear.

Here we thought we'd outwitted our enemies and escaped their clutches, but we were still a step behind them. Meanwhile, Jake has gone through his shoes and found one as well.

Jake slams it on the ground and then starts pacing the small room. "We don't have much time. We could just leave the tracker here and try outrunning them."

"Except you can't forget that you're still not one hundred percent. What if your stitches break?"

I crack open the door and peek outside. My heart slams into my throat when I spot our pursuers entering the courtyard's corridor. They are looking carefully at their tablet. I suck in a deep breath.

"They're coming," I whisper, and scan the room we're

in. That's when I notice there are two other doors on the other side of the room. "Is there another exit here?"

Jake rushes to the far side of the room and throws open a door, revealing a supply closet cluttered with an old desk, room dividers, and dusty picture frames. He shuts it and tries the next one. I let out a breath of relief when it opens into another hallway. It's empty other than a group of tourists heading up a wide stone stairway.

Jake is about to toss our trackers into the room we just let, but I stop him.

"I've got an idea." I grab the trackers. "Meet me at the end of the hall."

Before he has a chance to respond, I race down the corridor, pumping my arms toward the stairway, gasping for air. If I ever get back to Florida, I promise to start running every day.

I take the stairs two at a time. They're worn as if they've been stepped on by thousands of feet for hundreds of years. A domed ceiling arches above in an intricate web of carved-out triangles in the wood, unlike anything I've ever seen. But I don't stop to take in the beauty, instead, when I reach the first landing, my eye is drawn to the second story where a wooden railing runs along the edge.

I've no idea how much time I have, or if this is the right idea, but I toss the trackers upstairs. No time to second guess my decision. Instead, I race back down the stairs, nearly stumbling on their slickness. Once I reach the first-floor hallway, I don't pause, but careen around the corner.

At the far end of the cream-colored walled corridor, Jake waves at me to hurry.

A voice calls out from behind me, saying something in a language I don't recognize. Crap! They found us. I wasn't fast enough.

I stagger up to Jake just as he's picking up a massive golden candlestick that was positioned by the door.

"Get inside," Jake tells me, nodding to the low doorway behind him.

I hesitate and as I do, fingers swipe at my back, pulling on my shirt. I scream and Jake lifts the candlestick and heaves it down on my hunter. I spin around to watch the guy crumple to the ground in a heap.

"Is he dead?" I choke.

"Probably not," Jake mutters. "Hopefully he'll have a bad headache for a week though. Come on. Help me drag him inside so his buddies don't find him."

It takes both of us to slide the man into the entryway of the small room that we were going to enter. Jake grunts in pain.

"Be careful," I warn. "We can't have you bleeding."

"Good point," he says and wipes the sweat beading along his forehead. "Can't leave a trail."

I frown. I know he's trying to joke it off and keep things light, but I can't stop worrying about him. Jake starts digging through the guy's pockets, tossing aside tickets and random slips of paper. Seeing what he's doing, I join in, even though the whole thing feels wrong.

But when I pull out a phone from the inside pocket of his jacket, my heart soars. "We can call home now."

"If you can get that phone unlocked," Jake says sharply. I get his frustration. Even if I can get the phone unlocked and we call home, it doesn't mean we'll survive the hour.

"I've got an idea." I point to the guy's eyes. "Hold open his eyelids for me so I can unlock his phone."

Jake shrugs. "Can't hurt, but we need to hurry."

I'm half-surprised that my idea works because the moment I hold the phone in front of the guy's blank eyes, the phone flicks to unlock. Quickly, I tap on settings and select Never Auto-Lock.

Meanwhile, Jake finds the guy's wallet, pockets the money, and then inspects the rest of the wallet. He holds up a slip of paper written in a foreign language. "No ID, but a random guess is this note was written in Russian."

"What have we gotten mixed up in?" I whisper.

"Nothing good."

Voices outside of the hallway send my instincts into overdrive.

"They're coming," I whisper, fear curdling up my spine.

"Come on," Jake says. "There's an opening and stairs behind you. Let's see where it takes us."

We abandon the knocked-out Russian and stoop through another doorway, taking another set of flights deeper into the monastery. The moment I reach the bottom step, it's like I've entered another place entirely.

Brick walls stretch out in a network of long passage-ways, each one arching above to create the appearance of ghostly tunnels. Torchlights hang along the wall and pale beams cast a deathly pallid light across the area. But as I take in the contents of the tunnel, I nearly scream in horror. Bones, piles and piles of them, are stacked in neat precision in brick-lined storage bins. Skulls line the walkway and are stacked up on the dead-end stairwells, their eye sockets boring into me as if they're still alive.

I shiver in the sudden coolness of this underground section of the monastery.

"Oh, wow," Jake breathes. "This is a crypt. I wondered why that sign outside of the building said catacumas."

"As in catacombs? This can't be good. What do we do?" I ask, but I already knew the answer. "We need to keep going, don't we?"

He nods grimly. "We have to see if there's an exit on the other side."

"Right." Taking a deep breath, I slip my hand into his, soaking his warmth and strength, and we take off along the dusty stone floor.

I try to ignore the ancient containers each stacked with hundreds upon hundreds of human bones white as tomb-stones. How many people were buried here? Who would build a place like this?

It doesn't take long though before we hear voices echoing through the chambers like ghosts of the bones. And they aren't oohing and awing like tourists. Instead, their tones were urgent, determined. We pick up our pace and enter a room with nothing inside except for a waist-high circular wall that opens up into what appears to be a cistern.

"Maybe we can hide inside that," I say.

But when I peek over the edge, I gasp. Below, hundreds of bones are laid out in a macabre pattern of rings, alternating between rows of femurs and skulls. I press my hands over my mouth to keep from throwing up.

"We're definitely not hiding in there," Jake says. "Talk about morbid."

We wander on. The passage twists and turns about in so many directions that soon I lose track of where we are. All that I can focus on are the sounds of those pursuing us.

"We're going to get lost in here," I finally say. I pull out the Russian's phone and start a Google search. "Maybe I can find some kind of map of these catacombs to help us out."

We huddle on the floor beside a low brick wall, our backs leaning against a barred-off vault stacked high with more eerie-white bones. I try to ignore them and focus on getting some information about this place.

"Find anything?" Jake whispers, peering over the brick wall.

"Other than there are 25,000 buried bodies here?" I shudder at the thought.

"Yikes. That's a lot of bodies. Hopefully, we won't add ours to the count."

"And apparently we should be on the lookout for ghosts wearing dark suits who levitate through these passageways, calling out in chilling voices."

"Think we've got the dark suits trying to kidnap us already covered."

"Oh, wait! This article mentions there are secret passageways from here to other parts of the city. If only we could find those."

"Whatever we do," Jake says, "we should keep moving."

I tuck the phone back into my pocket, and we skirt through two brick pillars just as organ music strikes up, drifting down through a grate above, echoing through the catacombs like a haunting melody. I peek up through the bars to discover we're directly below the front section of the chapel. People are walking inside and sitting down.

"If only we could get through that grate," I murmur, but it's obvious that the grate is cemented into the brick ceiling.

I'm about to have Jake hoist me up so I can call out for help when a man bursts into our hallway and calls out something I don't understand. But then he lifts up a gun and points it at us, this time speaking clearly in English.

"Do not move." He grins a crooked smile. "Or I shoot."

TWELVE
THE SECRET PASSAGEWAY

I stare down the barrel of the gun, my pulse throbbing against my temples. The Russian cocks his head, grin widening as if he can smell the fear pooling off me. He's enjoying this way too much.

Instinctively, I back up until my heels hit against the brick-walled bin packed full of bones.

"There is nowhere for you to run," the Russian says, stepping closer to us.

"Hey, man." Jake holds up his hands. "Why don't you put the gun down? We can have a little talk about whatever it is you want. We are unarmed."

"What do you want from us?" I ask.

"You will come." The Russian nods at me.

"She's not going anywhere with you," Jake says, his tone switching from easy-going to a low growl.

"You forgot. I have the gun." The Russian chuckles

and waves the weapon about like it's a toy. I choke back a gasp, terrified it's going to go off accidentally.

"Trust me," I say, desperate to draw out this whole interaction. Maybe some tourists will show up. Or if we're loud enough, the priest might hear us. "We haven't forgotten. But why me?"

"I take you to Sadir Gesner," he says. "You are the key to the next stage of the Great Plan."

"Right." I glance over at Jake. His jaw clenches, and there's a fierceness in his eyes. That looks tells me he would do anything, *anything*, to keep me safe. And that is a little terrifying as well. I can't let him get hurt.

Then Jake's eyes flick to the bin of bones that our backs are pressed against. He can't possibly think we can fight against this armed Russian with a femur.

"Distract," Jake whispers.

Great. He *is* thinking of using these bones as weapons. But what other option do we have? So with a nod, I refocus back on the Russian who's eyeing us intently. His brown hair has fallen over his dark eyes, and he's got a scar that runs from his lip to his cheek.

"Okay, I'm coming." I step forward and slightly to the right so I'm standing in front of Jake. "But who exactly is Sadir Gesner? I've never heard of the dude."

"Dude?" The Russian's face darkens. "He is one of the greats. Soon you will know him. Once he rises to his true place of power. Come closer."

"Gesner seems like an interesting person," I continue,

deciding to milk this guy's star-struck thinking. "Lau sure seemed afraid of him. Why do you think that is?"

I feel Jake's presence, hovering right behind me, and then something presses against my spine.

"Lau?" the Russian spits out the name like he's tasted something sour. "She should be afraid."

"Oh? Why?" I slip my hands behind my back, pretending I'm thinking. As soon as I do, Jake presses something smooth and slick into my palms.

It's a bone, I realize. I shiver, thinking about how I'm holding a dead body part. But this person that lived hundreds of years ago is about to save my life, I tell myself. They would be cool with that, wouldn't they?

"We waste time." The Russian huffs and reaches out for me. As he does, the gun lowers slightly, angling left as his body shifts.

That's when Jake springs to action. He shoves me to the right, yelling, "Run!" and then smacks the bone he's holding down on the Russian's gun. The weapon snaps free and clatters to the ground. The Russian growls and swings his thick, beefy arm at Jake. But Jake ducks and whacks the bone hard against the Russian's temple.

The guy teeters as if dazed from the impact, but then he snakes his arm out and grabs Jake's wrist, twisting it. Jake grunts but rams the bone he's holding in his other hand onto the other side of the guy's head.

I spring into action, hefting up the femur Jake gave me and slamming it into the back of the Russian's head. His grip must have loosened on Jake, because instantly, Jake frees his arm and slams a solid punch to the guy's jaw with his uninjured arm. The large man teeters, but Jake doesn't wait for him to retaliate. He slams the bone once again down on the guy's head with a solid thump.

"Wow," I say, staring at the second Russian we've knocked out in the last ten minutes. "I've got to say. That was impressive, baby."

Jake's breathing heavily, sweat dripping down his face. His eyes dart around the area until they land on the gun. He snatches it up just as we hear more voices in the distance.

"Anton?" a voice calls out, and then he says something else in Russian.

"They're looking for him," I whisper to Jake.

"We can't get a break," he groans, and then he takes my hand. "Come on, I think I saw a place we can hide."

He leads me back down a passageway we recently left and stops at a section that looks like an excavation site. At first glance, it appears to be a dead end. Rubble is piled up along the walls along with a cart loaded with tools. A chain separates us from what looks like a dead-end section of the tunnel. A sign hangs from the chain. The top is written in Spanish, and the bottom is in English.

Keep Out
Excavation in progress

Jake ducks under the sign and darts over to the wall.

"What are you doing?" I whisper. "It's a dead end."

"Is it though? Look how the brick here is a different shade and pattern than the rest of this corridor."

He moves to a section that's hidden in the shadows. A tarp covers one part, and when he pulls it aside, it reveals a hole.

"Quick." Jake waves me over. "I think this opens to a space behind the wall. Someone must have barricaded off a section of the tunnel system down here. We can hide there until they leave."

I scamper under the chain but hesitate at the hole. "What if there are rats or dead bodies in there?"

"It's either that or hang out with your Russian buddies."

I glare at him, but the voices are coming closer, so I take a deep breath and squeeze myself inside. Sticky cobwebs cling to my face, and I bite back a scream as I feel something skitter across my arm. I huddle in the shadows as Jake squeezes in next and then drags the tarp back over the hole to hide it.

"Do you think this will work?" I ask.

"Maybe." I can't see his expression un the muted light, but I can tell from his voice that he's not convinced.

We hunker in the semi-dark with only the glow from the Russian's phone illuminating the area. I crane my ears for any sound on the other side of the tarp.

"Let me see that phone." Jake holds out his hand.

I pass it to him, and he presses on the flashlight mode. Then he pans the area we're in. It reveals that we're crouched in another tunnel, this one so narrow with rubble along the sides that it's obvious the archaeologists aren't even close to completing the restoration of this section of the catacombs.

"What if this is one of the secret passageways you read about online?" Jake wonders. "It might lead us out of the catacombs."

"Or it might be a dead end. Plus, you saw the sign. There's a reason it says keep out. The ceiling could collapse on us."

I'm interrupted by footprints clattering over the stone floors not far from where we're sitting. Men are speaking in Russian so I've no idea what they're saying. Except then a voice cuts through the foreign words as one of the men starts speaking in English with an American accent.

"You're worthless!" the voice says. "Untrained teens managed to knock out two of your men?"

"It is hard to capture them without hurting them," a voice with a thick Russian accent says.

"Try harder then. I'm headed back to the embassy since I suspect that's where they'll head next. Hopefully, you'll have good news for me before I reach my office. If not, I'll be sure to pass on the news of your incompetence to your superiors."

Then there's the sound of shoes clipping away at a brisk pace. It's silent for a brief moment before the men start speaking in Russian again, this time their tones are harsher, angrier.

I whip around to face Jake, grabbing his hand. In the pale phone light, I see the horror in his eyes.

"The embassy isn't safe," I whisper.

"Which means we're on our own," Jake says grimly.

"Oni zdes'?" a voice says, startling close to where we're hiding. The sound of the chain dropping terrifies me, and I jerk upright, clinging to Jake.

Wordlessly, he points to the dilapidated tunnel, and suddenly, a collapsing ceiling and cave-in seems like a great idea. I nod vigorously. Holding the phone as our flashlight, he leads the way. We squeeze through the small space, stone and brick scrap against our bodies and snag at our clothes, but we press on, twisting through the narrow cavity of rumble.

Dust coats the air, and I have to press my hands over my face to hold in a sneeze. Behind us, the tarp crackles through the darkness as if its being pulled back. Quickly, Jake tucks the phone into his pocket, thrusting us into darkness.

The air smells stale and heavy. The brick and stone seem to press against me, making it hard to breathe. Jake wraps his good arm around my body, and I lean my face against his chest so I can hear his heartbeat pounding against my skin. The rhythm of it and the strength of his arms soothe me. We wait for a moment until there's more movement. They are trying to squeeze into the hole!

Jake must realize this too because he drops his arms from around me, turns back around, and continues shuffling deeper into the darkness. Though the air is cooler down here, I'm still sweating, probably from panic. Dirt coats my body, clinging to the sweat. That feeling I'm being buried alive threatens to overwhelm me. What if we come to a dead-end and the Russians find us? What if we trapped ourselves?

What if the ceiling collapses and my bones are tossed into the bins just like all the other twenty-five thousand bodies before me?

But then after what feels like an eternity, a horrible stench fills my lungs.

"Oh, my gosh." I gag. "What's that awful smell? Tell me we haven't found a pile of decomposing bodies."

Jake pauses to snap back on the flashlight and creeps forward tentatively. After a few more twists and turns, a stream of pale light fills the rubble around us, revealing that we're standing about five feet above the edge of another arched brick tunnel. But this one is lit, larger, and the bricks look newer.

"We made it to a sewer system," Jake whispers excitedly. "This is good. Very good."

"I never thought I'd be so happy to be in toilet water," I say.

But he's right. If there's a sewer, it means we aren't at a dead end, waiting for the Russians to find us.

Jake drops onto the ledge below that runs along

sludgy, dark water. He then turns around and reaches up to me. I slip down next and he steadies me with one arm. We take off running along the edge of the putrid water. It's dimly lit, but light enough to allow us to slip along at a faster pace than when we were walking by phone light. The air reeks but as I scurry on the slick, brick stones, I feel so close to freedom that I don't care about the smell.

Suddenly, there's a strange shift in the air.

"Is it me or does the air smell different here?" Jake asks, pausing to study a rickety metal ladder.

"That's not necessarily a bad thing," I mutter, and my gaze follows the ladder climbing up to a grate in the ceiling.

"Let's see if that grate is unlocked," Jake says.

He scampers up the ladder, and to my relief, the grate lifts up. He squeezes himself through the opening and then peers down at me from above.

He waves. "Come on up. It's safe."

I don't need to be convinced. I scramble up the rungs and crawl into what looks like a storage room. Boxes are stacked on shelves and large burlap bags fill the center of the room.

"Where are we?" I ask. "And why does this place smell like chocolate?"

THIRTEEN

THE CHOCOLATE SHOP

Jake pushes a crate over the grate we just came through, blocking the entrance. "Just to be safe," he says. "Can't hurt to watch our backs."

"Smart move." I scan the boxes stacked on the shelves. Each is labeled with a different type of chocolate. "Wow. This place has a lot of chocolate. Looks like we entered a storage room of some sort."

I pick out a bar of 70% cocoa, taking a deep whiff. It's got a rich, chocolatey scent that makes my stomach rumble. "Do you think they'd know if we ate a few?"

A grin passes across Jake's face. It's the first time I've seen him smile since we sat together at dinner in New York. He pushes back a strand of hair hanging over my face and then cups my cheeks with his hands. His blue eyes are warm, and he's looking at me with such intensity as if I'm the most important person in the world.

"When the Russian pointed that gun at you." He takes a shuddery breath and leans his forehead against mine. "I was about to lose my mind. I can't lose you, Aria. I'll do anything for you, you know that, right? We're going to survive this. Together."

"Together," I whisper back.

His lips find mine, soft, and yet, there's an intensity there. A passion that's ready to explode between the two of us. I reach up and trail my fingers along his arm and he sucks in a deep breath at my touch. His tongue slips into my mouth and I melt beneath his kisses. His hands drag along my shoulders and down my back, squeezing me tighter against him.

I sink in deeper to his kisses, letting the world around us fall away because right now we're here, together and safe. Maybe that's what happens when you realize you nearly died and have been given a second chance.

Someone shouts just on the other side of a shelf. I wrench myself free, gasping for air, flushed and disorientated.

"Someone's here," I whisper, my whole body tightening ramrod-straight.

We peek through the shelf. It's just a worker wearing an apron over a uniform. He's come into the storage area to grab a box while talking to another person through the opened door.

I let out a breath of relief and sag against the metal shelf.

"We need to find a place that's safe," Jake says. "Somewhere we can rest and eat without worrying about someone jumping out of nowhere ready to kill us."

I nod, taking deep breaths. "This must be some sort of store. If we can slip through that door, we can pretend we're just shopping."

Slowly we creep up to the door that's still cracked open. I dart through it and step into what feels like a completely different world.

I blink a few times, trying to orientate myself. One wall is lined with bamboo stalks where chocolate bars of all different types are shelved in neat stacks. Baskets dangle from the ceiling and quaint signs hang about the room. A large tree with beans hanging from it rises in the center of the store. It must be a cocoa tree.

Jake takes my hand while I snag a shopping basket stacked against the wall. We begin strolling around the room, pretending we're shoppers.

"We could be Americans on holiday," I tell Jake. "Or two college students studying history."

"Two vagabond Americans," Jake mutters.

A mirror to our right gives me a glimpse of what I look like, and it's a little shocking. My clothes are dusty, and my cheek is smeared with black soot. I stop to pull out a cobweb from my hair.

"You might be right about the vagabond part," I whisper. "I look like I just emerged from the garbage bin."

"Whatever. You look like a badass." Jake squeezes my hand. "Because you totally are."

We wander to a table covered by a geometric-shaped pattern tablecloth. Cocoa beans and chocolate pieces fill different wooden platters. Small white teacups are set out, ready for visitors to try the cacao tea samples.

"Hello, there," one of the workers greets us with a smile. "Would you like to try our chocolate?"

All of it, I think hungrily. "That would be great," I say and pop a piece into my mouth. It melts on my tongue, rich and creamy.

We both sample the cacao tea, but the reality is we need water. Like a lot of water. My throat is dry and dusty.

"Is there a place where we could buy a lot of this?" I ask. "And food. We're starving."

The worker points to the back of the shop. "Our cacao cafe has all your chocolate needs."

"Gracias," I say.

We find the bar at the back and discover they have all sorts of food. We order a bag of empanadas to go and water bottles along with a stack of chocolate. As much as I'd love to sit down and eat under the cute cocoa trees, I know we need to get as far from this place as we can.

"Where is a good place to stay that's affordable?" Jake asks the cashier as he pays for the food.

"There are many close by." The cashier pulls out a flier that's written in both Spanish and English. "This brochure lists all the hotels and restaurants in this area."

"Thanks," Jake says, taking the bag.

I grab an empanada and practically inhale it in two bites as we head toward the front of the shop. I peek out of the window. I don't know what to expect, but I know we aren't necessarily safe. The Russians could be following us. Experience has unfortunately taught me this.

"The Hotel Diamond is close," Jake says, after studying the map. "Five-minute walk maybe? That might be a good option."

"Is that too close? They might check out the place."

"Wherever we go, we just need to hope they'll take cash and not ask for our passports."

I bite my cracked lips. "I hadn't thought of that."

Jake does a quick count of the wad of cash we've collected. "Looks like our Russian buddies are paying for tonight's hotels and food. But we don't have much. We have a day or two before we'll run out."

I pull out the phone I stole. "I'll try to call Dad again." I dial the number and wait, listening to it ring over and over. When no one answers, I try to leave a message, but the mailbox is full. "Why isn't he answering?" I ask Jake in frustration.

"That's not a good sign."

My chest tightens in worry. Quickly, I stab in Sun's number next. It only rings twice and suddenly, I hear Sun's voice on the other line.

"Tell me this is Aria," Sun says.

I close my eyes in relief. Just hearing her voice calms my racing heart. "Sun! I'm so glad you answered."

"Aria!" Sun practically yells. "What the hell is going on? Where are you? That message you left me on Insta is freaking me out."

"We're in trouble." I glance around the store making sure no one is listening. "I can't get in touch with my parents and the embassy...it's not safe either."

"This is all bad. Why are you in Lima? I don't understand."

"Lau. She kidnapped us. We escaped but now there's this other person who seems to want us too. Some Russian guy named Sadir Gesner."

"We should get moving," Jake whispers to me. "We've been here too long. It can't be good."

"Danny and I will come get you." Sun's voice sounds breathless like she's walking quickly.

"Sun, no," I say. "I can't ask that of you. I just need..."

"I already asked Danny after I got your message. He says he's getting the jet prepped. You know I have a beef with Lau, maybe even more than you do. She's messed with the wrong family. Also, I just got off the phone with your mom."

"I was too scared to call her," I say. "They're watching her. You need to be careful, too."

"I am, but she's worried sick."

I press my fingers to my temples. "Please tell her I love her."

"I will. Where are you?"

"We're going to stay at the Hotel Diamond," I say and give her the address. "But we don't have passports or much money. And I need to get rid of this phone, too. I don't know if it's traceable or not."

"Right," Sun says. "Stay low and I'll be at the Hotel Diamond by morning. We'll get you out of there. I'll try to get your passport. Hang tight. And yeah, definitely get rid of that phone."

Tears edge my eyes. "Thanks, Sun. You're the best friend."

"Oh, girl. We're so much more than friends. We're family. And family sticks together. Now stay safe."

I hang up and look over at Jake. He rubs his forehead like he does when he's thinking hard.

"You're right," he says. "That phone is probably traceable."

"Should we throw it out or destroy it?"

Jake stares out the window and then the corner of his lips curls up. "No. We get it as far from where we are as possible. Come on."

He heads through the door with me trailing after him. He runs up to a bus stop and then turns to me. "I'm going to hide this somewhere on the next bus. You find a way to hold the bus from moving, and then we'll get right back off."

"Look at you." I grin. "All espionage and sneaky."

A bus rumbles up, and the moment the doors swing open, Jake rushes inside. I step onto the first stair.

"Excuse me," I say to the driver. "Do you know where this bus goes to?"

The driver shakes his head, obviously not understanding my English.

"I'm looking for other cool places to tour in Lima," I continue, pretending I don't see his frustration. "Maybe you have some recommendations?"

Before the guy answers, Jake scampers back down the bus aisle and joins me in getting off the bus. The driver says something about Americans, obviously frustrated, and shuts the door. I watch the bus take off, heading in the opposite direction we're going, and my shoulders relax in relief.

"That was a good idea," I say. "Although it's hard knowing we just got rid of our one means of communication."

"We just need to make it until Sun gets here," he says and takes my hand.

We clip down the street, trying to blend in as best as we can, but the reality is my red hair sticks out like a sore thumb here. If only we were in the Dreamscape, and I could change my hair color.

Finally, we arrive at the hotel. It's a rectangular building set on the edge of the street with the front made entirely of glass windows. Inside is a lobby of white marble floors, leather couches, and turquoise chairs that overlook the street outside.

Thankfully, the attendant doesn't require our passports for check-in and takes the cash without blinking an eye. We head to the room, and the moment the door shuts behind us, my muscles relax. Suddenly, I'm so tired I think I could collapse on the wooden floor and not even care.

"Uh-oh. Only one bed." Jake nods to the king-sized bed filling the center of the room. "I forgot to request for two."

"Oh." I glance at Jake and notice his smirk. "Are you sure you forgot, or did you do this on purpose?"

"Or maybe I just wanted to keep you safe," he says, grinning.

"Right." I roll my eyes. "I'm going to take a shower."

"Do you think you'll be safe in there alone?" He moves to follow me, his smile widening.

"Nice try, buddy." I push him back and shut the door in his face so he can't see me laughing.

"I'll sleep on the floor," Jake yells to me through the bathroom door.

"Good," I yell back, trying to calm my racing heart. It's one thing to be traveling with a guy that I'm head over heels for, but a whole different thing staying the night in the same room.

I know that's what we did in the Philippians, but things are so much different between us now. It's almost like I was a different person then.

But what do I tell him? Sleep on the floor even though you were shot less than forty-eight hours ago? Or, it's okay for you to jump in bed with me because you're super-hot, especially without a shirt.

I shake away those thoughts and step into the shower. The hot water runs over me, washing away the grime of the catacombs and spider webs clinging to my hair. It's the most wonderful feeling, and I just stand there as the pounding water soothes and relaxes my tense muscles. The hotel shampoo smells like sandalwood, and as I rub it over my body, its scent calms me. It's the first time that I've been able to let myself relax since before the Night Show interview in New York City.

My mind starts processing everything since that interview. How did this all even happen to us? Dad had been so careful and even the police had been involved in ensuring our safety. More than anything, I want Sun to get here and take Jake and me back home to safety. Except, will we ever really be safe?

Sadir's men obviously wanted me alive. I mean, they could've shot me at any moment, and they didn't.

But why?

Unless there are still glitches in Reasner's Dreamscape that Sadir stole. After all, that's why Reasner initially kidnapped Dad and took him to Macau, China. Because he needed Dad to fix and finish the Dreamscape.

Which would also mean that to find out what the issues are with the Dreamscape, Sadir would need to rescan my brain. That's the only reason I can think this is all happening.

I press my fingers over my eyes, trying to shut out the memories of being in Reasner's Dreamscape in China. The feeling of being shot and thinking I would die. And then Jake and I agreeing to destroy the program, knowing full well that we could also be destroying our brains in the process.

It had been worth it because that was the only way of escape for us. It was either that or allow our minds to slowly be altered and destroyed in the Dreamscape. But isn't that exactly what's happening to those agents that Operative Joe had been talking about? Right now they're stuck in that Dreamscape, unable to escape until they give over precious intel.

And who knows how much more time they have before their minds give up the information that could potentially threaten millions of people's lives? I let out a shuddered breath, hating that I'm feeling responsible for all of this. I know it's not my responsibility, but I can't let go of the fact that I'm a part of all this. The problem and maybe even the solution.

If I don't destroy this copy now, it will never end. Someone will always try to use it for their own selfish reasons.

How did Dad's brilliant scientific discovery go from saving people's memories to using it as interrogation tactics? Even now, he's still working on his original version, and he's so close to finding the way to unlock a person's memory vault. My stomach clenches thinking about Grams, and I lean against the shower, letting the water pound against my shoulders. She was the reason we started all of this. How can Dad and I possibly help her when we have this threat hanging over our heads? Her time is running out, too. Every day we delay in our work, her memories are slipping away.

Finally, I turn off the water and dry myself off, pushing away the million worries that snap at the edge of my mind. I need stop worrying and take time to prepare myself for what tomorrow brings. Because I need to be one hundred percent ready for anything that I'm faced with.

Once I'm finished, I wrap myself in a towel and step out of the room, feeling like a new person. Jake is arranging a blanket and a pillow on the floor. He looks up at me and lets out a long breath. "Wow."

"What?" I ask, frowning. "Everything okay?"

"You're um... yeah. Great. You look...great."

"Oh." Suddenly I feel my cheeks flush, and I look down at my bare toes. "My clothes are nasty. I couldn't think about putting them back on. I was going to call the front desk and see if I can get them washed here."

"Right. Great idea." He swallows. "I should do the same. I'm going to shower now."

I step aside to let him in and try not to think about him in the shower. Or without his clothes. My whole body warms. What am I even thinking? I clear my throat and go to the phone, determined to stay on task.

I call up the front desk and request for laundry service. Then I find the laundry bag in the closet and put my clothes into it.

I knock on the bathroom door when the water from the shower has been turned off. "Jake," I say. "I'm putting a bag outside of the bathroom door. Put your clothes in it and then set it…"

Before I can finish, Jake throws open the door. Steam rolls out, drifting over me, smelling of sandalwood and soap. Except it's suddenly hard to breathe. Because Jake is standing before me wrapped only with a towel around his waist. His blond hair is damp, hanging over his eyes and water still glistens over his toned chest.

"Hey," he says softly.

My brain spins, trying to remember what I was going to say. Clothes. Bag. I grab it, trying to still keep my towel tightly wrapped around me, and hand it over to him. "Your dirty clothes."

He takes it with a lopsided smile. "Thanks."

"Just put it outside in the hall by the door. House-keeping will pick it up." I back up, knowing I need to put space between the two of us because more than anything I want to close that space.

To feel his body against mine. His lips on my skin. His hands trailing across my back.

I spin around and practically launch myself into the bed. It's huge, wide enough for me to lie in any direction and still not reach either end. I tuck the covers around me, soaking in their soft coolness. The door to our room opens and closes and then Jake is back inside and walking over to his place on the floor.

Suddenly, the fear that some Russian or Lau with her henchmen might suddenly come bursting into our room clenches my chest. And even though I know there's no way they could find us here, I'm still paranoid.

"Did you bolt the door?" I ask, fingering the edge of the sheet.

"Yep."

"Maybe we should move something in front of the door to block it," I suggest. "Just for an extra safety precaution."

He lifts his eyebrows and looks around the room. "The only possibility is the dresser. Except, it looks like it doesn't want to move."

He has a point. The dresser is large and from the wooden construction, it looks heavy. Still, there isn't much else to move other than a single small chair. "We could try?"

"Bring over those muscles, Supergirl."

I slip out of the bed and try to secure the towel tighter. It's not really cooperating, I think blushing as I twist and adjust it. Jake just chuckles and shakes his head at me but joins me at the far end, and together we push it across the carpet, so the other end butts up against the door. I check the door and try to open it as a test. Thankfully, the dresser holds the door securely in place.

"Happy now?" Jake asks.

"Very." I give him a satisfied smile and clamor back into the bed while Jake settles on the floor. I lie there for a few minutes staring up at the ceiling, wondering how Jake is doing sleeping on the floor. So, I sit back up and peer over the edge of the bed. "Are you okay down there?"

He grins at me and gives me a thumbs up.

"Make sure you don't lie on the carpet. There could be bugs or stuff in it."

"If I get bitten up, you can be responsible for rubbing cream on me tomorrow. The positive is it's not as hard as the wooden floor in the Philippines' bungalow."

I bite my lip. "I feel awful that you're sleeping on the floor. Why don't you sleep in the bed? We could put a pillow between us."

"A bed does sound nice." Obviously, he needed zero coaxing because before I have a chance to blink, he's bounding into the mattress.

"Just don't let that towel come off," I warn.

He chuckles as he tosses the covers over him. Then he cradles his hands behind his head on the pillow, saying, "Don't worry. I'll behave. Besides, I'm an injured guy so you have the upper hand."

He points to where he got shot. I frown and move to lie on my side, staring at the stitches that run along his arm. "Does it still hurt?"

"A little." His face turns more serious. "But it could've been a lot worse. I got lucky the bullet just grazed me."

Unable to resist, I reach out and trail my finger over the bandage. "I'm sorry you got dragged into all of this. Your life really got messed up the moment you stepped through MaxLife's doors. It's not fair."

Now it's his turn to turn sideways and face me. "That's the farthest from the truth. The reality is my life started the moment you entered my dream. I wouldn't go back and change a single thing."

He takes my hand and kisses my fingers. My heart skitters at his touch. Then he leans in closer, and his lips find mine. It's a sweet, tender kiss. One promising of his love for me. I know we've never verbalized our feelings, but I know it's there. We've proven it over and over. And I have no doubts about how I feel about him.

Maybe now is the time to tell him.

"Jake," I say, pulling back and sucking a deep breath.

He frowns and a flash of hurt washes over his face. "What's wrong? Should I put the pillow in place?"

"We've been through...a lot to say the least. And honestly, after everything that has happened so far, I can't know what tomorrow will bring us or if we even have a tomorrow. So I wanted to tell you that well... I love you. You've not only been there for me through literal life and death situations, but you're someone who I can't stand the thought of ever losing."

A warmth fills his blue eyes, changing them to the color of midnight. "I feel the same way, Aria. I love you, too. So much. You know that I'd do anything for you, right? And I'll do everything in my power to make sure you get back home."

His hand caresses my cheek as his eyes stare into mine. Then his hand trails down my neck and arm as he kisses me again, this time with more intensity. His tongue slips inside my mouth, sweeping across every inch of it. I'm breathless as his lips move down my neck and he softly kisses my bare skin on my shoulders.

My hands slip into his hair, pulling him closer so our hearts are beating as one.

I don't know what tomorrow will bring, but I know that amid all this pain and terror, I've found someone who makes it all worth it.

I'm woken by a ringing sound. My nerves leap into hyper-awareness, and I jerk to sit straight up in bed. It takes me a few hazy seconds to realize it's coming from the room's phone. At first, I hesitate. I mean who could be calling our room?

A peek to my left confirms that Jake is soundly sleeping through the phone ringing.

"Some watch keeper you are," I mumble at him.

But I close my hand over the receiver and answer the phone, crossing my fingers that this is the right choice and there won't be a voice thick with a Russian accent on the other end.

"Hello," I say tentatively.

"Good morning, Ms. Congeniality," a man's voice says on the other line.

Ms. Congeniality? Then I roll my eyes, remembering

that's the name Jake gave the receptionist when we checked in. Ever since I made him watch that old movie twice, he's been teasing me about it.

"There's someone here you would like to speak—"

He's cut off as someone else jumps on the call. "Tell me I flew all the way from Florida and arrived in time."

I sag against my pillow. "Sun," I breathe. "Thank god, you're here."

"Are you still in bed?" she asks, her voice rising in skepticism. "Because I was expecting you to be waiting in the lobby ready to bolt."

"I uh—" I secure my towel and toss off my covers, swinging my feet to the floor. "No. Absolutely not. Jake and I were just waiting patiently for you."

I glance over at Jake who's just blinking awake. Then his mouth crinkles as he holds back a laugh as I fumble with keeping the towel secure and managing to hold the phone that's got an extremely short cord.

"Riight," Sun drawls out, and I know she's not believing a single word I'm saying. "Just get down here pronto. Oh, wait. The receptionist says your clothes should be arriving at your room any minute. Now I see how it is."

She giggles, and I hear Tony beside her whistling.

"It's not like that!" I say, which I'm sure only makes things sound worse. "Nothing happened!"

Meanwhile, Jake sits up and stretches, completely

distracting me from my argument. He really does have great abs.

"So how was your niiiight?" Sun's voice has suddenly switched to sing-song and teasing.

"I think I hear someone at the door," I say. "Got to go. See you soon!"

I hang up, eager to end this conversation, get myself out of this towel, and safely back home.

ONCE DRESSED, Jake and I leave the room and head down the corridor. I try not to think about how less than twenty-four hours ago, we were being chased through a similar hallway at the JW Marriott by men with guns.

"How are you feeling today?" Jake asks, pressing the elevator button.

"Better, I guess. I know it sounds silly but having that dresser in front of the door helped me sleep better." I step inside the elevator and push LOBBY. "But honestly, I don't know if things will ever be the same again. Just because we're back in Florida, it doesn't mean we will be safe."

He steps closer to me and places his hands on my arms, leaning his forehead against mine. "Yeah, those were my thoughts, too. Will we ever be safe? I don't know if I can live like this. Always worried you could be kidnapped, or someone comes to you with a request that they have no right to be asking of you."

The doors to the elevator slide open, and there, waiting on the other side, stands Tony and Sun. Tony's wearing one of his Hawaiian shirts and sneakers. His arms are crossed, and he's got this massive I-knew-it grin on his face.

Meanwhile, Sun is dressed in a smart, chic black suit with a gorgeous silver necklace and spiked heels. Her shiny, dark hair frames her face. She looks like she's an executive ready to land a big merger or sign a multi-million dollar deal. Her eyebrows are raised, and her lip is quirked up.

"Now I see what you two have been up to," she says. "Are you sure you don't want me to delay your rescue mission?"

"Sun! Tony!" I race out of the elevator and give them both hugs. "You have no idea how glad we are to see you."

"You two are our heroes," Jake says as we head to the lobby. "I don't know what we would do without your help."

"Javier came along for the ride, too," Sun says and points to him sitting in the lobby's alcove. "Danny stayed at the airport and is working on the flight details for the ride home."

Upon seeing us, Javier rises and shakes his head like he can't believe we're actually here. Even though we're not at work, he still feels like he's our boss, and from the look on his face, I can tell he's worried.

As usual, he's wearing jeans and a button-down shirt, but one big difference is that he's grown a goatee.

"Amigos," he says as he gives us a hug. "Why is it that trouble keeps finding you?"

"You've grown a goatee," I point out, avoiding his question. "It actually looks good on you."

He rubs his chin. "Gracias. I might keep it for a while. It's a whole lot easier to manage than you two. Have a seat and tell us exactly what's going on and what happened."

We all settle down in the alcove, and Jake and I tell them everything that has happened so far.

"Man." Tony whistles in shock. "That is some serious stuff that went down. I can't believe you got shot!"

Jake rubs his arm as if mentioning the wound brings back the pain. "It could've been a whole lot worse, and Lau's nurse did good work stitching me up. But I'm definitely still not 100%."

"I just don't get why they had to kidnap you to get the information on her husband's whereabouts," Javier says. "Why drag you all the way here and not hire professionals to find him?"

"She's on all my blacklists," Sun mutters, drumming her manicured nails on the seat's armrest.

"You have more than one?" Jake jokes.

"She tried hiring people but hadn't gotten results," I explain. "That's why she had me go into the Dreamscape.

She wanted to see if I could get the facility's location from a guy they were interrogating."

"That is messed up!" Tony says. "Your father didn't design the Dreamscape for this sort of thing."

Sun takes my hand. "I'm so sorry you had to do that."

"I didn't find out much from Locket—he's the guy's dream I went into. Only that I should ask for Mono and then I'll know the way."

"Mono?" Javier asks. "That is an odd thing to say."

"Right? So of course that got us nowhere. But then I was yanked out of the dream when Locket was killed."

"No!" Sun gasps. "You were in his dream when he was killed? How did you find your way out?"

"It's like I was booted out." I grimace. "But when I came out of Locket's dream, Lau's hotel room was under attack by a guy named Sadir Gesner."

"That name sounds familiar." Javier frowns and pulls out a laptop from his bag beside him.

"From what I could make out," I say. "He came to kill Locket so the guy wouldn't talk and then take me. His men managed to steal the tracker Lau planted on us and follow us."

"Since they didn't shoot Aria," Jake adds, "we think they need her for something."

"Maybe something is malfunctioning with the Dreamscape they stole from Reasner," I offer.

"Which is why they'd need you," Javier says. "To rescan your brain."

"Exactly," I say. "And the way these Russians were hunting us down, I don't think they'll stop searching for me until they get what they want."

"So what you're saying is they'll follow us to Florida," Sun says with a groan, leaning back in her chair.

"Or anywhere." Jake scrunches his face up as if just saying that out loud makes him sick to his stomach.

Then I explain what Operative Joe told me about the U.S. agents and Lau's husband.

"I just looked this guy up," Javier says, still staring at his computer. "Sadir is a wealthy Russian obsessed with power. He's been bent on trying to become Russia's next leader but failed on every attempt."

"Sounds like the perfect guy to be getting attention from," Tony says sarcastically.

"From what I can tell," Javier continues. "Since he can't rule his own country, he plans on taking over another."

"Is that even possible?" I ask.

"And then there's another article here that says he's been excommunicated from Russia," Javier says. "And he bought some land in the Amazon to settle down."

"If I could get my hands on a computer," Jake says. "I could ask around and see what he's really up to. Maybe get some inside information."

"Here." Sun pulls out her tablet from her purse, unlocks it, and holds it up to him. "Just don't go through my stuff, got it?"

"Loud and clear, boss," he says, and she passes it to him with a stern look.

"When I was in Locket's dream." I wrap my arms around myself. "It looked exactly how I would imagine the Amazon to look like."

"What are you saying?" Sun asks. "That you think the facility that holds Lau's husband, and the U.S. agents is located in the Amazon?"

"It's a guess." I twist my hands, remembering each detail in the dream. The people shooting at us, the boat, the piranhas. "Honestly, it was more like a nightmare than a dream."

Sun takes my hand and squeezes it. "I'm sorry I asked."

"No, it's fine." I press my lips together. "That is nothing compared to what the U.S. agents are suffering right now if they're in Reasner's Dreamscape. Gesner's definitely taking torture to a whole new level. As much as I hate to say it, Operative Joe was right."

"What happened to him?" Sun asks.

"He got shot trying to protect us," Jakes says, grimly. "We don't even know if he survived. He was trying to rescue his team that was being held hostage by Sadir. Apparently, they know information the U.S. government can't afford to get into the wrong hands."

"Wow," Tony says. "So what will they do now?"

"No clue," I say. "But the real question is what will we do?"

"What do you mean?" Sun frowns. "What we're going to do is let the U.S. government worry about the hostages, jump on my plane, and go home."

"Uh oh." Jake looks up from Sun's tablet. "Bad news."

My heart sinks. "What is it now?"

"Someone sent me a message on my secure network this morning." He rubs the back of his neck. "It says to hand over Aria, or they'll start killing everyone on the list they sent me one by one."

"What?" I leap to my feet. "Who sent it to you? Why?"

"It's from Sadir. And the worst part is every one of you is on this list."

SIXTEEN
DISSECTING THE CLUES

"I don't care if Sadir has me on his hit list," Tony says. "There's no way I'm helping the dude. We need to protect Aria at all costs, not put her in more danger."

"True, but now all of our lives are at stake," Javier points out. "Did he give a deadline when he wanted us to hand over Aria?"

"By midnight in two days." Jake rubs his head. "At that point, he'll start killing us off one by one on the hour."

"He acts like he's some god that can just kill us with the snap of his fingers." Sun rolls her eyes. "There's no way he can follow through with that."

"You can't risk your lives for me," I say. "I won't have that. So the way I see it is, I'll turn myself in, they'll scan my brain, and then we'll all be free from these schemes."

"Except for the fact that once he gets his Dreamscape

up and running again properly," Javier says. "He'll use it to gather intel and gain more power right here in the Americas. This kind of technology is unprecedented."

"Not to mention that there's no way I'm letting you turn yourself in," Sun says. "There's no guarantee he will release you and leave you alone after you help him."

"Agreed." Jake nods, typing furiously on Sun's laptop. "One of my guys on the Dark Web says he thinks he can get us more information on Sadir. We'll see if he comes up with anything."

"People! We need to send that list to the feds like yesterday." Tony leaps to his feet. "They need to know what's going on."

"On it," Jake says. "But keep in mind that Sadir is safely tucked away in another country out of their reach and jurisdiction."

"Besides," I add. "I'm sure the dude's already on their hit list, and they've been searching for him based on what Operative Joe was telling us. You know things are bad when the U.S. government is coming to me to try to get this guy's location."

"I say we head to the airport and get back to the United States," Sun says. "Then we can figure out how to deal with Sadir."

"If only we knew where Sadir was holding those hostages." I start pacing in front of the couch. "Then we'd know where his Dreamscape was being kept. If we could find this place, we could release the prisoners and destroy the Dreamscape. Then he wouldn't have any chances of fixing it or rebuilding it."

"Are you serious?" Javier asks. "You're really thinking of finding that place? Aria, you know I want to keep you safe, but that's like the least safe thing you could do."

"We're not equipped to rescue hostages," Tony adds. "Like I can hardly rescue my cat when she gets herself stuck in the cabinet."

"We're so over our heads with this," Sun agrees.

"What exactly did Locket tell you in the dream?" Jake asks, looking up from the computer. "He said for you to ask for Mono, right?"

"That's right." I close my eyes, trying to pull back the memory. "We were kayaking to an island, and he said, 'If I don't make it. Ask for Mono. Then you'll find your way.' Do you think there really is a person named Mono?"

"Maybe." Jake starts typing again, his forehead creased in concentration. "I'll do a search and see if there's a connection between Sadir and that name."

"Something that might help," Javier says, rubbing his goatee. "Mono can mean monkey in Spanish."

"Monkey?" Sun asks. "How's that helpful?"

"What might help." Tony rises to his feet and swivels in a circle, searching the lobby. "Is if we could get some food. I'm starving and I can't think properly on an empty stomach."

"You're not the only one, man," Jake agrees, rubbing his stomach. "Okay, so my preliminary search doesn't bring up any connection between the names Mono and Sadir."

I suck in a gasp as a new idea hits me. "Wait. What if the island Locket was trying to get to was actually the *place*? A place where Sadir's secret facility is located. Maybe Locket was being cryptic when he said *finding* Mono would help me find my way. Jake, look and see if there are any places in the Amazon called Mono."

"On it." Jake's fingers fly over Sun's laptop. "That said, if I had more time or a faster computer, I'd get better and quicker results."

"I found something." Javier looks up from his laptop. "Except it might be nothing."

"What is it?" I drop onto the couch beside him.

"There's an island in the middle of the rainforest." Javier points to an article. "It's called Monkey Island."

"Monkey Island?" Sun scoffs. "Sounds like a tourist trap. Locket was either pulling your chain or was dreaming about his favorite travel destination."

"It is famous for its monkeys," Javier agrees.

"Are there any pictures of it?" I ask. "I wonder if it would look at all like the place I was at in Locket's dream."

Javier clicks on Google's image tab. Instantly, I'm met with images of a small island overflowing with palms and brush, free of beaches or any sort of habitation. Its coast is steep and the land drops directly into the dark waters of a river. My skin grows cold, and I pull the computer closer to me so I can get a better view.

Not that I need to. Because there's no doubt in my mind that this is the very same place that Locket was trying to take me to in the dream.

"That's it," I whisper. "That's the island in Locket's dream."

"Let me see it," Jake says, and when I turn the computer to face him as well as Sun and Tony, they're all silent, first assessing the image and then me.

"But what if it's not?" Tony finally breaks the silence. "I mean there's got to be a lot of islands in the Amazon rainforest, right?"

"Considering the Amazon is over 1.6 billion acres," Jake says. "Yeah, a lot."

"It could be a coincidence," Javier says, but he's got this weird edge to his voice. He knows me, and he also knows my hunches have always been right on target.

"I don't get why we're even having this conversation," Sun says. "Why bother finding the place when we're obviously returning to Florida?"

"After we get some food," Tony points out.

"Except maybe we're not supposed to go back yet," I say. "Maybe we need to put an end to all of this once and for all."

"You can't be serious!" Sun exclaims. "We don't even

know what we're doing. We're scientists. Dream therapists. We aren't secret agents who can go on missions and rescue people."

"Hold up," Jake interrupts. "One of my contacts on the Dark Web just sent me a photo. It's of Sadir. And he was last spotted in Puerto de Maldonado."

"I take it it's not in Florida," Sun says, dryly.

"It's a town on the edge of the Amazon Rainforest." Javier shakes his head as he studies something on his computer. "Not far from Monkey Island by the looks of it. Maybe an hour boat trip."

"See?" I leap to my feet. "We're onto something here! Do you want us to be looking over our shoulders for the rest of our lives? Wondering who they will kill next just so they can get me? I lost count of how many times they've tried to kill Jake and I barely escaped being captured. Not to mention that Lau kidnapped me already, which is why I'm even here. It's only a matter of time before they are successful. We don't have time for the U.S. government to come and save us. We have to act now."

My voice has risen and the staff at the receptionist counter has glanced up to stare at me. I lick my lips, settle back onto the couch, and lower my voice. "I vote that we go on the offensive. We scope out this island and see if Sadir's facility is there. If it is, we let the U.S. government know what we've found so they can go in, destroy the Dreamscape, and rescue the hostages. Sadir still thinks

Jake and I are here in Lima, which means we'll be the last people they will be expecting at their door."

The four of them stare at me like I've grown a second head covered in eyeballs.

"So who's in?" I ask. "Because I think it's time we took this party to the Amazon."

SEVENTEEN
PLANS IN THE MAKING

Our group is quiet as the taxi bumps and zigzags through the streets of Lima. After our long discussion, we put it to a vote. Everyone except Sun was in favor of heading to the Amazon Forest to investigate the situation and gain surveillance. She ended up agreeing with us with the condition that if we do discover Sadir's facility, we provide the U.S. government with evidence of where he's at.

It's a start in the right direction.

My head still spins from the enormity of our decision, and yet, there's a sense of relief threading through me knowing this will give me the chance to make everything right. At least, I hope it will.

In the end, hunger is what spurs us to head out of the hotel and grab a taxi.

"I want to get us out of the historical district," Sun

says, breaking the silence. "We need to leave the area your pursuers last saw you."

"I'm good with that as long as we can find a place with food sooner than later," I add, my stomach rumbling.

"Agreed," Jake says. "Aria and I haven't eaten a solid meal in days."

"Good point," Javier says, and then talks to the driver in Spanish. "I asked for our driver to take us to a place near food and where we can shop for a computer for you Jake."

"Can I use your phone, Sun?" I ask. "I want to call my dad and mom."

"Of course!" She hands me the phone and I stare at it for a moment, preparing for what I'm going to say.

I try calling my dad first, but I'm sent to voicemail.

"Dad," I say, leaving him another message. "I know you said you're going to try to come get me. I can't get a hold of you, but I wanted you to know that Sun and the gang are here. We're going to use her plane to check out a lead we got. I don't want to say much in case someone hacked your phone messages. We're just going to do a little surveillance, but don't worry, we'll stay safe."

I lick my lips, knowing that hearing this message will make him worried. "Please call this number when you get this, okay?"

I dial Mom next.

"Sun!" she answers. "Tell me you found her."

"Mom!" Tears spring to my eyes, hearing her voice. "It's me. Aria."

"Oh, my sweet, baby girl. Are you on your way home? How are you doing? Tell me you're okay."

"Be careful," Jake warns me. "Lau or even Sadir probably has your family's phone tapped."

I think about the video Lau showed me of Mom working in her garden. If they have video surveillance on her, the odds are heavily in favor that they are listening to this conversation right now.

"I'm good," I tell Mom. "And safe. We are planning on coming home really soon. I tried calling Dad, too, but I couldn't get a hold of him."

"He's been frantic. In fact, he's flying to Lima right now to go find you. As soon as he heard what happened, he's been doing everything he can to try to get to you."

Tears stream down my cheeks, thinking about both my parents worrying.

"Can you tell Dad that we think Sadir Gesner has a copy of Reasner's Dreamscape? That's what this is all about."

"I will," she says. "When should I pick you up at the airport?"

I bit my lip, hating that I can't tell her the full truth. "I don't think it's safe for me to say anything on the phone. But I'll see if there's a way I can get a message to you."

"Be careful, okay? I love you, and I'll be praying for you to get back home safely."

"Thanks, Mom. I love you, too."

I hang up. Everyone in the car is silent as the gravity of what we are doing hits home.

"I guess I should call my parents, too." Jake cringes as if he's worried about what to tell them. I hand him the phone and he says, "Wish me luck."

THIRTY MINUTES LATER, we stop at a small restaurant. Its exterior is painted in a cheery, bright orange with umbrella tables scattered about outside. Scents of grilled meat and steamed rice wash over me. My stomach rumbles from hunger as we step through its doors.

"I'm so hungry," I mutter. "I'll think much clearer once I get some food in me."

Upbeat music plays over the speakers as we cross the tiled floor and settle down at a quiet table at the back of the restaurant. Picture frames clutter yellow-painted walls and the wooden beams running across the ceiling remind me of the old section of the city we just left.

A server bustles over bringing water with freshly squeezed lime slices and piping hot fried plantains. After she takes our orders, I eagerly gulp down the water and gobble down a plantain in a few bites, licking my fingers of the juicy sweetness.

Once the server leaves, Javier pulls out his laptop.

"If we're going to do this," he says. "We need a plan of action and supplies before we leave. Puerto de Maldonado might be a good-sized town, but it definitely won't have what we will need. I talked to our driver, and we're not far from Cyberplaza, which will be a great place to pick up cell phones for Aria and Jake as well as a computer for Jake."

"How are we going to get the money for this kind of stuff?" Tony asks.

"I'll take care of it," Sun says, rising from her seat. "But first, I need to call Danny and let him know about the change of plans. Or more likely, convince him of it."

She ducks into a corner as she makes the call to her brother.

"Cyberplaza sounds like it will work." Jake polishes off the last plantain. "My biggest priority is a solid laptop and internet access. If I can have that, I have a better chance of seeing what we're dealing with. And if we do find the facility, I'll need something that can hack into the system and investigate how secure their alarm system is. The more information we can pass on to the government, the better so we all know what we're dealing with."

"We'll need appropriate clothing to blend in," I add.

"Don't forget snacks," Tony says with a grin. "But also, add in bolt cutters to your list in case we have fences to get through."

Javier does, but adds, "We shouldn't need to if we do this right."

"Radios because I doubt there's going to be good data out there," Jake says. "Flashlights, a drone to get surveillance of the area—I recommend the Blue Jay drone —and I remember reading about MTA hair clips, which have all the supplies we might need in case things go wrong."

"Wait." Javier pauses from his notes. "Did you just say hair clips?"

"I was reading about them when I was studying up on gadgets Batman might use."

"Batman?" Tony lifts his eyebrows at Jake, lips quirking as he leans back in his chair.

"Laugh all you want." Jake tips back in his chair. "But these small hair clips also double as a ruler, screwdriver, trolley coin, and cutter. Trust me. If you get yourself in a bind, you'll be wanting one of these."

"As long as they come in fuchsia," Tony says, grinning.

"I'm adding it to the list." Javier sighs. "But the likelihood of you all finding specialized hair clips and whatever brand drones you are dreaming of is about as far-fetched as me getting a vacation in Fiji."

"Did someone say vacation in Fiji?" Sun asks as she pockets her phone and slips back into her seat. "Because that sounds good right about now."

"How did your conversation go with Danny?" I ask.

"Not well." Sun shakes her head and then sips her drink. "Danny isn't happy, but when I mentioned that Lau was involved, he agreed. So when you see him, best keep quiet about the Sadir business. If Danny gets a whiff of danger from this, he's going to turn his plane around and head back to the States. Got it?"

We all nod in agreement.

"He's getting the plane fueled up and the flight plan ready," she continues. "If all goes smoothly, and the flight is approved, we should be able to take off this afternoon. It's about an hour and a half flight to Puerto de Maldonado."

Once the food arrives, everyone quiets, focusing on the early lunch. Javier ordered ceviche and shares it with the group. It has a light, refreshing taste to the fish with a bit of spice to it. I'm surprised at how nicely the citrus and cilantro pair with the shrimp.

Meanwhile, Tony and Jake both dig into their lomo saltado, a stir-fried beef meal of marinated sirloin strips, onions, and peppers along with thick, golden French fries. My meal is a simple one of seasoned chicken, steamed rice, and vegetables flavored in freshly squeezed lime. It might be the best meal I've ever had; I am that hungry.

Sun picks at her food. From the crease on her forehead, I can tell she's worried. Which I get after everything we've all been through.

Once I'm finished eating, my head clears, allowing me to think better. I start running through all the situations that we'll be facing on our trip.

"We'll need to book accommodations," I say, "preferably somewhere that's hidden away where we can use a different name and pay cash."

"Good point," Javier says. "I'll do some research and find a place for us to stay and book it. In the meantime, there's a shopping area not far from Cyberplaza where I think we'll find some of the other supplies we'll need. How about you all head that way and we can meet back up here in an hour."

"Should we split up to save time?" I ask. "We could divvy up the list that way."

"I don't like the idea of splitting up." Jake sets his fork down, a pained expression filling his face. "If anything were to happen to you—"

"I'll be careful," I say. "Besides, right now, Sadir and Lau's people have no idea where we are."

"Except that's what we thought that last time we got away," Jake says. "Until we found those trackers."

"That might be true, but I'm feeling like time isn't on our side," Sun adds. "If we want to fly out this afternoon, we need to make the best use of every moment. Which means splitting up."

"I say, Tony and Jake, you head to Cyberplaza and pick up the electronics we need," Javier says, taking on our team leader role in stride. "Aria and Sun, you two gather up everything else. I'll stay here and work out all the hotel and airport pick-up logistics. Let's plan on rendezvousing back here in an hour."

"Sounds like a plan to me." Tony rubs his hands. "And if you ladies happen to spot some chips along the way, could you pick up a bag for me?"

"It depends on how much of my money you're spending today," Sun says dryly.

"It's good to have the Dream Team back," I say, staring around at my friends, glad to have them close. "Nothing, not even Sadir Gesner is going to stop us."

Sun and I make our way down the concrete sidewalk. Cars zip past us and a slight breeze rushes through the tiny, planted trees along the roadside. I can't help feeling jittery at every loud bus barreling past or honking car. I know that neither Sadir nor Lau's men are here, but after they were able to track us last time, I just can't put my guard down.

"You okay?" Sun asks, glancing worriedly at me. "You look a little jumpy."

I cross my arms and peer over my shoulder. "I guess after everything that happened these past few days, I'm not myself."

"That's totally to be expected. You both went through some serious stuff over the past few days." She wraps her arm around me and gives me a side squeeze as we head to the closest mini-mall, according to GPS.

This area has a mixture of quaint, Spanish-style buildings with fluted rooftops, arched windows, and cute balconies similar to what we saw in the downtown area. But there's also the addition of the more industrious and practical, flat-sided buildings void of decoration. We finally reach the mall and stride inside.

"You have the list?" I ask Sun.

She nods, pulling it out. At the top is Tony's handwriting scrawled in large letters: CHIPS!

"If we don't come back with chips," I say, "Tony is going to be so disappointed."

Sun snorts. "No kidding. He gets his hopes set on things too easily."

We step into a wide-open atrium filled with benches and small potted plants, and shops ringing its perimeter. Above, three floors circle the atrium, each level sporting different types of shops.

"There are so many places." I try to read the signs, all in Spanish. "Hard to know where to begin."

"When in doubt, just dive in."

And with that, we start our shopping. We comb through the racks, checking off each item and making sure the sizes are correct for our team members. We even find a suitcase to put the items inside.

"Wait a second." My whole body freezes as a terrible thought hits me. "If we're flying, Jake and I are going to need some sort of identification even if it's a domestic flight. Please tell me you got my passport?"

"You mean this thing?" Sun smiles mischievously as she whips it out of her hip pocket and hands it to me.

I run my fingers over the smooth surface of the passport. Just having it in my hands gives me a sense of freedom.

"I'm glad you mentioned it on the call," she says. "Before we left, I stopped by both of your houses. Your moms were more than eager to hand them over to us when I told them we were going to get you."

I let out a long breath of relief. "You are brilliant."

"Why, yes I am." She beams. "Although from the way you and Jake act together, it seems like you wouldn't be too upset being stuck in a foreign country as long as you had each other."

"Trust. We definitely want to go back home."

"You both seem like you're getting pretty serious. Am I right?"

I grab a pair of pants. "I mean we've been dating for a while. But..." I finger the price tag as the memory of Jake getting shot ricochets through my mind. "Watching him get shot and blood pooling across his shirt... it was...everywhere."

Sun's eyes grow wide. "I can't imagine."

"Then I woke up on Lau's plane." I close my eyes as if to shut out the images. "I couldn't even think straight between fury and terror. I didn't know what happened to Jake. I wasn't even sure if he was alive."

"That must have been horrible."

"It was." I tuck a black shirt that I think will fit Jake into our cart. "I just know now that I can't lose him. I don't know if I could handle it."

"I think he feels the same way about you," Sun says. "You two have been through a lot, and that's pulled you together in ways that nothing else could have. I just hope we can get this problem with the Dreamscape under control, so you don't have to keep living like this. It's not fair to you or any of us."

"Sometimes I get so angry. I mean, all Dad and I wanted to do was try to help and heal people. And now his technology is being used to interrogate and hurt others. It's just so wrong."

"Speaking of which." She pushes our cart brimming with clothing, flashlights, and boots to the checkout line. "How and when are you going to tell your parents that you're not going directly back home? She thinks you're on your way back to the States right now. And I know Dr. Hale. He's totally going to freak out when he realizes you're heading directly into danger."

I don't look at her, instead, I focus on loading the items onto the conveyor belt. "After we find out what we're dealing with in the Amazon, then I'll tell them."

"You sure that's a good idea?"

"What about you?" I push back. "Are you going to tell your dad that you're here and Lau is involved? Won't he also freak out?"

"Touché." She rolls her eyes. "Still, I'm twenty-six. You're only nineteen."

"Okay, *mom*. Way to make me feel like I'm five."

Sun laughs and hugs me. "Don't worry. I've got your back. You know that."

"Yeah, I don't know what we would've done if you hadn't shown up. You are literally a life-saver."

"That's right. I'm amazing, aren't I?"

She grins, and I know she's joking around, but tears edge at the corner of my eyes. I duck my head, focusing on our purchases as once again it hits me how close we came from things going really sour really fast.

After gathering up our purchases, we head to the grocery store to pick out some snacks. Even though the products are different from those back home, it's also fun to try to find things we might like to eat. Most of the fruit I don't recognize, but we grab some chirimoyas, which according to Sun's Google search are like apples as well as bananas and water. We even find chips for Tony called Plantanitos Fritos.

"Do you think he'll like these chips?" I ask as I toss them into the cart.

"The package does say Fritos." Sun shrugs. "Besides, maybe he'll want to try something Peruvian while he's here."

By the time we finish shopping, our hands are too full to hardly carry it all.

I groan from the bag handles digging into my palms as

I prep myself to haul the bags down the busy sidewalk. "How are we going to lug this all down the street back to the restaurant?"

"Wait," Sun says. "I'll call Javier."

When the minivan pulls up, the others are already inside, waiting for us.

"What took you so long?" Tony asks, grinning.

"Shut up," Sun says as we stuff all the clothing into the new suitcase we bought and then place it next to the tech gear the guys picked up. "It's all your fault for making us get chips."

But she smiles as she hands him the bag. He whoops upon seeing it.

"Peruvian Fritos?" Tony exclaims, and he seems so excited that I'm surprised he doesn't hug the bag. "This is the best. You are the best."

Meanwhile, I slip in beside Jake, and he takes my hand, squeezing it. The worry lines on his face smooth out, and his shoulders relax as I settle in closer to him. I guess that's what happens when two people go through something like this. Every time we separate, there's the risk that will be our last goodbye.

It feels like only moments before we arrive at the airport and the taxi pulls up to the curb. As soon as Tony slides the van door open, my muscles tense up.

"We should be careful," I tell the group. "It would make sense if Lau or Sadir had people stationed at the airport to keep an eye out for us."

"True," Sun acknowledges. "But my guess is they will likely have their scouts stationed at the international terminal. I bet they won't suspect that we're going to be taking an internal flight. Oh, and speaking of flying, this is for you, Jake."

She hands him his passport.

"Is this real?" Jake flips his open to inspect it.

"I stopped by both of your houses before we left," she explains. "Your mom was freaking out, but she seemed calmer when I told her we were picking you up."

"Thanks for this," he says. "I owe you big."

"And here we are." Tony hops onto the sidewalk and pops open the van's hatch. "Heading closer to danger rather than flying safely home. Because who would be stupid enough not to go home?"

Sun heaves a sigh as if she agrees with him while I roll my eyes.

"Or maybe that's why we're so smart," Jake offers. "We're two steps ahead of our opponents."

"Let's just get these bags unloaded," Javier says. "We've got a flight to the Amazon catch."

We unload the baggage and bustle into the domestic airport. My stomach twists while I scan the area, trying to keep a sharp eye out for anyone paying special attention to us. The problem is we all stand out like sore thumbs. The only two in our group that sort of blend in are Javier and Jake. There isn't a Black or Asian person that I can spot in the whole airport, and no one has red hair.

"I should've gotten a wig," I whisper to Sun.

"Just pretend you're a tourist," she says. "If anyone asks, we're going on a boat trip down the Amazon."

"Boat trip," I say. "As long as we don't encounter piranhas."

"So morbid!"

Once we get to the security inspection,

"Come on," Javier says. "Let's pick up the pace. I don't want to linger in this lobby longer than we need to."

We scurry to the private flight section of the airport. As we stride out onto the tarmac and up the flight of steps to take us onto the plane, I glance over my shoulder one last time.

I don't notice anything out of the ordinary, so I step through the doorway and into Danny's private jet.

And cross my fingers I'm making the right choice.

NINETEEN

THE GATEWAY TO THE AMAZON JUNGLE

Puerto Maldonado, Peru

"Okay, friends," Danny's voice called over the plane's intercom. "Fasten those seatbelts because we're making our landing into Puerto Maldonado."

I lean against the back of my seat, gripping the armrests as the airplane begins its rocky descent. The cabin shudders and everything rattles about while my stomach flip-flops in nervousness. Beside me, Jake somehow managed to fall sound asleep during our short two-hour flight.

Rain beats against the window, rivulets of silver. But even with the rain, I can make out the patchwork of vibrant green stretching as far as my eyes can see below. Endless trees, a mix of palms and pines, create what looks like a velvety soft blanket.

A strip of open land cuts through the forest like a knife and our plane bullets down toward it, landing on the ground with a hard thud and a screech of engines. Jake jerks awake and shakes his head as if trying to take in his surroundings.

"Sorry about that," Danny's voice pops up over the intercom. "That was a short runway if I ever saw one. Wasn't sure I had enough space to land. Had to come in hot and quick. Otherwise, I was going to have to do a touch-and-go landing and redo it."

Tony breaks into applause and cheers while Sun yells across the small plane at how horrible his flying skills are becoming. Meanwhile, my attention is pulled to the small airport we're taxiing to. It's a one-story building that spans out across the tarmac with a white strip running along the edge of the roof and white walls that race halfway up along the sides of it, leaving the rest of the building open-aired.

Our plane finally parks in the middle of the tarmac, and we all start unclipping our seatbelts. I swipe at the beads of sweat on my forehead and focus on gathering my bag. Danny steps out from the cockpit, a frown firmly pulling at his handsome features.

"Why are we here again at this god-forsaken place?" he asks. "Tell me they have a fancy resort on the Amazon River that I'm going to be sipping a cool drink at because this airport needs modern updating."

"Dude," Tony says. "We're in the jungle."

"Don't be spoiled and open the door," Sun snaps as she touches up her makeup and smooths down her hair.

"Sun looks stressed," Jake whispers to me. "I hope we made the right choice."

"I'm feeling the same way," I say. "This excursion is starting to feel like we've reached the outer edge of civilization, and it's the last place that Sadir would pick as his home base of operations."

We gather up our few belongings while Danny opens the clamshell door of the aircraft and lowers the airstair. As I step outside and work my way down the steps, thick, warm air drenches me. Right away, I'm reminded of Florida on a hot summer day, full of humidity that tangles the hair and soaks the skin.

Thankfully, I changed into cargo shorts and a comfortable hiking shirt Sun and I picked up while at the store. I also braided my hair so it stays out of my face.

Unlike the airport in Lima, buzzing with the roar of engines and rumbling trucks, this place is strangely quiet. Bruised-blue clouds hang low in the sky, and I wonder how much time we have before they dump buckets of rain upon us. Thick foliage of heavily leafed trees and palms circle the perimeter of the tarmac as if barring us from going anywhere other than the single building before us.

"Yikes," Sun mutters, her eyes widening as she takes in our situation. "I sure hope this is the right place."

"What are you talking about?" Tony's face lit up like

he's just discovered a new flavor of pizza. "This place is awesome. It's like something from the movies."

"That's fine." She grimaces as her heel steps into a puddle. "As long as the movie is a romantic comedy and not a horror film."

"Let's find a taxi driver and see if we can make it to our accommodations," Javier breaks through our group huddled at the base of the stairs, and takes off across the tarmac, following the line of cones into the airport.

"He's right," I say. "We've got to stay focused and keep our heads about us."

What I don't say is my greatest fear. That we're not going to make it out of this place alive.

I hurry after Javier, scurrying along the edge of the building that consists of waist-high barriers and the rest being a meshed wire that stretches all the way to the ceiling. Finally, the cones lead us inside the open-aired airport. Other than the conveyor belt in the center and a few checkout counters for money exchanges and taxi services, it feels more like a large warehouse. The skylights above provide most of the lighting for the place, and besides a few people strolling about and a guy slouched in a chair sleeping, we're the only ones here.

We trail after Javier as he beelines it through the airport and out the front entrance. A few rickshaws and taxis are parked in the lot, the drivers huddled by the building, smoking. Javier pulls out his phone and heads over to them. One of the men tosses his cigarette to the ground and waves to our group perched at the edge of the entrance.

"This way!" he calls to us. "Come along."

He directs us to a car, which must be his, and pops open the trunk. We start loading in the few belongings we have but there's just not enough space.

"I suppose we can carry some of the things on our lap," I offer.

"Yes, very good." The driver smiles at us. "My name is Carlos. Welcome to Puerto Maldonado. I count only five. I was told you had six?"

"My brother is dealing with the plane right now," Sun explains. "He's meeting us later."

Tony opens a door and chuckles as he peers inside. "This is a car for six? Because it looks more like a tight squeeze for five."

"Yes, yes." Our driver nods happily and jumps inside, cranking a tired engine. "This is it. Or you can pay for two trips."

"We'll squeeze," Javier says, hopping into the front seat.

"No way, man," Tony grumbles, opening the backdoor. "I wanted shotgun."

"Since I speak Spanish," Javier says. "I should be the one in front to help with any questions he might have."

"The dude sounds practically fluent in English," Tony grumbles but squeezes his large frame into the back seat.

As the group slips inside, I spot the guy who was sleeping in his chair stumbling out of the airport, his hair sticking about with a hat in his hand as if he rushed outside in a hurry.

He pauses abruptly when his eyes land on our taxi as we cram into the small confines of the car.

"It's a bit of a trip to where you are going," Carlos explains. "The roads are rough this time of the year with all the rain and mud. Hold on tight."

But my eyes are glued to the guy on the curb who is pulling out his phone and striding out to where our driver still is urging his taxi's engine to turn on. I grip Jake's hand and nod to the approaching man.

"You think he's a scout for Sadir?" I whisper to Jake.

Jake's eyes narrow, and his lips press together. My pulse quickens the closer the guy gets. But then our taxi finally bursts to life and speeds away from the airport.

I glance over my shoulder, wondering if the hat dude will follow us, but he remains standing stock still in the center of the nearly deserted parking lot, gazing after us. We stop briefly to pay the airport parking fee, and then we're off again, bumping and rumbling along a hard-packed dirt road that actually is more puddle than dirt.

"He's not following us," I tell Jake.

"Maybe." Jake runs his hand through his hair. "Or maybe he doesn't need to."

The driver is unfazed by the conditions of the road. He careens and weaves around the puddles and potholes like he's memorized every crook and cranny of this road. American rock music plays from his speaker, and he sings along to it as he drives.

The thick forest surrounding the airport thins out as small concrete houses start popping up along the roadside. Goats are penned up at some houses and laundry is strung out, I'm guessing to dry between rain showers.

Soon the flat front homes start cluttering closer together, some painted in cherry reds, sunlight yellows, and emerald greens. Music plays through opened doors of homes as people gather around tables. Though it's only six o'clock, the sun is starting to dip below the treeline, casting the town in a golden glow.

"You here to visit the Amazon?" Carlos asks us as he makes a turn that takes us away from the streets of houses.

"That we are," Javier says. "Always wanted to see the nature of the area."

"Yes, yes." Our driver grins widely. "Nothing quite like our home. Puerto Maldonado is considered the gateway into the Amazon jungle. You will not be disappointed with your stay. Though... you may get a little wet this time of year."

"Guess we hadn't thought to bring rain gear," Javier says. "It was so dry in Lima."

"That is because Lima is a desert." Carlos pauses briefly to hum along with the song. "But here, it is very wet and very rainy. But the rainy season is nearly finished so your stay might not be so bad."

He pulls onto a muddy road where a wilderness of brush and trees encroach on either side. Thunder rumbles in the distance and droplets of rain patter on the roof of the car. We come to an old one-way wooden bridge that forces the car to ride on two slabs of wood. No guard rails are on either side to prevent us from going over the edge.

I hold my breath as the driver carefully drives up and along the slabs of wood. Outside, I fasten my eyes on the brown, muddy river that gushes under the bridge beneath us. One little slip of the tires and we'd plunge into its depths.

On the other side of the car, Tony is praying under his breath while Sun clamps her hands over her eyes, proclaiming that she just can't watch this. But the driver, seemingly oblivious to the rushing river below, belts out the chorus of his song.

Finally, we cross unscathed, and all of us let out a long sigh of relief. It feels like we've driven forever when the driver finally slows the car and halts before a wide-open gate.

"This is your stop," he proclaims.

In the fading light, I can barely read the sign by the entrance. It reads Tambopata River Bungalows and Tours and has an emblem of the parrot painted above the name.

The car rolls through the gate, bumping along until it stops before a large bungalow-style building practically buried in the jungle growth. We all clamor out of the car and the driver yanks out the luggage and plants them on the muddy drive.

I'm eager to stretch my legs. Right away, I'm struck by the freshness of the air. It smells like sweet flowers and fresh greens along with the rich scent of the dirt after the rain.

The jungle feels alive around us with sounds that I've never heard before. Strange birds, buzzing insects, and some animal calling out in the twilight hour. I'm not sure if I should be terrified or enthralled by the wilderness.

Sun gapes at the area, her body seemingly frozen in place. "Please tell me this place has hot water."

"Can't say that there is," Javier says as he pays the driver and waves goodbye.

"No way!" Tony is holding up his phone, moving it about as he stares at it. "No internet service?"

"That's going to make things tricky for us," Jake says.

"Wait!" Sun drops her suitcase in the mud, racing after the departing taxi, yelling, "This is a mistake!"

But the taxi just keeps chugging along with the driver belting out a new song at the top of his lungs.

"I don't think Carlos hears you." I put my arm around her, staring at the retreating headlights as the taxi disappears into the jungle road.

"Why did I agree to this?" Sun wails.

"Maybe being out in the wilderness is a good thing," I offer. "It makes it less likely for Sadir to find us."

"Or more likely for him to send in his people and

murder us all in our sleep," Sun mutters. She trudges to her mud-caked suitcase and picks it up, grimacing.

I gulp. "Let's hope I'm right, and you're not."

Because if she's right, we're in the middle of nowhere with no chance of escape or a means of help.

TWENTY

AMBUSHED

The Amazon Rainforest, Peru

I sling my backpack filled with the equipment we purchased earlier today and trudge up the worn steps of the hut before us. Inside, a lantern hangs from the rafters, illuminating the open room in a flickering hue. There isn't much here other than two picnic-style tables and a bar to the right where dusty bottles line up along the back wall as if they're more for show than actual use.

Spider webs cling to the thick wooden beams crossing our over heads above and something skitters in the jungle outside the mesh windows.

"Hello, there," a man greets us as he enters from behind a cloth doorway. "You must be the guests who reserved a bungalow today."

Javier steps up to the man, speaking to him in Spanish, while the rest of our crew piles in.

But just before Jake shuts the front door, the rumbling of motorbikes fills the tranquility of the rainforest surrounding us. Bright headlights cut through the darkness of the resort's entrance. I stiffen, all my senses on edge.

Because my first thought is that they're Sadir's men here for us.

"Is that Danny?" I ask hopefully. Or maybe these guys are tourists? It's not like everyone is out to get us. I must be overreacting.

"Danny doesn't ride bikes," Sun says, frowning as she squints into the darkness.

The bikes skid up to the entrance, kicking up mud in their wake. They are riders wearing dark clothing with helmets and visors to hide their identity. But when they all whip out guns, pointing them at the hut, my body turns cold.

"Guns!" I scream and dive under one of the tables.

The rest of our group springs for cover as bullets ricochet across the hut, piercing through the mesh windows and thin wood of the building. The owner who came in to greet us, races back through the curtain, screaming.

Javier kicks the door closed while Sun crawls to join me beneath the table.

"That's one way to say hello," Jake grumbles, pushing

the table down so it creates a barrier for us. "We need to move."

"Crap," Tony says, his eyes wide as moons from where he's hiding behind the bar. "What do we do?"

"Why are they here?" Sun asks. "How did they even know how to find us?"

Jake and I glance at each other and I know he's thinking about the guy on the phone in the airport parking lot.

"They want Aria," Javier says.

"But they were shooting at all of us!" Tony points out.

"That was a warning," Javier says. "Those bullets weren't targeted. And if they were, they'd be aimed at all of us except for Aria. The rest of us are disposable."

"What do we do?" Sun's voice quivers.

But my mind is on our equipment. "We leave everything behind other than must-haves. Frantically, I open Sun's suitcase. "Is there anything we need?" But as I toss out clothing, my eyes land on a kit stowed inside it.

It's a Dreamscape kit.

Sun swallows. "I brought one just in case."

Jake swears under his breath. "We can't let them get their hands on that."

"Like hell, we won't." I snatch it up, stowing it in my backpack.

The sound of boots clomping on the wooden stairs draws our attention to the door.

"Hey," Tony calls to us from the bar. He's holding some of the dusty bottles. "Catch!"

Then he tosses a bottle to each of us.

"You want us to fight against their guns with whiskey bottles?"

"Hey, man," Tony says, fear evident in his eyes. "Whatever it takes."

Jake grumbles under his breath but grabs my hand and tugs me to the back door. Except halfway there, I spy some guys creeping along in the shadows on the wooden walkway outside. I yank Jake back.

"They've surrounded the hut," I whisper.

Suddenly both the front and back doors are kicked in at the same time. Men, this time without their helmets, leap into the room, guns outstretched.

"Throw your bottles!" Tony screams.

As one, we toss our bottles. Glass shatters across the hut. Liquid goes flying. Javier and Jake start throwing chairs next.

Tony continues throwing bottle after bottle while Sun and Javier rush for the cloth door the owner escaped to. But as I dart to follow, my whole body is yanked backward. Someone has gotten a hand on my backpack and is dragging me toward him.

Jake smashes a bottle on the guy's head. It's enough of a distraction for me to twist out of my attacker's grip. I spin around, scanning the room for an exit, but there's nowhere to go.

Except... my eyes drift to the rafters and the open-aired ceiling.

My heart slams against my ribcage. Pure adrenaline courses through my veins. It's a crazy idea, but the only option I can think of at the moment.

I leap onto the counter of the bar.

"Esa es ella!" one of the men shouts, pointing at me.

As Javier predicted, no one shoots. Instead, they all move in as if to grab me. I scamper along the bar until I reach the wall where a rug hangs. I don't know if it will hold my weight, but I give it a try. I grip the heavy material and start climbing.

Behind me, I hear grunting, glass shattering, and the sounds of a struggle.

I don't pause but keep climbing until I'm nearly at the top of the wall. I reach out my hand to grab onto the wood-beamed rafter, but it's just out of my reach.

One of the attackers has managed to snatch up a large pole and heaves it at me. The metal smashes against my side. Pain wracks through my body. I cry out and nearly let go of my hold on the rug.

Below, another attacker yells at the pole guy and rips it out of his hand.

I blink back tears. Someone obviously wants me unharmed, which I need to use to my advantage. Next, two guys race into the hut with a ladder. And that's when I realize I don't have much time.

My eyes focus back on the beam and suck in a deep

breath. I push off the wall, reaching for the beam just in front of me. For a brief second, it's just me and the air, my hands outstretched.

And then my hands are grabbing onto the rough wood. I tuck my legs around it, so they, too, are hugging the beam. My vision swims just a little as the realization of what I just did. I don't even want to think about how many bones I would've broken if I fell.

I pause for a heartbeat, recovering from the jump, but then the ladder props up against the beam. I scamper along the rafter until I reach the ladder where a guy is scaling its rungs. Without hesitation, I push the ladder off the beam and away from me, so it goes crashing against the far wall. Then I keep moving until I come to the other side of the building where the eaves open up into the night. Before I leave the main room, I glance over my shoulder to check on my friends.

Tony and Jake are still below by the back door, fighting off two guys.

"Get out of here, Aria!" Jake yells as if sensing my hesitation to leave. Then he punches one of the guys.

"What about you?" I ask.

"Call me when you're safe," he yells, and with that, Jake and Tony race out of the back door.

And now I'm alone. Some of the guys run off, chasing Tony and Jake, but the others merely turn their focus back on me. The ladder is back into place on the beam and one of the men is climbing the rungs.

My heart pounds against my chest like a hammer. I continue crawling on the beam out into the eaves and outside the main wall. Suddenly it dead ends and I realize that below are bushes and the ground.

"Psst," someone says below. "Climb down."

Another ladder hits against the beam where I'm at.

I pause, my heart not trusting the voices. But then the clouds part just enough so the moon illuminates Sun and Javier below.

"Hurry!" Sun whispers.

Quickly, I scamper down the ladder and then jump down the second half onto the soft ground. I nearly trip over two men who are lying still as stones against the wall.

"They were problematic," Javier mutters.

"But we took care of them." Sun hands me a frying pan. "We found the kitchen. Quite a useful place for weapons."

"Oh." I suck in a shuddery breath as I take the pan.

Javier motions for us to follow him, and then takes off down a trail into the jungle.

The darkness cloaks us, but it also makes it nearly impossible to see anything or where we're going. I try to calm my pounding heart so I can listen to the sounds in the forest. Brush and trees press from every direction, and the strange sounds of the jungle animals startle me. Javier stops for a brief moment to listen.

Something drops from the tree above with a thunk,

and I choke back a scream. I pick up the round object and hold it up in the shadows.

"Mango," Javier says. "They're falling from the trees."

Mangos. Right. It seems like something so ordinary but when every noise has become life-threatening, a falling mango truly is terrifying.

"Hold onto it," Sun whispers. "Might come in handy."

We continue on until the path butts into the river-bank. The clouds have shifted even more to allow the moon to have a full range. They illuminate the river rushing below us and the path that we're on.

"What do we do now?" I ask. "How are we going to find Jake and Tony?"

"We're not," Javier says. "We're going to get as far from this place and keep you safe."

"I'm not leaving them." I grip my frying pan tighter. "I won't. Isn't that our team motto? Leave no team member behind?"

Javier sighs. "They don't care about Tony or Jake. They only want you. So you'll be doing exactly what they want."

I push past Javier and start jogging down the path that runs along the river. I pass a few bungalows and nearly have a heart attack when I disturb a chicken and her chicks nested in the brush by the trail. Thankfully, Javier and Sun must have decided to follow along because I hear their footsteps and panting behind me.

I'm crossing over a wooden bridge when gunshots

echo through the jungle. A strangled cry erupts from my throat, and I stumble to a halt and listen.

Did they shoot Jake and Tony? Are they okay?

"Oh, my god. I can't handle this." I lean over, bile filling my mouth. "I can't lose Jake."

"You need to stay strong for him," Sun says.

"Where did those shots come from?" I turn, grabbing her arm for support.

"From that direction." She points to a path that leads away from the river and back into the jungle.

"Don't go," Javier begs me. "Stay here. I'll check it out."

And that's when the sound of bike engines roar back to life. My heart seizes. "What does that mean? What is happening?"

"They're leaving," Javier says, grimly.

"But why?" Sun wonders.

I break into a sprint down the path. Now that the moonbeams wash across the forest, I'm able to see most of the way, allowing me to move at a faster pace. I leap over thick tree roots and duck below branches.

That is until I hear the clomp of footsteps and someone breathing heavily. I jerk to a standstill. Sun runs into me, nearly knocking me over.

"What is it?" she whispers.

"Someone is coming." I prep my mango.

The person barrels around the corner, and that's when I throw the fruit.

It smacks against Tony's chest, and he cries out in pain, halting and holding out a broken bottle as his weapon.

"Who's there?" he demands. Sweat glistens against his dark skin. His clothes are shredded.

"Tony!" I say as Sun and I run to him.

"Are you okay?" Javier asks. "Where's Jake?"

Tony shakes his head and pauses, leaning over and gasping to take in air. Finally, he looks up, his eyes watery.

"We almost had them," he gasps. "Only three left. But they had guns and...oh, god. They took him."

"What?" I clench his arm. "What do you mean?"

"They left," Tony said. "And they took Jake."

My knees finally give out on me. My whole body starts shaking in shock.

"No." I sink to the ground. "Please, no."

"I'm so sorry, Aria," Tony says.

TWENTY-ONE

DESPERATE PLANS CALL FOR DESPERATE ACTION

"What do we do?" I ask, my words choking me. "We have to get Jake back."

I think about when Reasner had Jake hooked into his Dreamscape. That had been terrifying. I wasn't sure if he would survive.

"It's happening all over again." I curl my arms around my body. My stomach twists and I throw up.

Sun rubs my back.

"They couldn't find you," Javier says, his words bitter and curt. "So they grabbed him knowing you'll come after him."

"We can't stay here." Tony's eyes are wide, glancing fugitively into the forest. "We should find someplace safe to hide until we come up with a plan."

"Yes." I feel Sun's hands trying to help me to my feet, but my whole body is numb. "Come on, Aria. You have to move. For Jake. Here, let me take your backpack. I'll carry it for you."

My mind takes hold of what's in my backpack. It gives me the motivation to climb back to my feet. Dully, I shuffle after Javier's shadow with only the moon guiding us. To any other person, it would seem like a beautiful evening in the Amazon with the palms shifting in the moist breeze that's blowing in from across the river.

But not for us. Not after we've been chased, shot at, and one of our own kidnapped.

"I'm betting the owner called the police," Tony says.

"They'll be here soon," Javier agrees, taking charge as if we were on a Dreamscape mission. "I noticed an old, abandoned resort just down the road on our way here. We'll go there and hunker down where it's safe. I'll make some calls. We'll get this figured out. It's going to be fine. We're going to get Jake back."

He's acting like everything is going to be okay. Like we're just dealing with a minor inconvenience of Jake getting lost. I suppose Javier's doing this to keep us all calm. But I also know that this is a bigger problem than he's letting on. Because even if we can get government operatives here, it would take time.

There would be paperwork and approvals.

Flights and transfers and off-road car trips to where we are at.

Jake doesn't have that kind of time. He has hours.

We need to act and now.

We skirt along the edge of the road, careful to keep hidden in the brush until we come up to a grand, white gate. Except, the left side hangs loosely on its hinges. The paint is peeling off.

"Whoever built this must have had big plans," Tony says as we slip between the gates, "but ran out of money."

He's right. The road cutting into the wanna-be resort has overgrown and tall weed brush against my legs as we head toward the first building.

It's also a hut similar in style to what the other resort had, but the thatched roof sags at the center, and the front porch has collapsed on one side so the whole front resembles more of a slide than a porch. Palms rise up on either side of the building and cobwebs stretch across the entrance, shimmering in the moonlight.

Javier holds out his hand for us to wait, and then creeps up the wooden steps of the porch. He peers into the window and then tries the door.

The knob turns. Slowly, he pushes open the door and slips inside. Moments later, he pokes his head out the door and whispers, "All clear."

We scramble up the steps, which groan and wobble a bit as I climb them. The interior of the hut is merely an open room with a single table against one wall. Rafters stretch out above and beyond that is the thatched roof. Like the main hut where we were attacked, the sides of the ceiling open outside to allow a breeze to flow through.

The windows have no glass, only mesh coverings and

moth-eaten curtains to give a sense of privacy. But even still, without the constant breeze, the hut is stiflingly hot. I'm already sweaty from racing through the jungle, but now my clothes stick to me like glue.

"We'll need to be quiet," Sun notes. "This is an open hut so anyone passing nearby can hear us."

"I'm going to make some calls." Javier digs out a phone from his backpack. "You three rest up as best as you can. Just make sure you stay quiet."

Once he leaves, Tony checks the bathroom, only to return to tell us that there's no running water. Sun pulls out her phone and presses it to her ear. After a few moments, she hangs up.

"I can't get a hold of Danny," she says, her voice quivering. "You think he's okay?"

I can't answer her because I don't think she wants to hear what I think. My feet are still rooted in place, my mind unable to get off the fact that the answer to finding Jake and solving all our problems is tucked away in my backpack.

Slowly I slip the pack onto a carved wooden seat. I peek out the window to watch Javier stride away, I suppose trying to put some distance between him and us in case his voice might lead someone here.

"I have an idea," I tell Tony and Sun as I watch Javier settle onto a fallen log at the river bank.

"Uh-oh," Tony says. "I have a feeling I'm not going to like this."

I lick my lips and turn to face them. "I want to go back to the first resort."

"That sounds like a stupid idea." Sun frowns and plants her fists on her hips. "Why would you do that when we're safe here?"

"I want to see if any of those guys we knocked out were left behind," I explain and then turn to Tony. "Do you remember if there were any motorcycles left?"

Tony shakes his head. "I... I don't know. I was so upset. Maybe, maybe not."

"We have to find out," I say. "Which is why I'm going back out there."

"Wait a second." Sun grabs my arm. "You aren't thinking of doing what I think you're thinking of."

Her eyes narrow on my backpack. The one holding the portable Dreamscape she brought.

"At first," I say, "I was worried and upset about bringing the Dreamscape here. But now, I'm glad. This could be our way of finding where they took Jake."

"You can't be serious." Tony throws up his arms, realizing now what I'm insinuating.

That we find one of the men we knocked out, hook him to the Dreamscape, enter his memories, and find the location of where they took Jake.

"Shhh!!!" Sun snaps at Tony. "You can't yell like that!"

Tony rolls his eyes but switches to a whisper. "We can't do this whole entering people's dreams again without their permission. It's against who we are. And it's dangerous!"

"The moment they took Jake and shot bullets at us, everything changed," I say. "Who knows how long it will be before Javier finds someone from the government to come here? And even after they agree, think of all the paperwork and time it's going to take to just get here. We're in Peru, in the middle of the jungle. I can't wait around for some bureaucrat to get here and rescue Jake."

"She's right," Sun says. I stand straighter, surprised at how quickly she agreed with me. It's a relief, too, because I can't do this without her. "But if we find someone, we bring him back here, not do it out in the open where we could get caught."

"Did you bring the Temazepam?" I unzip the backpack to check.

"Who do you take me for? An amateur?" She huffs and takes the pack from me, pulling out a black case. With a snap, she pops it open and pulls out a vial and syringe.

"If we find one of Sadir's men," Sun says. "It should keep them unconscious."

"Tony," I say. "We're going to need your help with the body."

He crosses his arms, his jaw working as indecision swims across his features.

"For Jake?" I press. "Who knows how soon it will be before they start torturing him. I don't know how long his mind can handle it."

Tony's face softens at that. He sighs, rubbing his forehead. "Okay, let's do this."

We slip back outside, checking the path for any movement. But all I hear are the occasional sounds of hooting and insects buzzing. Clouds scuttle above, ghostly tendrils trailing across the moon's surface. The jungle is strangely peaceful after what we just experienced.

"The entrance is back this way." Tony points right. "And then we'll need to take our first right back to the main hut."

Sun and I stare at him impressed.

"What?" He lifts his eyebrows. "I'm good with directions. You should know that by now after all the Dreamscape missions we've been on."

We take off, following Tony's instructions until I spot the sign to the resort and the outline of the main hut steeped in the shadows of the jungle. I hunker down in a crop of shrubbery and wave for the other two to join me.

I listen, trying to find out if there's anyone else nearby, but the area is deathly quiet.

"I don't even hear the owner and his crew," I note.

"They may be in hiding, too," Sun whispers. "Or waiting for the police to arrive."

"Then we should hurry," Tony says.

"Right." I nod. "Let's check outside the kitchen where we knocked those guys out."

"It's a starting place," Tony mutters.

I take off down the path, my heart pattering like the

sound of rainfall. I just hope I'm making the right choice going back to the scene where everything went down. Each crunch of my footsteps and brush against a branch of leaves makes me cringe in worry that I'm being too loud. I've never thought of myself as a noisy person, but here in the quiet of the forest, I feel like a stampeding elephant.

My breath is ragged by the time I reach the side of the hut where the kitchen is located. I pause, trying to control my breathing to keep it quiet and even. Besides me, Tony and Sun also seem to be having the same issue.

Tony taps me on the shoulder and then points to the side of the porch. There, half-covered by a bush, sticks out a set of boots.

"They left one behind," he says.

Sun pulls out the syringe from her pocket while I scan the area for any other sign of life. I'm rising back to standing when I spot a figure walking slowly down the boardwalk that leads from the hut to one of the other paths.

I duck back into the bush and press my hands on both of my friend's arms, nodding to the retreating figure. "I bet they're searching for him right now."

"We need to hurry," Sun says.

I wait until the guy disappears down the path and then take off toward the boots, Sun and Tony following at my heels. The moment we reach the bush, we hunker back down, listening once again.

Tony stands up, scans the area, and then gives us the

thumbs up. We yank the guy out of the bush where he must have fallen into I'm guessing by the way the bush's branches are bent up. He groans as we move him.

Without wasting a moment, Sun plunges the syringe into his arm. The guy shakes his head and lifts it, staring blearily at the three of us. He opens his mouth as if to say something, but the Temazepam must have hit his system because suddenly his head flops back and his eyes flutter closed.

"On the count of three, we'll put this guy over my shoulder," Tony says. "One, two, three."

We scoop him up and then toss the guy over Tony's broad shoulders like a sack of rice. Once the guy is settled in place, Tony gives us a nod. We skirt around a tank of water and an outdoor sitting area before slipping back into the forest.

As I retrace our steps back to the other resort, my heart continues to thump so loudly, I'm sure it must be as loud as a drum, announcing to everyone where we're at.

Then, before we know it, we're back at the hut, darting inside. Tony drops the guy onto the floor with a grunt.

"The dude weighs like two hundred pounds," Tony says, his skin dripping with sweat. He grabs a towel and mops his face and neck.

Meanwhile, Sun grabs the Dreamscape kit and sets it on the bedside table. "Since we've got no electricity here, we'll be running the Dreamscape on battery," she tells us.

"I hadn't thought of that," I say. "Will we have enough time to get into the dream and find out our information?"

"Hard time say." Sun doesn't look up from the computer. "I'll give you a five-minute signal. You'll need to fade ASAP at that moment, or your mind could seriously get messed up."

"Great," Tony says. "So now we don't have much time before our brains are fried."

"We?" I ask Tony.

"You're not entering this Dreamscape alone." Tony rolls his eyes like that was obvious. "I'm going in with you."

"Do you have earbuds and masks?" I ask Sun.

"Just two." Sun's fingers fly over the computer keyboard as she configures the Dreamscape. "You know if Javier finds us, he's going to freak."

"Then we should hurry." I grab the equipment and drop onto the dusty floor.

Tony grumbles under his breath. "I can't believe we're doing this again. I thought we were done with all this illegal stuff."

"Stop focusing on that." I plug in the earplugs and take a deep breath. "Focus on finding where they were planning on taking Jake."

"Okay," Sun says. "I'm initiating the Sound Oasis."

I suck in a deep breath as I slip on the Neuro-Read sleep mask, and blow out a long breathe to calm my beating heart. The Sound Oasis kicks in, and my muscles relax as the familiar cry of seagulls and crashing waves reach my ears.

I imagine Jake standing in front of me, his blond hair blowing in the breeze and hands reaching for mine.

I count down, "10, 9, 8, 7..."

TWENTY-TWO
THE MIND OF THE ENEMY

The world shifts and swims before me, a vibrant sea of greens rising and falling around my body. I fix my gaze straight ahead and allow my mind to settle into the dream.

Deep breath, I remind myself. Soon, the rolling of the dark-green waves settles until I find myself standing in a thick forest. Above, trees taller than a two-story building stretch toward a stormy steel sky.

There's an odd tension in the air as if at any moment the world around me might snap and splinter into a thousand pieces. Or maybe it's just my nerves. Because I know that if I can't find answers, there's no hope of discovering where those men took Jake.

I spin in a circle, scanning the thick foliage. "Tony?" I whisper, knowing that the dreamer should be close by as well. "Are you here?"

"Give me a second," Tony's voice mutters from nearby.

The bushes before me rustle. I push aside the branches to find Tony tangled up in vines and spider webs.

I grin, shaking my head. "What did you get yourself into this time?"

"Shut up," he grumbles and thrusts a hand at me. "Help a brother out, will you?"

I haul him out of the bush but grimace as sticky strands cling to my fingers. "Yuck. Why does it have to be spiders?"

"Shhh." Tony lifts his eyebrows and nods at something over my shoulder.

I turn to find our dreamer standing just behind us, still and oddly silent. He's got his biker helmet on so I can barely see his face behind the clear visor. He stares at Tony and me through angry eyes as if we've done something horrible to him.

Which, okay, we might have hit him on the head, drugged him, and forcibly entered his dream, but he's the one who joined the kidnapping crew, right?

"I think he's upset at us," Tony whispers to me.

My mind whirls as I try to review our protocols at MaxLife. The only one that pops into my mind is if the dreamer becomes antagonistic to the Dream Walker, we're supposed to Fade from the dream ASAP. Which is not an option until I have a clue as to what's going on with Jake.

"Do you remember the consequences of staying in the Dreamscape when the dreamer is upset at the Dream Walkers?" I ask Tony.

"Uh, yeah." Tony shifts to stand beside me. "Let's just say, we need to get this guy to like us."

As if in confirmation, things start to happen. Wind kicks up, oddly cold for the jungle around us. I shove back a flurry of tremors and plaster on a smile, giving a little wave. "Hey! We are uh...out hiking."

Helmet Dude frowns and his eyes narrow.

"You're acting sucks," Tony tells me, and then he flashes the guy a grin. "We're just checking out the wildlife here."

"Yep," I jump in. "That's us. Tourists who love the wild. But one of our friends is lost. You wouldn't happen to have seen him? He's about six feet tall, blonde hair, and blue eyes."

"Don't say hot," Tony jokes softly.

"I wasn't!" I cross my arms, but inwardly my heart warms. Tony is trying to keep things light and carefree as usual. As my best friend, he always knows when I'm stressed. And while we're dream walking, it's important to defuse tension in the dream.

The man starts speaking, but of course, it's in Russian so I've no idea what he's saying other than his words spit out harsh as the cold air tugging at my hair and clothing.

Above the branches dip and quiver as if they're shaking their fists at us while the sky darkens into a deeper, more ominous gray. I swallow down the worry creeping up my throat.

"I think we need a Plan B," I say.

Before I can think of a new strategy, Helmet Guy turns to stare down the path that snakes out before us. The ground quivers, and then patches of dirt begin to break up as if something sinister is growing out of the forest floor.

"Why does this feel like a bad dream?" Tony asks.

I grab Tony's arm, bracing myself. Wooden posts rise out of the ground. I stifle a cry of shock as fingers emerge, clawing for freedom, followed by heads attached to bodies bound to posts. It's as if the dead are rising from the earth.

Except these aren't dead bodies. They are definitely alive, and they aren't strangers.

All the air inside my chest is sucked away. The people tied up to each post are my friends.

My heart dives. "This is bad."

"Very, very bad," Tony says along with a lot of other words that I can't focus on because all I can see are Sun, Javier, Jake, Tony, and even myself.

The five of us are covered in grime as if we'd been buried underground, sputtering and choking like we'd swallowed dirt. Sun starts wailing and Jake and Javier start yelling, "Help!"

"We have to help them!" I say, but Tony holds me back.

"No, we have to hide. We can't let the dreamer see that there are two of us."

He has a point. If he turns around and realizes he's dreamed up two Tonys and two Arias, it could make him end the dream.

Except, I can't stand watching my friends in agony. "Even though I know they aren't real," I say. "It's terrifying to see the people I love look like they're being tortured."

"No kidding." Tony's mouth twists in horror.

I'm about to take off to help them when Tony hauls me back into the bushes.

"Wait," he says. "We need to time this out."

"But we have to help them," I argue, biting my lip as I watch Dream-Jake frantically wipes his dirt-smeared face back and forth as if expecting something horrible to emerge.

Meanwhile, the dreamer decides to turn back around and face us with a wide, gleeful expression, except the moment he realizes we're gone, his grin falters. He picks up a stick and starts beating at the bushes near us like he's searching for our location. My heart rate picks up and uncertainty floods me. I need to do breathing exercises to keep my pulse in check so Sun, who's monitoring our heart rates, won't freak out back in the hut, but it's tough.

The air grows even colder. I shiver in the muted light and huddle with Tony in the brush. Suddenly, something sticky starts creeping over my skin. I glance down to find glistening spider strands curling around my arms and hands. The ground at my feet loosens.

Panic seizes me. "Move!" I grab Tony's hand, but he doesn't budge.

"Oh, crap." Tony eyes the ground where his legs are already half sunk into the dirt.

"You've got to Fade," I choke out. *Stay calm. Stay calm!* I inwardly order myself. "It's too risky otherwise. We don't know if your mind will be able to handle being..."

I can't say the words.

"Being buried alive?" he finishes for me with a grimace.

"Yeah, that."

"Okay, you might have a point," he concedes. "But I'll come back if you stay in this dream too long."

"Deal." I eye his body, which is now buried up to his waist. "Hurry and Fade already!"

His hands vanish from mine and then his whole body is gone. I scramble away from where we'd been hiding, yanking my feet out of the shifting ground. I snatch up a branch and use it to attempt to break the sticky spider webs off me, but they don't come off.

The dreamer seems to have abandoned the idea of looking for me because he's backing away from the bushes, holding his stick as if it's a weapon, eyes wide and body stiff as if expecting something to appear.

"Okay, dude," I mumble. "You're really starting to freak me out."

Dream-Sun continues to wail, fighting against her bindings. The others scream louder for help as if they too are feeling the press of time. Jake starts rocking his post back and forth and I realize he's attempting to free it from the ground.

"Quiet!" Helmet Guy yells at them, surprising me with his English. If I try to talk to him, maybe he'll be able to understand me.

We've been in this dream long enough for me to know that it will either end soon or things will start to derail. I need to get answers, or it will be too late. I'm desperate enough to forget all protocols and just show myself even if there are two of me in the dream.

"Where did you take Jake?" I ask Helmet Guy, stepping into his line of sight. "What have you done with him?"

"Jake?" The guy's forehead bunches in confusion, and he glances over his shoulder at Jake who has nearly managed to yank his post out of the ground.

Before I get any answers from Helmet Guy, grunting and screeching sounds echo through the jungle, yanking our attention to the canopy above. Dark black forms skitter along the branches and swoop down on vines.

Monkeys.

They drop down onto the path we're standing on, eyeing us with fierce intensity. Their bodies are posed as if they're planning to spring on me and rip their sharp claws across my skin. Beside me, Helmet Guy whimpers.

"Ah!" I say. "So this is what you're so scared of. The monkeys."

These are not the cute ones munching on bananas that you watch from behind the safety wall at the zoo. These are feral, wild, untamable.

Fierce.

I gulp down my fear as the terrifying creatures surround me, grunting, pawing at the earth. Their lips are twisted in snarls.

This isn't a dream. This is a nightmare.

TWENTY-THREE

THE NIGHTMARE

I back away from the creatures, my pulse throbbing against my temples. I've been fortunate to never enter someone's nightmare before. Another team once encountered one, but they were pulled out of the Dreamscape right away. There's no need to risk someone's mind getting confused and letting them get lost in the horrors of another's dream.

But I can't leave this one. I have to stay. I have to find Jake's location.

A deep guttural growl rumbles from the creatures as they creep closer to me. The cries of my friends continue to echo through the jungle while Helmet Guy starts thrashing his stick in front of him as if that will keep the creatures at bay.

The monkeys' faces whip around to face him, snarling in response. I take the distraction he's unknowingly given me to creep away to where my friends are struggling against the ropes holding them to the stakes.

I reach Sun first, and with shaking hands, I start working on her rope. "I'm going to get you out of here. Don't worry."

But she doesn't even glance my way. She's staring off into the thick foliage, screaming, tears creating rivulets through her dirt-covered face. Except, no matter how hard I work on her bindings, it's like they refuse to budge. In fact, the more I work, the tighter the rope becomes.

From the corner of my eye, I see Jake has finally yanked his stake out of the ground. He tumbles to the forest floor but manages to scramble back to his feet. He whirls around, eyes full of terror.

"Jake!" I yell and rush to him.

My heart aches at seeing him right before me. He looks so real, it's hard to process that he's just a Dream-Jake. I grab hold of his hand, but it hangs limply in mine. It's another reminder this is not his dream, but Helmet Guy's. Dream-Jake only can do what his dreamer dreams him to do.

But I refuse to give up. "Jake!" I clutch his cold, lifeless hand tighter. "Where did they take you? Are you okay?"

My words must have gotten Helmet Guy's attention because I feel a shift around me. The wind shudders and the branches of the trees stretch down like claws reaching for me. I glance back to where Helmet Guy stands still holding his stick, and sure enough, he's staring straight at me through his helmet visor.

A shiver curdles through my body.

A rumbling like a thousand footsteps fills the air. The ground shudders from the impact.

Another swarm of monkeys erupts from the dark shadows. There must be hundreds of them, racing with the intensity like they're being controlled by something or someone else.

There's no room for me to run.

No place to go.

What should I do? I've got to get this nightmare under control, but how? I have no idea how to deal with nightmares. That was never a part of our training.

The monkeys swoop down, and in a coordinated effort, take hold of each of my friend's posts with them still tied to it. Last, the monkeys surround Jake, grabbing a hold of his arms, legs, and his post.

"Stop that!" I scream, scanning the ground for a stick like Helmet Guy has.

Except there isn't time as the creatures start dragging Jake across the ground into the jungle.

"Aria!" Jake calls my name, his voice full of terror. He reaches for me and then he disappears into the forest. My heart rips in half. I choke back a sob.

He's out of view of the dreamer so the rational part of me knows he had to have vanished from the dream. But another part of my mind refuses to let him go.

I break into a sprint, chasing after him. Any second, I know I'll Fade since I'm so far from the dreamer. Yet, strangely I don't.

Up ahead, I spot Jake's feet slip into some foliage and I press on harder. My breath shudders out of me in heavy gasps. My chest burns like it's going to explode. But I barrel through the brush, desperation pushing my mind beyond anything I've ever experienced before.

Suddenly, I'm being passed by the monkeys dragging my friends on their posts. The strangest and most unsettling part is my friends are being dragged face down in the dirt, none of them making a single sound. My steps falter as I try to process it, and I glance behind me. That's when I see Helmet Guy is only just behind me. Why is he following me?

Or is there something more happening here?

But I don't have time to worry about Helmet Guy's intentions. Right now I have to follow Jake.

Spinning back around, I take off at a speed even faster than before. It's almost like I'm in control of the dream. Like I'm able to do things I normally wouldn't be able to do. But soon my steps slow as I realize I lost Jake.

No. No, no, no!

Which way did he go? I can't...and then a flash of red from Jack's T-shirt flickers through the world of dark greens and muted shadows.

And I'm running again, faster than humanly possible, branches snagging at my clothes and palms slapping against my face, but oddly, I don't feel anything. Only the desperate need to find Jake.

Within moments, I stagger out of the brush onto a well-worn dirt path where the sides are neatly trimmed and tall, thick-trunked trees twined with hundreds of roots grasp for the sky. Just ahead, I spot the monkeys dragging Jake who is bouncing along behind them like a rag doll. They halt at a flat circular, metal plate planted in the center of the path.

Suddenly, Helmet Guy appears beside the object like he's magically transported himself to that location. I have seen dreamers do that from time to time, yet I'm so caught up in the terror of this nightmare that it startles me.

The monkeys hoot and dance around the plate like they're performing a ritual and then Helmet Guy grabs a handle in its center and lifts it up like a lid of a...

I gasp. "It's a hatch."

Could this be the secret location of Sadir?

It has to be!

But my shock has made me too slow because the moment this revelation hits me, the monkeys have already dropped Jake inside. It's his screams that yank me out of my shock. Meanwhile, Helmet Guy leaps inside the hatch and slams the top shut.

Then the monkeys turn and face me. They attack in a rushing wave of claws and sharp teeth, ripping at my skin like knives. I scream as pain rages over my body.

In a swoop, the darkness rushes across the jungle, enveloping me.

When I open my eyes, I'm met with pale light. I blink a few times only to realize I'm back on the floor in the hut. Safe from crazed monkeys. Safe from the ground desperate to suck me into its depths.

My hands shake a little, the dream still hovering at the corners of my mind as Sun pulls off my mask and earplugs.

Quickly, I run my hands over my arms, checking for the blood and injuries that I surely must have. But there are none there.

"I'm safe," I whisper.

"Yes, you are." Sun's face hovers over mine, lines furrowed across her brow. "But girl, you can't do that anymore. You completely freaked me out when you wouldn't come out of the dream. Your heart rate was through the roof."

Pain presses against my temples. Slowly, I push myself to sitting, groaning from the effort.

Moonlight illuminates the hut. When I twist myself on the wooden floor, I find that Helmet Guy is still sleeping while Tony is no longer lying where I last saw him before I entered the Dreamscape.

"Tony?" I ask Sun.

Suddenly, a retching noise like someone throwing up comes out of the tiny bathroom. She nods to the sound, rolling her eyes. "He's having a tough time. His body is missing our sleep pods."

"He's not the only one." I grimace. "It was a rough dream. Actually, it was more of a nightmare."

Even though I'm sitting here in the warm hut, safe for the moment, I still can't quite shake the chill of the dream and the complete terror I felt. Sun's frown deepens, but she wraps her arm around me.

"You need one of those blankets that Nurse Debbie always gave us when we had a bad Dream Walk." She rubs her hands along my arms. "Still, you should've come out of that dream if it was a nightmare. You know better."

"I think I found out where they took Jake," I whisper as if spies watching us from the rafters above.

"Okay, so why do I feel like I'm not going to like what you have to say?"

The door to the hut cracks open, spilling moonbeams across the dusty hut, and someone steps inside. Both Sun and I tense, and she reaches for a rock she must have found along the way, prepping to throw it. Tony steps out of the bathroom, half-bent over, but pulling his fist back, ready to punch whoever entered.

"Chill, everyone. It's me." Javier holds out his hands, chuckling. "Save the battle for the enemy."

He's about to turn around to close the door when his eyes land on Helmet Guy sleeping fitfully on the floor.

"What in the—?" Javier points to him, and even though the shadows shroud his features, I know his face is twisted in anger.

"He's one of Sadir's men," I explain, trying to sound like it's just a normal thing that happens when we're hanging out in a hut in the jungle.

Javier launches into a string of Spanish words that are probably not G-rated. I finally manage to pull myself to standing, wobbling a bit from the effort. Man, that nightmare really did a number on me. Not going to tell Javier that. No need to offer him more ammunition.

"Before you flip out," I say. "Just hear what we have to say."

"Before I flip out?" Javier practically yells. "Too late for that. I flipped out when we were attacked back at the resort. This is—this is way beyond flipping."

"Shh!" Sun reminds us. "We need to keep our voices down. Plus we can't wake *him* up. I've given him Temazepam, but he's a fighter and isn't taking it well."

"Speak." Javier crosses his arms, leveling his gaze at me. "And fast."

Quickly, I summarize what we did and why, leaving out the details of the nightmare. Once I'm finished, his eyes drift to Tony.

"What's wrong with you?" Javier narrows his eyes skeptically on Tony. "Did something happen in the dream?"

Tony shrugs. "Rough night. You know running from men with guns and demented monkeys."

"Monkeys?" Javier asks.

"It's a long story," I say, shooting Tony a look as if to tell him not to say that we entered a nightmare. Javier's already ballistic enough as it is. "But I think I know where they've taken Jake."

"Let me guess, Monkey Island," Javier says.

"Exactly," I say. "Now we have a clearer picture of where on the island they took Jake."

I'm about to tell them more details of the dream but hesitate. If I tell him what I saw, I won't be useful anymore. He could very well run off and find this place without me. And there's no way I'm sitting around waiting for someone else to help Jake. My boyfriend needs me, and I know he'd do the same for me.

Javier's eyebrows lift incredulously. "A path? *That's* the lead you have?"

"This path is the entrance to the facility. I'm sure of it. If I saw the place, I could take us there."

"It's a possibility." Javier crosses the hut to where Helmet Guy is sleeping. "But we can't forget that you entered a dream. There's a high chance that the events and things you saw symbolized reality but aren't actually real."

"It's the only lead we have right now so I think we should take it seriously." Tony slumps to the ground. "How about you? Did you come up with anything?"

"I did," Javier says and pulls out some fruit from his pockets. "And I brought some mangos. It's not much but it should get us through the night."

As if hearing Javier's words, my stomach growls in agreement. We all settle on the floor and start munching on the fruit he brought while he gives us an update.

"There's this guy who reached out to me through my MaxLife email," Javier begins. "Says he knows you, Aria. Calls himself Joe and apparently is a U.S. operative."

"Wait." My heart skips. "When did he send this email?"

"About an hour ago. So you do know him?"

"Yeah, he literally saved Jake's and my lives. But we thought he might be dead. The fact he sent the email means he's okay."

I let out a long, relieved breath. Finally, some good news!

"He's very much alive," Javier says. "Maybe it was a mistake, but we're in a desperate situation right now, and he seemed legit. Plus, I remember you telling us about him. So I called the guy."

"That was risky," Sun says. "It could be a trick."

"It was a risk, but it's not like we have a lot of options. Especially since I can't get a hold of your dad, Aria, and no one else from the U.S. is taking me very seriously. I left a message but I'm still waiting for a response. Dr. Hale might still be traveling. We don't have time for bureaucrats to follow the proper legislation channels. And Jake sure as hell doesn't have time."

"What did Joe say?" I ask, suddenly feeling hopeful.

"He said he could get a team to our location in less than three hours if I told him where we were. He's on his way now."

Sun sucks in a breath, but I nod saying, "You made the right call. I was skeptical of him at first, too, but as I said, he nearly died saving Jake and me."

"So he should be here soon then?" Tony says.

"In a few hours." Javier tosses the pit of his mango out the window. "I'm going to head to the road and make sure they find us without any issues. I need you three—" He pauses and glances over at Helmet Guy. "You four, to stay here and not get into any trouble. No more Dream-scapes, no more sneaking off and picking up assassins. In fact, try to get some sleep. We have a long road ahead of us."

I really don't like the idea of sitting around waiting here, but Javier's right. It's the safest option. Plus, even though I don't want to sleep, I'm exhausted from every-thing that's happened in the last few hours.

Javier slips out of the hut, and through the wide

window, I watch him disappear into the folds of the jungle.

"Should we take turns guarding our prisoner?" I say, trying to keep the situation light.

"You both get some sleep." Sun sinks to the floor, pressing her back against the wall. "That nightmare has got to have taken it out of you. Besides, right now I can't even think about falling asleep."

Suddenly, sleeping sounds like a very good idea. The adrenaline must be leaving my body.

I barely manage to nod. I feel myself drifting off into an exhausted sleep the second my head hits the hard floor.

I WAKE to the sound of voices. My head feels a little fuzzy and my body screams at me to just roll over and go back to sleep. But then I remember that Jake's been kidnapped, and they could be torturing him right now to get information from him on what he knows about the Dreamscape.

"My men are securing a boat to take us down the river," a voice is saying. "But it would be helpful if I could talk to Aria. Get details on the dream."

Hearing my name snaps me to being fully awake. I push myself up to find Operative Joe standing in the hut with Sun and Javier. Another guy is busy tying Helmet Guy up, which is a bit of a relief.

"Joe," I say, my voice sounding weaker than I'd like it to. "You're alive!"

I stand up, wanting to give the dude a hug or something. He saved Jake's and my life already and nearly got himself killed in the process. But instead, I find myself standing there awkwardly, jamming my hands in my short's pockets.

"Very much alive," Joe says. "It takes a lot to kill me. Especially when I've still got a job to do."

"Guess you better make sure you don't run out of jobs then," I say, but my eyes go to his side where I remember blood pooling out across his shirt. "Are you okay to you know...walk?"

He chuckles. "I'll manage. But right now Sadir Gesner's still got your friend, my agents, and probably even closer to getting highly sensitive information from them. There isn't time to not be okay."

I swallow, nodding. Nothing is more sobering than knowing how high the stakes are for us.

"Now Aria." Joe's voice is urgent. "We're securing a boat to head out ASAP to Monkey Island, but Javier here says you've gotten more intel for us from a dream. Is that right?"

"That's right." I lift my chin. "But I'm coming with you. I'll take you to the spot that I saw in the dream."

"Afraid that can't happen. It would be too dangerous."

"Then I'm going on my own. I'm not sitting here to wait around, hoping that you can understand all the details I saw in my dream. So if you want to know where Jake and your people are, you're going to have to take me."

Javier throws his hands into the air, muttering again in Spanish while Joe rubs his head, clearly frustrated.

"Listen, Aria," Joe says. "I don't have time to convince you or make some kind of deal. I need you to tell me what you saw in the dream and then let Wayne here drive you back to Lima where we've got transportation back to the U.S. being set up. I don't trust the airport here in town, and it's our best option to keep undercover."

"I'm not budging." I cross my arms. "And I'm not leaving Jake."

"Same here." Tony raises his hand like we're voting. "I'm staying."

"Me, too," Sun adds and then looks pointedly at Javier. "Leave no team member behind."

"That's a low blow," Javier mutters. "This is a completely different situation than leaving someone behind in the Dreamscape."

"Is it?" Sun asks. "The Dreamscape has its dangers, too."

Joe pulls Javier outside and the two start talking. Soon their tones turn heated. Meanwhile, the Wayne dude is hauling Helmet Guy across the floor and down the steps toward the Jeep parked outside.

Finally, Joe leaves Javier outside and steps back into the hut. He sighs, rubs a hand over his eyes, and says, "Fine. You all can come. But while we're on this mission,

I'm your leader. You will do everything I order you. No exceptions. Understood?"

"Understood," the three of us say.

"Now get in the car," he says, briskly. "Dawn is in four hours, and we need the darkness to hide our approach."

TWENTY-FIVE
THE RESCUE MISSION

Darkness cloaks us as our group tumbles out of Operative Joe's van and scurries up to the gate of what looks like another deserted resort. Above, the clouds wreathe the moon, and the air has stilled almost as if the wildlife is holding its breath for us. My nerves zing through my body, part anticipation, and part terror. I mean, it's not like I just go out on covert operations every day.

Or ever for that matter.

"I'd feel a whole lot better if I were blinged out in shiny black gear like Joe and Wayne have," Tony mutters beside me. "I'm guessing it's water-proof, bulletproof, and for all I know, explosive proof."

"Please don't say explosive," Sun says. "It makes me nervous."

Still, Tony's right. They're decked out while we look like vagabonds in our tattered, muddied clothes.

Three flashes blink from inside the abandoned building, and instantly Joe comes to life, waving one hand to indicate for us to move. Wayne pushes open the small wrought-iron gate and races across the open lawn. I don't hesitate but rush after him, my shorter legs struggling to keep up with Wayne's sprint.

The front door to the resort opens as if by magic and we all stream inside. We're met by another of Joe's men who must have opened the door. His eyes take each of us in with skepticism. He rubs his bald head.

"Follow close," he whispers, and then turns, leading us at a jog down a stone-arched ceiling corridor.

Leaves and sticks litter the marble flooring and cobwebs stretch across the hallway, sticking and clinging to us as we run along.

Soon the corridor spits us outside onto a long series of steps that trail down a hillside to what looks like a river below.

"Remind me to start running every day if we ever make it home alive," I say, breathlessly.

"Or maybe just don't ever leave home again," Sun says.

"Someone tell me why I agreed to this," Tony complains, panting heavily.

"Hush!" Wayne stops to cut his hand through the air. We all stiffen at his tone.

He continues on, and I gulp down the fear pushing up in my throat as I shadow him. Finally, we reach the bottom of the hill, my legs aching from everything we've been through in the last twenty-four hours. A boat bobs in the water, hugging a long wooden dock. It's long and flat looking, and even in the darkness, the sides look weathered as if it's been around longer than I have.

Two other men are already inside it, moving about as the bald man joins them. Wayne climbs into the boat and indicates for us to follow. As we each enter, he passes us a lifejacket.

"Sit," Wayne instructs, and we all quickly settle on the wooden benches in the back, securing our lifejackets.

"This boat isn't going to sink halfway there, will it?" Sun asks.

Wayne just ignores her, and instead, starts unwrapping the rope keeping us tied to the dock.

"I don't think he's happy about us coming along," I whisper to Sun.

"Can you blame him?" Javier asks. "This is a big risk."

As soon as Joe steps inside the boat, the driver turns on the engine and we take off, whizzing through the dark waters of the river. A cool breeze cuts over my face and whips my hair behind me. I'm surprised at how fast the boat moves, considering that my bench is cracked down the center. The moist air is thick and fresh, drenched in the scent of river water and mossy forests.

"This is the Madre de Dios," Javier explains to us. "Translated as "Mother of God" and one of the tributaries of the Amazon River."

Soon, the clouds part, revealing the moon and a few bright stars. Moonbeams illuminate the river, wide and empty of any other boats. Meanwhile, thick forests shroud the shorelines in darkness. The boat rises and falls from the light waves as if it's mimicking my growing terror.

Sure I'm scared of what lies ahead of us, but the memories of how I nearly lost Jake at Dr. Reasner's lab in China only add to my worries.

I can't lose him. I won't lose him.

"I feel like we're the only people in the world," I whisper to Sun, and she takes my hand and squeezes it. "Do you think they'll be able to find the right island?"

"They're professionals," Tony consoles me from my other side. "If anyone can find it, it will be them."

Despite my fears, my eyes keep trying to shut thanks to the drone of the motor and the cool breeze. A jerking motion wakes me, and I realize I must have fallen asleep. The boat is slowing down, and the air suddenly feels still. A dark shape rises from the center of the river.

It's an island.

The shape and the curve of the shoreline, along with its steep and nearly impenetrable banks cause my pulse to throb. This is the same island from my dream with Locket back at the hotel.

I rise from my seat and stumble along the stretch of our boat until I reach where the driver and Joe are standing. Joe is staring through binoculars while Wayne is rigging up what looks like a drone.

"This is the island," I say, clutching the side of the boat as I squint to see it better. "I'm sure of it."

"According to the locals, it is Monkey Island," Joe says, but he sounds unconvinced. "We're not spotting anything on it yet. Wayne's going to take a closer look though."

The drone lifts off the side of the boat and buzzes across the dark waters, heading directly to the island. Meanwhile, Wayne flicks open a tablet, and with a few touches, the screen bursts to life, displaying gray shadows.

"The drone's camera has infra-red" he explains. "It will pick up any heat signatures on the island if there are any at all."

We wait in silence, and I hold my breath, watching the scenery below the drone change from water to the foliage of the treetops. Endless leaves. Endless branches.

Once it reaches the end of the island, Wayne maneuvers the controls to do another run in the other direction, but after a few passes, the drone comes back with no information, so he drives it back to our boat.

"Looks like it's a dead end." Joe's shoulders sag a little. "Should've known better than to be chasing after things in dreams."

A surge of panic rushes through me. "We can't just leave. We haven't even investigated the island properly. What if that camera missed something?"

But Joe has already turned to speak to the boat driver. "Turn us around. We're heading back."

"No!" I grab the driver's arm to stop him.

He stiffens, but his hand wavers on the wheel.

"We can't waste time and energy running around some island in the middle of the jungle." Joe pulls out his phone and starts tapping on it.

"If there were people underground," I finally say. "Would Wayne's camera be able to pick them up?"

Joe's eyes snap to mine. "Why do you ask?"

I hesitate, wondering if I give away too much then I won't be useful anymore. But at the same time, I don't want them to just give up because I never said anything. "In the Helmet Guy's dream, there was a hatch and he dragged Jake inside it."

Joe swears under his breath and pinches his forehead. "This information would've been helpful to know beforehand."

"I think I can recognize the path this hatch is located on," I continue.

"What are you saying?" Joe crosses his arms. "You want me to take you on that island so you can wander around until you can find a specific path? That's a large island. We'll be searching all night in complete darkness for this hatch you saw in a dream."

"I'm willing to give it a try," I say. "What else are you planning on doing tonight? Movie and dinner?"

"You've got a smart mouth on you," he grumbles. "But fine. We'll give it a try."

The driver turns on the engine and we glide along the

water, but just before he pulls up to the steep embankment, I stop him with my hand.

"Wait," I say. "In one of the dreams, we were paddling on kayaks toward a specific section of the island. Can you just drive around the island's perimeter so I can see if I spot anything familiar?"

The driver hesitates and looks to Joe for confirmation. Joe gives a slight nod. As we putter around the island's edge, I squint at the shoreline, searching for the familiar embankment that I saw in Locket's dream. I'm about to give up and just pick any spot to pull the boat up to when I spot a steep incline of the island with a dark muddy section that runs from the top of the embankment to the water. My heart leaps.

I point out the section to the driver. "That's it."

Joe doesn't say anything, but he's quiet so I'm guessing he's not totally upset with me. The boat slips up to the edge of the muddy ground. I'm about to scramble out when Joe stops me.

"Not so fast," he says. He tosses me a heavy black jacket that's just like what the other guys are wearing. "Put this on. You're not getting killed on my watch if I can help it."

I tug it over my shoulders. It hangs halfway down my thighs and dangles over my fingertips. "It's a little big but it works."

"The rest of you are staying here in the boat with Captain Zeed. And that's an order."

When my three friends start complaining, Joe lifts up a finger. "Nope. You agreed. As long as you're with me, you follow my orders without question. Understood?"

They nod miserably while Joe and two other guys step out of the boat and slosh their way to the muddy path. My heart stutters a little when they stop on the path and spin around to face us. Yikes. They are holding very large guns.

"The moment you step ten feet off this boat," Wayne warns us, "our cloaking devices won't hide you. A tracker may be able to pick up your movements so be careful and always be on the alert."

"Keep an eye aerial visual on us at all times," Joe orders Wayne. "Call if there are any issues."

"Yes, sir." Wayne nods and resumes work on putting his drone back into the sky.

I swing my leg over the side of the boat and slop through the muck to join the other two on the path. Once there, we carefully climb up the slippery rocks to the top of the embankment above.

The moment I'm in the thick forest, everything feels familiar and yet also much more realistic than Helmet Guy's dream.

That should make me feel better, but the guns which Joe and his men are holding out in front of them, ready to use at a single command, make my insides all twitchy and fluttery.

I eye the trees, half expecting a horde of wild monkeys to come screeching and rushing out, ready to rake their claws across my body. But other than a few hooting sounds, bug noises, and the wind rushing through the leaves far up above, it's eerily calm. Almost as if we were in a place that time forgot.

We creep along the narrow forest trail, every unusual hoot causing me to jump just a little. Branches stretch out, scraping at my arms and legs, and mosquitoes buzz around my face, nipping at any part of my skin that's exposed. The air feels hot and constricting compared to being out in the open breeze of the river.

"Are you sure this is the right way?" one of the guys asks.

"Probably not," Joe mumbles.

"If this isn't a goose-chase," one of the men mutters. "I don't know what one is."

My shoulders dip.

Maybe I got confused. Could it be that all the parts of the dreams I thought were clues, were actually not clues after all? But then we come to a sign planted in the middle of a quadrant where four paths converge into one large opening.

Monkey Island

"I've seen this place." I inspect the sign until I'm sure of my next steps. Then I take off down the path, jutting to the right.

Joe's men whisper-yell for me to stay with them, and

they quickly run to make sure they're flanking my sides. Soon, I come to a part of the path that is terrifyingly familiar to the dream I was in only a few hours earlier.

My steps quicken, which only makes the men even jumpier as they give me annoyed side glances. But when the path widens even more, that's when I see it.

Gleaming silvery in the moonlight and lying on the path is none other than exactly what I'm looking for.

The hatch.

I sprint to the hatch despite Joe's harsh whisper to stop. I have to touch it. Feel it for myself to know that what I saw in the dream was real. My knees hit the soft, jungle floor first, and I reach out, touching its gray surface.

The latch feels hard against my skin, a harsh contrast to the forest around me. Before I can wrap my fingers around it, Joe pushes me away from the opening.

"What the hell are you doing?" Joe barks at me. "What if there was a trip wire or land mine? You could have been killed on the spot."

He glances about, quick and sure, taking in the situation. Then he orders the two other men to scout the perimeter before returning. Unlike his cool composure, sweat drips from my forehead, and my breathing is hitched and shuddery.

We're so close to Jake. I can feel it. I know it.

"Can you open the hatch?" I ask. My voice quivers, betraying my desperation. "I think this is where they took Jake."

"In the dream?" Joe's eyes lift skeptically.

Okay, so I know I must sound like I'm a lunatic, relying on a dream so heavily, but it's all I have. Besides, dreams have served me well in the past when I needed to find my dad.

I lift my chin. "Yes."

Meanwhile, the other two men silently rejoin us with word that the perimeter is clean. They position themselves so their backs are to us, guns and eyes pointed into the thick jungle. I can't decide if I feel safer with them nearby with the weapons or more terrified. The clouds have blanketed the moon, leaving us to the dark night.

"Sir." The bearded one flicks on a small penlight, pointing it on the silvery hatch cylinder. "Should I open it?"

Joe hesitates, eyeing the hatch and then the path. Thunder rumbles in the distance, and boney fingers of light flash across the sky.

Suddenly, he presses his hand to the black device in his ear and says, "Copy that." Then to our group, "A storm is coming in hot. We'll take a quick look at this and then get back to the boat. I don't want us to be out on the water when it hits."

A weight replaces my excitement. He doesn't think this hatch is where they're holding Jake. They're just following this lead because we have no other options while his mind is already back to returning to Puerto Maldonado.

"Yes, sir," Beard says and twists the hatch's handle. It clicks, but after much pulling and grunting, it doesn't move despite his efforts.

Droplets of water patter against my cheeks. I try to remember how Helmet Guy opened up the hatch in the dream. He did something strange with it, but what?

"Try pulling it up," I offer.

Beard and Joe glance up at me, hovering over them like a little child wanting to open a present. Their eyebrows lift in question as if they don't understand what I'm talking about. I lick my lips and crouch down beside them by the hatch. This time, Joe doesn't push me away. My hand closes over the lever, and I pull up and back on it.

The top pops up, and my heart does a little flip.

I hold my breath and back off as Joe pushes the lid up the rest of the way.

The three of us peek inside, but we're only met by utter darkness plunging into the earth below. A medal ladder just like the one I remember Helmet Guy scaling down clings to the edge of the hatch. Rain starts falling in earnest, wetting my body, pinging off the hatch, and falling into the dark abyss of the hole in the ground.

"This is it," I whisper, twisting my hands in excitement. "It's just like the dream."

The operatives glance at each other again, seeming to be able to communicate without speaking, which is annoying. Do they believe me? Or do they think we're on a goose chase? Finally, Joe pulls a glow stick from his vest pouch, snaps it so it turns green, and tosses it into the hole.

It plummets into the darkness, tumbling into a circular tube until it finally bounces onto what looks like a concrete floor. It appears there's a doorway at the bottom of the shaft.

I shiver, blinking against the water that's running down my forehead. The two other men guarding us continue to stand stoically, their silhouettes lit up only by the occasional flashes of lightning.

Finally, Joe shrugs and tells Beard, "Head on down and check it out. I'll follow." Then he points at me, his face hard as stone. "You stay here, understand. Do not follow."

"Okay," I say, swallowing the lump in my throat. Is it wrong that I'm a little glad they don't want me to go? There is something a little creepy about plunging into a dark shaft with only pale green light as a guide.

With smooth agility, the two slip into the hole, scaling down the metal ladder with ease. I grip the edge of the hatch, the metal cold and biting against my palms. I wait. Joe's penlight pricks a pale light against the smooth, metal tube they're descending into. I hold my breath in anticipation of what they might find.

But when another flash of lightning streaks across the forest, something catches my attention from the corner of my eye. Startled, I whip my gaze to the space between the trees where I thought I'd seen something.

Darkness and rain drape over the forest once again, leaving me to wonder what I saw, if anything.

I focus back on the hole in the ground, except Joe's light has vanished. "I can't see them anymore," I tell my stoic guard. "Do you think they're okay?"

He presses a finger to his ear, saying, "Everything okay down there?" He listens for a moment. Thunder crackles through the jungle. How can he hear a thing?

Finally, he nods. "Copy that." He looks at me and says, "Joe needs you below."

"He wants me to go down there?" My heart stutters a little. I mean, a part of me is desperate to go down there, but as I stare down into the swampy-green glow from the glow stick, a cold fear curls around my chest. "Are you sure? Because right before Joe went down, he said for me to stay here."

"Guess he changed his mind." He shrugs. "Don't worry. I'll keep watch from above."

"Right." I suck in a deep breath. "Here goes."

I reach for the top rung of the ladder and swing my leg over the edge. My heart slams against my chest as my palm slips a little on the rung's wet surface.

You can do this, Aria, I tell myself. *Be brave!*

I take another deep breath, reminding myself that this is for Jake. He wouldn't hesitate for a moment to climb into the darkness for me. I plant one foot onto the ladder, and then another, pushing out all thoughts of slipping and falling to my death below.

"Be careful going down," the guy warns, his forehead bunching up in concern. "The rain will make that metal slick."

No kidding, I think, trying to calm my thudding heart.

Raindrops hit the top of my head and shoulders as I descend. I take one rung at a time, focusing on the cold metal surface of the ladder instead of the distance below. Right foot down, right hand down, left foot down, left hand down. At this achingly slow pace, it will take days for me to reach the bottom, I think morbidly.

Suddenly, I plunged into darkness, and the cool flow of rain abruptly stops. I glance up, to no longer see the stormy sky above. I freeze on the ladder, unable to move. Darkness presses against me, choking on my lungs. I close my eyes, telling myself to stay calm.

Finally, I manage to croak out, "Hello!"

No one answers. Panic shoves my body into action, and I quickly scale back up the ladder at twice the speed. It's hard to see as the light from the glow stick doesn't quite reach up here. But when I get to the top, my head hits the hatch's lid. Someone closed it.

My fingers frantically try to find a latch or button to open it, but all I find is a smooth surface.

I pound on the top. "Hey! Open up!"

When no one responds, a wave of dizziness washes

over me. What does this mean? Am I trapped inside? How will I get out?

But then I remember that Operatives Joe and Beard Guy are here, too. They'll know what to do. And they have comms so they can communicate with the guys above. Maybe the guy shut the hatch to keep the rain off me and make it easier for me to climb down the ladder.

Yes. I suck in a shuddery breath. That's got to be it. I'll just find Joe. He'll know what to do. Spurred on by a purpose, I resume my descent. I refuse to think of anything else or I might lose it.

This time, I move faster, eager to get out of the dark confines of the shaft I'm in.

When my foot finally touches solid ground, my legs crumble beneath me, in part from fear and part from relief. I push my wet hair out of my face and blink as if that will bring on more light than the tiny glow stick affords. But nothing happens.

I pick up the green stick and grope through the emptiness until my palm slaps against a hard, ribbed surface. Suddenly, a flicker of muted light pops up to the right of what appears to be another tunnel.

"Joe!" I call out, suddenly not caring if I'm quiet or not. "Hello? Are you there? I'm coming."

Keeping one hand on the wall, I creep along the tunnel until soon it turns right, and I can see the light ahead of me. My steps quicken as I hurry along until I find its source. It's not Joe's penlight but a bulb attached to the wall. The corridor I'm standing in dead ends.

Nothing is here.

No Joe. No Beard Guy. Not even a sign of them having come this way.

I spin around, wondering where they went. Did they go in the other direction? But when I backtrack the way I came, I'm met with another dead end. I stare at it, my heart sinking into the pit of my stomach.

This was the way I came, wasn't it? I rub my forehead, confusion filling me with panic. I should've left a trail of some sort except I don't remember any other tunnels along the way.

A grinding sound rumbles behind me. Quickly, I spin to face the sound, my pulse throbbing against my skin.

And that's when I realize this isn't a dead end after all. The wall is sliding open to reveal a doorway.

"Welcome, Aria," a voice greets me from an intercom just above the door. How had I not seen that before? "We've been expecting you."

TWENTY-SEVEN
THE HIDDEN FACILITY

Bright, harsh light cuts into the gloom of the tunnel. I shield my eyes, backing up as the door rumbles open while my brain scrambles to understand the man's words, "We've been expecting you."

Did I just walk into a trap? But they couldn't have known that we would've entered Helmet Guy's dream or that he would dream about this hatch. So how could they be expecting me?

My back presses against the cold metal wall, heart hammering in my chest as two men with guns step through the door. They grab my arms and literally pick me off the ground and haul me through the door into another hallway, white as ash.

My boots skim along the floor as the men ruthlessly drag me along.

This section is a startling sharp contrast to the grungy

tunnel I just left that I'm trying to process exactly what is happening. I glance about for the person whose voice came over the intercom, but no one else is in the corridor.

Is this what happened to Joe and Bearded Guy? Did they get kidnapped, too, or did they face a worse fate? Could they still be safe?

"Who are you?" I ask the two men. "Where are you taking me?"

Their faces are set into deep frowns. By the broad shoulders and brown hair, I'm guessing these must be Sadir's men since they look Russian not Peruivan. They're wearing camouflage that would blend well in the jungle above. But the stench of these men makes me gag. They really could use a shower.

"You're Sadir's cronies, aren't you?" I grimace when the guy on my left squeezes my arm harder. I'm going to have deep bruises from their grips.

We take a left turn along the alabaster hallway, which at first looks like a dead-end but suddenly turns into a door sliding open. My breathing hitches, and I start praying frantically for a way to get out of this situation.

I'd been so desperate to save Jake, and yet, here I'm being captive all the same. My great plans to fix this situation are racing out of control. As we come up to the door, the men toss me through the entrance. I crumple into a heap, smashing my cheek on the concrete. Stars flicker in my vision, and I groan.

"What is this?" a voice barks above me. "How could you treat my little treasure with such disdain."

I crawl to my knees just as a thick trunk of a man wearing a black suit slaps one of my guards across the face. The suited man's broad shoulders and wide arms warn he isn't to be messed with. That slap must've hurt.

"Apologies, Great One." The guard's expression remains stoic despite the red splotch spreading on his face.

Great One. My eyes revert back to the large man with graying brown hair. There's something about his presence that demands attention. This has to be Sadir Gesner.

As if to confirm my guess, he turns his attention back to me. "Greetings, Aria Hale. I am Sadir Gesner. It is an honor to welcome you to my humble abode. I have been eager to bring you here, but you have been quite difficult to find."

I gulp down the terror rising up my throat. I'm glad I'm not standing, or my knees would buckle beneath me. This is the man Operative Joe had been so worried about. The one desperate to set up his own country here in the Americas so he could slowly take control of this part of the world.

"This is not how I wish for you to be treated," Sadir continues. "You are to be well cared for. I cannot have you hurt or sick, but only in prime condition. You look as if you have had a tough night, yes?"

"No kidding." I glare at him. My wet hair clings to the sides of my face from the rain, and my clothes are splattered in mud and grime. "Considering I haven't slept much since I was kidnapped. That I've been chased, shot at, and dragged about by your men. Not to mention that my friend was recently kidnapped, and I can't remember when I ate last. So yeah, I'd say I'm having a rough week."

The side of his lips twitch. I'm not sure if it's from anger or a near laugh. But then he clucks his tongue and shakes his head sympathetically.

"This is completely unacceptable." He snaps his fingers, and a nurse comes running to his side. She's wearing blue scrubs, and her brown hair is twisted into a knot on top of her head. He barks at her in Russian.

She dips her head into a bow, not once looking at him in the face as if one glance might kill her. "As you wish, Great One."

I finally climb to my feet and cast my eyes about, searching for the operatives. But there isn't a sign of them. The only thing in this room are walls lined with computer monitors and TV screens. A control room perhaps?

The screens show visuals of the jungle, including footage of the entrance to the hatch, which is now empty of any humans. Not a good sign. I can only hope the guy I left up there is okay. On another screen, I spy our boat bobbing at the riverbank. My friends are sitting inside talking, probably debating what they should do. Find us or return to the mainland.

I want to yell at them to leave right this second. To get out of here and stay safe.

My heart sinks as comprehension of the situation falls over me. Sadir had been watching us the entire time. In fact, he probably arranged for the hatch to open and close. And that man I thought I'd imagined I saw in the jungle must have been real.

Maybe they hadn't expected us, but they definitely knew the moment we set foot on this island.

"Nurse Anya will make sure you are well-fed and cleaned up," Sadir tells me, interrupting my terrified thoughts. "You are destined for great things, Aria. I look forward to seeing you shine."

"Great things?" I lift my eyebrows. "If you think I'm going to help you, you are sorely confused."

Those words finally bring a wide smile to his face. "Once you see what I have planned for you, you will want to join me in my endeavors. Now, do not worry your pretty little head about anything, my treasure. The important thing is for you to be prepared to reach your mind's full potential."

"I'm not eating or resting until I know where Jake is," I say.

Sadir merely knits his forehead and clasps his hands together in front of him as if trying to understand me better. "Your commitment is to be commended. I will be depending on that when the time comes."

Ice-cold fear creeps through me. What is he talking about?

Before I can ask him to explain, hands clamp around

my arms once again and lift me off the ground.

"That hurts!" I exclaim, frowning. So much for not hurting his precious Little Treasure, I think morbidly.

Nurse Anya spins on her soft-soled shoes and pads across the room while I'm unceremoniously hauled after her.

This next corridor is lined with doors, and security cameras dot the ceiling like someone has real trust issues. We finally stop in front of one of the doors, and when it slides open, I'm hefted inside and dumped onto a hard hospital-style cot with scratchy sheets.

"Get your filthy hands off me." I push them away as I try to calm my racing heart.

What are they planning for me? Why did they bring me here?

The two men step away, but they don't leave. Instead, they stand by the door, hands hovering near their guns hooked to their belts. Meanwhile, Nurse Anya passes me a bundle of what looks like clothes. She points to another door.

"You take shower," she instructs. "Change clothes."

"I'm not doing anything until I know where Jake is."

"He is not far. If you want to see him, shower, change, and eat. Then you see him."

My heart skips. So he is here! But even still, should I do what they are asking me to do, or should I ignore them? At this point, I'm not sure. Every choice of mine so far has been riddled with errors.

Dizziness washes over me, and the room sways a little. My body is obviously telling me I need food and rest. I can't be in the right frame of mind if I don't prepare myself for what is ahead. So in the end, I take the bundle Anya offers me and stumble into the bathroom.

By the time I've stripped off my grungy clothes and showered, I already feel a little better and clearer of mind. But when I step out of the shower, my clothes have vanished, leaving behind only the bundle Anya gave me. There's no way I'm going back out there naked with those awful guards, so I slip on the white tunic and yoga pants she left for me.

I stand for a moment in the simple bathroom, scanning the smooth walls for any sign of escape. But there's none. Only a toilet, sink, and shower.

More than anything, I don't want to leave the bathroom and face my new reality. That I've been kidnapped once again, and there's a reason why Sadir needs me.

A reason I know I'll be completely against.

Suddenly, the bathroom door opens as if telling me it's time to leave. I suck in a deep breath and step into the coolness of the room, only to find the outer door shut and the room empty. It's a relief to not have those awful guards with guns standing in front of me, but at the same time unnerving knowing I'm now a prisoner.

I need to find a way out of this place. There must be something I can do.

A tray of food has been placed on my bed. The scent

of grilled chicken and rice fills my nostrils, and my stomach growls. The thought of eating their food is unsettling, but at the same time, I need to be smart about this. I'll need the strength and energy for whatever lies ahead. I settle on the bed and devour the food in minutes.

A deep weariness settles over me after I push the tray aside. Even still, I'm determined to search for some way out of the cell that I'm in. But after I scour the smooth pale walls of the entire room for some means of escape, I collapse back on the bed in frustration. Sadir must need me for his Dreamscape, I decide. It's the only reason I can think of that he wouldn't just shoot me on sight or bother to lure me into his lair.

I need to be prepared for whatever he springs on me.

My mind reviews the different scenarios I might be faced with and how I can overcome those, but soon my eyes flutter closed as weariness sweeps through me.

I'M startled awake as hands grab my arms once again. My two guards are back, yanking me to standing. I grimace in pain as they clench my arms hard in the same place as last time.

The room swims a little, and I try to orientate myself. I must have entered Stage 3 of the sleep cycle, which is deep sleep. The floor bites cold against my bare feet, snapping me awake.

"No!" I resist, digging my feet into the ground and pushing back against them. All the calm and level-headedness I felt earlier has vanished, replaced by panic.

The two grunt as they try to heave me forward, but I fight against them, kicking and twisting about.

Suddenly, the speaker in the facility crackles, and a voice calls, "Aria!"

Then it cuts off as if there were other words, but they've only allowed me to hear my name. Even still, my whole body freezes because I know that voice is Jake's.

"Jake?" I glance about, searching for him, and then louder, yell, "Jake!"

"Want your boyfriend?" one of the guards says gruffly. "You come."

I pause unsure what to do when the voice comes back over the speakers again. "Aria!"

I can't tell if it's a recording or if it's real. But it's enough to pique my curiosity and let the guards push me forward, out my prison door, and into an elevator. There's a single button, which one guard pushes and we plummet downward until we jerk to a stop. The door swooshes open, and I stagger out into another long white hall, trying to reign in my scattered thoughts.

I'm in Sadir's facility. Need to find Jake. See if the operatives are here. Hope my friends have escaped.

But the moment we step through yet another door, all my thoughts disintegrate. Because things are far worse than I could have imagined.

TWENTY-EIGHT
THE TROLLEY DILEMMA

My guards have brought me into a large laboratory that looks like it could be owned by Stark Industries from an Avengers movie. It's a collection of glass and chrome with large computer monitors dispersed about the place. A raised dais in the center of the room overlooks the entire laboratory while hospital cots ring it. People are lying on most of the cots, still as the dead. They're wearing sleep masks and hooked up with wires to computers like we had at MaxLife.

Except this isn't MaxLife, trying to save dementia patients' memories. This is intrusive, forceful, against a person's will.

It's terrifying.

"Ah!" Sadir moves away from where he's looking over a technician's shoulder at a computer monitor to stand near the ring of cots. "There is my Little Treasure. Just in time."

I swallow the lump in my throat. All those people sleeping on the cots must be in the Dreamscape right now. I wonder if they're in the same dream or different ones? And how much did Sadir change Reasner's Dreamscape? Because if he hadn't made many changes since he stole it then they are all dreaming a living hell at this moment.

"I'm not your treasure," I snap. "What are you doing with these people? And where is Jake?"

"Come, come." Sadir waves to me excitedly like he's my uncle who has brought me a Christmas present. "I have so much to show you. Of all people, you will appreciate it the most."

Once again, the guards tow me down a series of smooth steps to Sadir. Desperately, I scan the lab for Jake, but I don't see him anywhere. Which in some ways is a relief. At least he isn't one of the people on the cots. After all, he went through in Reasner's Dreamscape and nearly lost his mind. I can't have that happen to him again.

"According to my research," Sadir snaps. "Your father designed the Dreamscape after your brain."

Uh-oh. I definitely don't like the direction he's going with this. "This is an incredible lab," I say, trying to distract him. "I'd really love a tour of the place."

Anything to get as much information out of him while delaying what I'm terrified he's going to do to me.

"The new home of mine really is state of the art." Sadir nods thoughtfully but doesn't take my bait of a tour.

"What do you want from me anyway?" I ask, trying a new distraction. "And why is this Dreamscape so important to you?"

"Many leaders instigate change through brute force and massive armies. But not me. I use the mind as my means of success. I have much to be thankful for. Your father and you who have enabled me to rise to power with the ease that every leader in the world would be envious of."

His words twist into my stomach like a knife. "You are a sick man," I spit out. "We created the Dreamscape to help dementia patients recover their memories. It was never to be used as a weapon."

He laughs, and his lips curl into a sneer. "How many times has progress been the result of the military? Your precious digital camera's infancy began as spy satellites used to take pictures. The EpiPen wasn't created to help people with allergies. It was made for soldiers to inject themselves when they were exposed to chemical warfare toxins and nerve agents. Canned goods, weather predictors, even Duct Tape. All were military inventions that ended up bettering the lives of everyday people."

"I don't see how interrogating people in their dreams is creating progress." I point to the people sleeping on the cots around me.

"You have heard of the Trolley Dilemma, yes?" I

shake my head, so he continues. "Imagine you are standing in a tram station. A runaway trolley is careening down a track about to hit five workers. Beside you is a lever connected to the tracks. If you pull it, the tram will be redirected to a sidetrack, and you will save the five unsuspecting workers. Except, there is one problem. A single person is working on this sidetrack. What do you do? Pull the lever, saving the five, but killing the one? Or do you let the five die?"

I cross my arms and glare at him. "What does this have to do with me and the Dreamscape?"

"The Dreamscape is the lever." Then he waves at those lying on the cots. "And these people are the one worker. Their information and cooperation save many from death. They enable me to take power without destroying cities and economies."

"This is so messed up," I mutter. The guy really thinks he's helping people.

"So what is your choice, Aria? Pull the lever and save the five or let the five die?"

"Since we're making up stories. How about there's an alarm button beside the lever. I push it, making the alarm go off. The workers all hear it and get off the track just in time. No one dies."

Now it's his turn to glare at me. "You are missing the point entirely."

I clench my fists, wishing I had a lever that would stop Sadir and his madness. "Where is Jake?"

Sadir sighs in frustration but waves his hand. "Bring the boy in."

The doors behind me swish open, and two guards drag in Jake. My heart clenches tight at seeing him. His sandy blond hair is a little wild, and he's wearing what must be their standard white tunic and pants for all their captives. Blue coloring rings his right eye and his lip is swollen. But the thing about him that terrifies me most is the red streaks in his eyes. They warn me that he hasn't slept in a very long time.

"Jake!" I try to run to him, but I'm glued in place by my guards maintaining their iron grips on me. "Are you okay? What did they do to you?"

"Aria!" he says. "I was hoping you'd left the country."

Sadir snaps his fingers, and the guards forcefully drag Jake down the stairs to one of the empty cots. They start strapping him down. He kicks and twists his body, trying to escape.

"Stop this!" I scream at them, and I start fighting against my captors. "What are you doing? Don't hurt him!"

"Jake Sutherland is going to take a little nap." A wicked smile slips over Sadir's lips. "I think you wish to join him, yes?"

"What?" Suddenly it's becoming hard to breathe. I can't get enough oxygen as the panic sets in. "No. Don't do this Sadir. Let him go!"

Suddenly, my guards yank me forward to the last

empty cot. I'm thrown onto the hard mattress, and despite my best efforts, I'm unable to stop them from strapping me into place, too.

"I wish you weren't here, Aria," Jake says. "You should've escaped."

"I couldn't leave you," I say.

"You should've. They were just using me as bait to get you here."

Tears stream down my cheeks, and I shudder as a nurse steps to my side, a syringe in her hand. Crap. This is not good. Not good at all!

"Aria!" Jake calls, yanking my attention back to him. "This Dreamscape is different. It's not safe. And whatever happens in there, you can't trust me. Okay?"

There's real terror in his voice. And that scares me more than anything.

"You've already been in there?" I shift my attention to Sadir. "You can't put him back into the Dreamscape. That's not safe for his mind."

"Did you not pay attention to my lesson, Aria?" Sadir clucks his tongue as if I'm a very bad student. "The fate of one must be sacrificed for the fate of many."

Pain spikes into my arm. I whip my head around to see that the nurse has injected me with whatever liquid is in that syringe.

"Don't worry, Jake," I tell him. "I'm going to find you. We'll figure this out."

"Noooo, you caaan't." Jake's words slur and his eyelashes flutter. "Don't give theeemmm—"

His head falls back with a thump onto the mattress. The nurse attending him slips on a sleep mask over his eyes and starts hooking wires up to him.

"Her heart rate is high," my nurse tells Sadir.

Sadir strolls over to me, but my vision shifts so much that his face blurs as he leans over me.

"She is strong," he says. "She will survive long enough to pull the lever."

I can't believe I fell asleep in class. So embarrassing!

Slowly, I lift my head off of my arm, which also feels like it's having a nap with me. Inconspicuously, I check for drool and then make a quick sweep of the classroom. Crap. Not only did I fall asleep, but in Psychology class. The one class I need to nail an A to keep my GPA up.

The prison-gray walls of our classroom seem drearier today. Or maybe it's just that the windows could use a good cleaning from the grime coating them. Sunlight barely pushes its way into the room. The school really needs to research color therapy because colors stimulate the brain. One look at this place screams uninspirational.

Mr. Kores has his back to us, writing on the Smart-Board what appears to be the latest theories on dream interpretations. This means I don't think he noticed my less-than-stellar behavior. I'm really counting on him for a college reference.

"The Journal of Neuroscience has some compelling theories," Mr. Kores is saying. "They relate to dreaming and how dreams are tied to our memories."

My shoulders relax, and I lean back in my chair. He's talking about research that I know inside and out thanks to what I'm working on with Dad at MaxLife. To my left, I spy Tony whispering in Melissa Benson's ear per usual. Probably trying to convince her to join him for the sing-a-thon at Mel's Coffee Shop. I don't know how he gets away with anything and not get in trouble in class.

A paper airplane swoops gracefully onto my desk. A quick glance to my right reveals whom I'm guessing is the culprit.

Jake Sutherland.

He's slouched in his chair, wearing jeans and one of his gamer T-shirts. Blond hair hangs over his eyes as he stares hyper-focused on his laptop. But then his gaze shifts to collide with mine. His lips crook up in the corner, totally giving him away.

My heart does a little flip-flop. He totally wrote me a note. Maybe even a love note. I've never been given a love note before. That said, we haven't been dating that long. Only a few months now.

"The write-up on the topic is due this Friday." Mr. Kores turns to face the class. I quickly tuck the airplane under my laptop until I can find a safer time to inspect Jake's airborne note.

Suddenly, the steel gray door opens and a woman, I'm guessing in her mid-thirties, strides into the classroom. She's wearing a starless night black suit with matching shoes. Her dark hair is pulled up into a tight bun and she's gripping a clipboard as if she's here to complete an inspection.

"Oh! Hello," Mr. Kores says, not missing a beat despite being interrupted. "Can I help you?"

"Greetings, students," she says stiffly. As if she would rather be anywhere in the world but here. "I'm here for your Career Day."

No one responds. Most of the kids just sit there, blankly staring at her. Not that I blame them. I don't remember us ever having a Career Day before.

"Career Day!" Mr. Kores slaps his pale forehead. "How could I have forgotten?"

"I don't know," the lady says in a weird voice like she's being forced to respond. "I keep telling you I don't know."

"Students, I'd like to introduce you to today's guest speaker," Mr. Kores says. "This is Agent Carol Marzano, a secret service agent for the U.S. government. She's here to answer any questions you may have about working in a job like hers."

"Can she tell us if they're really holding aliens in Area 51?" Melissa asks and then blows a bright pink bubble.

Tony tries to pop it, but she ducks away before he gets the chance.

"Aliens are not my area of expertise," Carol replies. "You must have confused me with someone else."

Suddenly, hands pop up around the classroom as the students burst to life. Everyone has a question to ask Agent Carol Marzano. I decide to use this distraction to unfold Jake's paper airplane. Sure enough, I find a note written in his handwriting. My insides go all warm like I'm sipping hot chocolate.

Aria,
I've missed you. Go out with me tonight?
J

My lips curve, and I dare a glance at Jake. He's staring at the U.S. agent, but then he leans back in his seat, and his head shifts just enough for me to see his smile. Discreetly, I pull out a sheet of paper from my notebook and scribble a response.

J,
Of course, but it will cost you.
A

"What types of security measures do you use where you work?" the girl next to me asks.

"Where do you keep your intel on each of your clients?" another says.

"What is your favorite password that you've ever used?

I'm mid-folding my airplane response, listening to their questions, which are pretty intense when the agent seems to snap.

"These questions are highly restricted," she huffs, pushing back strands of hair that have fallen into her tired eyes. "I can't answer anything. You're not going to get information from me!"

Her bun starts to sag to the side as if it, too, can't handle the barrage of questions. Wow. She's about to lose it. Poor lady. Feeling sorry for her, I raise my hand.

"Aria," Mr. Kores says. "I'm sure you have a great question for Agent Carol."

"If you were going out with a guy," I ask, deciding to lighten the mood here. I mean, this place is dismal enough and she seems like she could use a break. "What would be your perfect date?"

The agent's eyebrows lift in surprise and her shoulders lower a little. "Well." She presses her lips together and pushes the loose strands out of her eyes. "I think dinner in the park. With candles and a telescope to look at the stars."

Everyone awes as if that's the most romantic thing. There's a shift in the room, and it's like the mood has changed. Everything looks brighter, crisper. Sunlight streams through the windows, casting its warmth across the room. The walls appear a pale blue now, and everyone's skin doesn't look so pallid and ashen.

I blink, startled by the transformation. Or maybe I'd still been in a sleep haze before, and now I'm finally waking up.

More hands jolt into the air now and the questions have turned less interrogating-like. Now kids ask questions like:

What's your favorite number combination?

Tell us about your workday schedule.

And, do you own any pets?

I use the chaos of my excited classmates raising their hands to shoot my airplane across the room to Jake. But I only have to wait a second before his response sails back to my desk.

How did he respond so fast?

I'm unfolding his note when the classroom door flies open once again. A man in a suit stumbles inside. There's something vaguely familiar about him with his dark-cropped hair and eyes that look as sharp as a hawk's.

My pulse quickens in panic, but I'm not sure why. I rise in my seat as if something tells me I need to go with this guy, but I can't figure out why.

"Agent Carol!" the man barks. "We have a situation that needs your immediate attention. I need you to come with me right away."

"I don't know who you are." Agent Carol backs up

against Mr. Kores' desk. "You have me confused with someone else."

"Wait," I say. "You look familiar. Is your name Joe?"

The man frowns at me as if he's trying to place me. "Have we met before?"

Abruptly, the bell rings, snapping me out of my confusion and signaling the end of class. I settled back into my seat.

"All right students," Mr. Kores says. "Great session today. We'll pick up tomorrow where we left off."

Simultaneously, everyone rises from their seats and grabs their backpacks like they're programmed robots. I freeze, startled by the strangeness of the situation. My mouth falls open as they exit the classroom, filing one by one in perfect synchronization. Never have I seen my classmates behave so calmly.

I rub my eyes, wondering if I'm seeing things. When I open them again, the students have all exited except for Tony who is strolling out the door with Michelle, not giving me a backward glance. I rise from my seat, frowning as he heads down the hall. We always meet up after class. Why would he ditch me for Michelle? But then I realize Jake is standing by the door, waiting for me with a smile on his face.

My heart skips a few beats as I think about spending a date night with him. Maybe we should take Agent Carol's suggestion. I snatch up my backpack and start across the classroom. As I weave through the rows of desks, I open Jake's note.

Don't trust me.

My feet falter and my breath catches as I stare at the note. A sinking dread slithers through me. Not because of the warning, but because somehow I know I've heard these words before.

THIRTY

DREAM GIRL

The note from Jake falls from my fingers, the shock of it cutting through me like a sharpened axe. What could he mean that I can't trust him? And why do these words seem so familiar?

The doorway where Jake stood only moments ago is empty. He disappeared! My pulse ticks in panic. Quickly, I rush out into the hall except when I step through the doorway, I'm not stepping into my school hallway, but someplace altogether different.

This is a long corridor of archways, snaking around a courtyard with a pool below. At the edge of the courtyard lies a cliff that overlooks an endless cerulean-blue ocean. White balloons and silver streamers decorate the area and light music fills the air. People dressed in summer wear mingle around tables piled with finely decorated cakes while servers offer platters dotted with appetizers.

I rub my head in confusion. "What is going on? I need to talk to someone."

I hurry down a set of stairs that leads into the courtyard. But suddenly, a haze washes over me and I stumble. Something isn't right, but I'm not sure what. A quick glance down at myself shows that I'm not wearing the jeans and T-shirt I had on in class. Instead, I'm dressed in a light blue sundress dotted with white flowers and sandals. I lift my hand to my hair and feel the twist of a long braid.

How did that happen? A chill slivers through me despite the warm air that's soaking into my skin. Something is definitely wrong. But what?

My eyes sweep the area, hoping to find something about this situation that makes sense. That's when I spy the guest speaker from class.

Agent Carol.

She sticks out from the other partiers since she's still wearing her suit and her bun looks as frazzled as ever. The plate in her hand shakes a little like it's too heavy to carry. Her eyes dart about in fear.

Maybe she knows what's going on here. Maybe I got drugged, and I've been kidnapped. If she's truly an agent, she would have some answers, right? I thread my way through the party-goers who fortunately don't even seem to notice my existence. Finally, I stagger up to the lady.

"Excuse me," I say, trying to keep my voice from sounding terrified. "You're Agent Carol, aren't you?"

Her eyes widen when she sees me, and she drops her plate. It crashes onto the stone pavers, splintering into a thousand pieces at our feet. The music goes silent, and all conversation stops as the crowd turning to stares at us. But then a server rushes over and hands her a fresh plate complete with a thick slice of chocolate cake.

"Chocolate cake always makes things better," the server says. "Enjoy and relax."

She eyes the cake and then me. "Do you think it's poisoned?" she whispers.

"I...I don't know," I say, a bit shocked at her skepticism. But then I guess that comes with the territory of being a secret agent. "Listen. I'm sorry I scared you and made you drop your plate. I didn't mean to surprise you. It's just, I don't even know why I'm here, and you're the only person I recognize."

"You recognize me? How do you know me?"

"From Mr. Kores' class. You were our guest speaker."

"I don't know who you are." She backs away from me, reminding me of her actions in the classroom. "You have me confused with someone else."

"No. I'm one hundred percent sure it's you." I grab her arm to keep her from escaping. Her slice of cake slips dangerously close to falling over the plate's edge. "Please. You have to help me. I need to get back home."

Her eyes dart about, but then she leans in and whispers in my ear. "I'm here on an undercover mission. I can't leave until I complete my mission. Maybe if you help me, I can help you. What do you say?"

"Yes!"

"What was the last thing you remember?"

I frown. "I was in class. When I last saw you. Only minutes ago."

She nods thoughtfully. "It sounds like you've been kidnapped by the owner of this mansion."

I follow her gaze and suck in a shuddered breath. This courtyard stretches out with one end reaching the edge of a cliff and the other part connected to a large three-story sprawling mansion, complete with balconies and two turrets. What is this place? I swallow hard.

"I need to get out of here," I say.

"That won't be easy. I've been scouting the grounds. Between the cliff on one side and the guarded wall on the other, the place is practically a fortress."

"What do we do?"

Her eyes furtively flit about the party. "Meet me in the library in ten minutes. We can't let anyone see us together. Be sure no one sees you leave. Got it?"

"Got it."

My breath catches as panic threatens to over-whelm me. She stiffly moves away from me while I wander around, trying to look normal. As I move to the other side of the pool, I'm startled by a row of lounge chairs under a pergola. A person is lying in each chair and they're all wearing dresses or suits. But what sends spider-chills up my arms is the fact that they're all still as stone. Are they dead or just fast asleep?

I back away from the strange scene. I'm about to turn and run to the library right away rather than wait the ten minutes, but one of the people in the chairs stops me in my tracks.

It's a tousled blond-haired guy wearing a crisp white shirt and black pants.

Jake? I've never seen him so dressed up. Could that really be him? And if so, what's he doing here?

I rush over to him and take his hand in mine. It's cold and loose.

"Jake." I shake him a little, trying to wake him up. "Jake, are you okay?"

His blue eyes blink open, and his lips quirk when he sees me. "Aria. You're okay. You look so beautiful."

That was a weird thing to say. Only moments ago he was standing at the door to the classroom.

"What is going on?" My words stumble over each other in panic. "Why are you lying here like..." I can't say the word, dead. It's too terrifying.

Then I remember the note that I shouldn't trust him. Except, how do I know that note wasn't a trick? The reality is, at this point, I don't know what to believe. Everything is so screwed up.

"We've got to get out of here," I say. "I found an undercover agent and she says she can help us escape."

He sits up and rubs his eyes as if waking up from a dream. "Where are we?"

"I don't know, but the agent thinks we've been kidnapped. Come on." I pull him to his feet. "She wants to meet at the library in just a few minutes."

But instead of taking off with me, he draws me to him and cups his hands around my face. "I've been worried about you. I've missed you so much."

I know I should be running toward the library right now, but his words hit a chord inside me. I've missed him, too. Which doesn't make sense. I just saw him in class a moment ago.

His lips find mine, and he kisses me softly as if he's been dreaming of kissing me for a long time. I sink into him, grabbing his T-shirt to pull him even closer.

The world around us blurs in a fog of perfect bliss. Soon all I hear is the crashing of waves and feel his arms wrapped around my body. The world fades away so it's just the two of us, nothing else.

Suddenly, I'm yanked back to reality when hot sand slips into my sandals. I stiffen and extract myself from Jake.

"Something isn't right," I whisper.

When I take in our surroundings, I discover we're standing on the beach. Frothy white-capped waves crash against the shoreline and smooth-multicolored shells are scattered about on the snow-white beach. Sharp rocky cliffs rise up on our other side.

"How did we get here?" I gasp. "We were just by the pool."

Jake's eyes are as large and confused as mine must be. "I...I don't know." He scans the beach and frowns.

My heart sinks as a wild thought hits me. "Do you think this is a dream?"

"Maybe. It kind of feels like that time we were in Reasner's Dreamscape."

"Except nicer, which makes me even more worried." I stare at the waves, crashing on the beach. My mind whirls, trying to process this. "Except that doesn't make sense. I've been wandering all around this place and I haven't seen the dreamer. Plus, I've been alone many times without the dreamer and haven't Faded, which means it can't be the Dreamscape."

"Unless you are the dreamer."

"I'm the dreamer?" I clench the side of my sundress, wondering how that would work. I've never actually been the dreamer in a Dreamscape before.

"If you were the dreamer," Jake continues. "You'd have the power to walk around, talk to who you wanted to talk to, change locations. Isn't that right? I mean, how else did we get from the pool to the beach?"

"Oh." I gasp, pressing my hands to my mouth. "You're right. That must be why my brain is so fuzzy, and I can't seem to think through things properly. I'm dreaming. But why do they have me in the Dreamscape? And who are they?"

"Beats me. You're the expert." He leans down and scoops up a handful of sand and then lets it trickle through his fingers. "Did you have some sort of protocol at MaxLife if your dreamer wanted to wake up? Maybe we could use that to get out of here."

"You have to wake up or be woken up." And that's when the real fear hits me harder than the waves crashing against the shore. "The thing is, every time the dreamer discovered they were having a dream, they'd wake up. We had to be careful to not spook the dreamer so the dream felt natural. That was the big difference in Reasner's Dreamscape. I'm guessing this place is the same way."

"So what are you saying?" Jake asks. "That we could be stuck here forever?"

I give him a hard look. "That's exactly what I'm saying. The bigger question is who is running this Dreamscape and what do they want from me."

"Hey!" a voice calls behind us.

I turn around to find a doorway has opened up in the cliff. And standing there is that Joe guy again, wearing a suit and sunglasses. His dark hair is combed to perfection and the buttons on his suit shimmer. But then my eyes drift down to what he's holding in his hand.

Grabbing Jake's hand, I pull him backward. "Watch out. He's got a gun!"

But the Joe guy doesn't lift his weapon. Instead, he waves at us.

"Hurry!" he yells. "If the guards see you on this beach, they'll shoot you."

"What guards?" I scan the tops of the cliffs, and that's when I spot a man patrolling in a dark gray uniform, clenching a large gun across his chest.

His eyes rove along the beach until they land on Jake and me. He whips out a walkie-talkie and says something into it.

"I think we've already been spotted," I say. Then the man lifts his gun and takes aim at us. I scream and grab Jake's hand. "He's going to shoot!"

The two of us race toward Joe's secret door as gunfire tears through the air, sand shooting up in our wake. We barrel through the stone entrance and tumble into a long tunnel carved through the earth.

Joe slams the door shut. Instantly near darkness sweeps over us. I blink a few times, and dizziness washes over me. What's going on? Or perhaps I'm waking up. It's the same sensation when I'm waking up from a Dream Walk. My training at MaxLife kicks into gear, and I remember how blinking in a dream can force you to wake.

But then a jolt hits me, and I'm thrown back in the tunnel, this time sconces set into the stone walls flicker pale light. They cast twisted shadows across the floor. I lean against the stone wall to pull myself together.

"Come," Joe orders. "We must keep moving."

"Wait." I hold up a hand. "I need to refocus. Get my mind back in order."

Had I been sleeping? If so, what was I doing right before I fell asleep? Who was I talking to?

An image flashes through my mind. Round face, stone-hard eyes, and a smirk pulling up his upper lip. I gasp, finally remembering.

Sadir Gesner.

"We nearly died just now!" Jake leans over, panting. "Why was that guard shooting at us?"

"I don't know." I touch his arm, trying to calm him. "But I do know that this is just a dream, remember?"

"A dream?" He frowns in confusion.

I don't blame him. Even trained Dream Walkers from

work sometimes lose themselves in dreams, forgetting what is reality. This is why we always worked in teams.

"I think I figured out where we are," I say excitedly. "I believe we've been implanted in Sadir Geanser's Dreamscape. I don't know why, but we need to do whatever we can to make sure he doesn't get whatever he wants from us."

"Sadir," Joe mutters, his frown somehow managing to deepen. "This is the worst possible scenario. Follow me and hurry! They will find us soon. I'm sure of it."

"I'm glad you showed us this tunnel," Jake tells Joe as we trail after him. "But who are you, and how do we know we can trust you?"

"I'm Operative Joe. I found a way out of this place."

"I feel like I've met you before," I say, but my brain is fuzzy on the details. Worry creeps over me. There's something very different about this Dreamscape. As if we're only able to access parts of our memories.

"I still don't trust him," Jake says from behind me.

"You're going to have to trust me," Joe barks. "Because if I'm right, Sadir would rather kill you than let you escape."

"You mean escape from this dream," I remind him as we weave through the tunnel. "If I'm right and we're in the Dreamscape, we've all been hooked into it. It also means we're in the REM sleep stage. So we just need to do one of the things that consistently wakes someone from a dream."

"We should do those right away then," Jake says. "What are they?"

"Call out for help, blink, fall asleep, or read."

"Read?"

"Apparently, reading activates parts of your brain you don't use while in REM."

"Blinking? Falling asleep?" Joe snorts and checks his watch. "We don't have time for this nonsense."

"Help!" Jake calls out, spinning around as he walks. "Somebody help us!"

Realizing he's using one of the methods, I join in, "Someone help us!"

"Will you two be quiet?" Joe hisses. "You're going to alert the guards that we're here."

"If this is a dream," I say. "The guards can't hurt us unless we believe that they can. Look at your watch again. You'll know it's a dream if the time constantly changes, but if you really are awake, the time will hardly change."

"This is ridiculous," he grumbles and stomps ahead. "Just stick with the mission and follow orders."

At the turn in the tunnel, I'm met with a section strung with spiderwebs, glistening silver in the pale light. They crisscross the entire passageway, blocking me from Joe. Cringing, I swipe at the strands, but they stick to my fingers and sundress.

Wiggling about, I try to get them off me. But the more I move, the more tangled I become in them. Soon, the webs are twisting and slithering around me as if they're living creatures, intent on suffocating me.

I scream, but it stays muffled in my throat. I turn to see if Jake is okay, but he's no longer there. Instead, it's just me and a world of webs. I thrash about only to have the strands spin around me, tighter and tighter until I'm cocooned in a sticky nightmare. I can't scream or even move.

Panic stifles me and my heart drums against my ribcage.

Except... this is just a dream, I remind myself.

Breathing deeply, I close my eyes and will it all to go away.

Sleep paralysis. That's all this is. Slowly, the suffocating sensation and the heavy pressing on my body releases. When I open my eyes back up, the spider webs have vanished. The stickiness has left my hands, and my dress now flutters in the chilling tunnel breeze.

Huh. I stare at the smooth walls, my mind whirling at what just happened. Maybe I have more power in this dream than I realize.

I take off down the tunnel again, wondering what I can do with this power. Could I use it to escape?

A new sense of clarity washes over me, allowing me to remember more details of Dr. Reasner's Dreamscape when I'd been in Jake's dream. It was through his coding skills that he was able to implant a virus into the dream, and then destroy it. It had been a huge risk, but when the

Dreamscape was gone, both of our minds were kicked out of it.

If my theory is correct and this is my dream, then I have control over what happens and I can be alone. Unfortunately, I have literally no coding skills so repeating that past method isn't an option. There must be something else I can do.

I quicken my pace until I catch up with Jake and Joe.

"We were waiting for you," Jake says. "I didn't want to lose you."

"Wasting time is what we were doing," Joe grumbles.

"Wait!" I grab Jake's arm, his words inspiring me. "That's what you need to do. Get as far away from me so you're forced to Fade from the dream. That's how you can escape."

"Why do you keep saying this is a dream?" Joe asks. "This is the real deal, and we don't have time to dilly-dally about. Our window of escape is closing by the second."

My eyes narrow on Joe. Could he really be Operative Joe that we know or is he an implant created by Sadir and his crew? Reasner had all sorts of people enter Jake's dream, intent on forcing us to do his wishes. But Sadir seems more cunning. What if he brought in people under the guise of someone else?

"How do we know you again?" I ask.

"You still don't trust me?" Joe's eye twitches. "I literally saved you from that gunman and you are wondering if you can trust me."

"I say we ditch this dude," Jake whispers in my ear. "He's avoiding the answer."

I rub my temples, trying to push through the haze in my brain. "What we need to do is go to the library. That's where Agent Carol told me to meet her."

"Carol?" Joe lifts his eyebrows. "You won't trust me, but you trust her?"

"Let's get moving," I say. "It's not healthy for our minds to be in the Dreamscape for too long."

I push past Joe but stop when I come to a split in the tunnel. Something is pulling me right, so I take off in that direction.

"Wait!" Joe yells. "That's the wrong way."

The tunnel dead-ins at a doorway. It opens on its own, and I step into a room with rows and rows of books stacked on dark mahogany bookshelves. They stretch all the way to the painted ceiling above where a chandelier hangs down, scattering light across the room. Soft couches are scattered about and tables paired with small lamps.

The library.

"I found it!" I exclaim. "This is the place..."

Except, if they are separated from me, then they'll be forced to Fade and be kicked out of the dream. They'll be safe.

I turn around and envision the door shutting.

Like magic, the doorway starts closing, responding to my thoughts.

"No!" Jake yells, his hand reaching for me.

My heart aches hearing his anguished cry, but I firmly slam the door shut with a thud. It's for his safety, I tell myself. Now hopefully, he'll be kicked out of the dream.

In a blink, the door vanishes, leaving behind only paisley green wallpaper, a picture of an old man, and a wooden bench.

My shoulders sag. I know I did the right thing, but the guilt of shutting Jake out still rips my insides up.

"You made it!" a voice says from behind me.

I spin around to find I'm face to face with a lady in a suit and tendrils of dark hair tumbling out from her bun.

"Oh! Hello." I push the loose strands of hair out of my eyes and take a deep breath.

"This placc is evil," she whispers conspiratorially. "I've been trying to escape it for a very long time, but it's like it has a mind of its own."

"Yes." I study her, wondering how long she has been in this dream. "I'm still trying to figure out this place and the programming of it. You look familiar. Have we met before?"

She holds out her hand and I shake it. Then glancing furtively about the room, she says, "Name is Agent Carol

Marzano. I work for the U.S. government, and I was sent here on a secret mission. I've been locked up in this mansion for years, trying to complete my mission."

I bite my lip, doubting it's been years. Time moves at a different rate in dreams. What feels like a long time in the dream can actually be only a few seconds or at most thirty minutes. Unless...she's been in here for weeks. That would feel like years in the Dreamscape. I can't imagine what that would do to someone's mind.

"But then yesterday," she interrupts my thoughts. "I found the code to escape."

Eagerly I step closer to her. "You did?"

"I hid it in a book, but it's on the top shelf above." She points to a shelf three stories high near the ceiling. "I just need your help getting to it."

"That shouldn't be a problem. There must be a way to access the higher-level books, right?"

I scan the room until my eyes land on a library ladder. Quickly, I rush to it and grab its sides. It's attached to a J-style hook at the top, so I'm able to slide the ladder along the track above that it's attached to. Gliding it along, I move the ladder so it's directly under the location Carol pointed to.

"That's a great start," she says. "But the ladder isn't tall enough."

I start scaling the ladder, but when I reach the top, I realize in disappointment she's right. I'm still one story away from the books on the top shelves.

"What's the name of the book?" I ask. "I'll climb up there and bring it down to you."

"The name of the book is *Birds of Paradise*."

Taking a deep breath, I reach for the edge of the bookshelf above me and pull myself up. Then I find a ledge below for my feet to perch on. Slowly, I start to scale the bookshelves, but soon, strangely, I realize I'm floating up to the book. I'm lighter than air, almost like I'm holding onto a balloon that's lifting up to the sky.

The only time I've ever flown in a dream was the first time I was in Jake's dream. This is so weird! But then flying and floating in dreams is a thing. It's a little surreal, but I allow the lightness of myself to buoy me to the top shelf where the book is shelved. Once I find it, I tuck it under my arm.

Except, my body keeps trying to rise higher, rather than go down. Gritting my teeth, I force my feet to plant firmly on the bottom shelf, mentally trying to keep it in place. Except my foot slips under me and all the buoyancy I once felt vanishes. I lose my grip on the shelf.

And fall backward.

I claw for the edge of the bookshelf, but my hands only find air. The book slips from my fingers. Wind whooshes around me and I scream as I plummet. I can only hope I'll fall on something soft.

Thump! I drop onto a velvety couch with a thud.

Bam!

The book hits me in the face, which scientifically makes no sense.

"Whew!" Carol hovers over me. "I wasn't sure if you were going to make it. But you did. Plus you found the book."

She goes to grab it, but I scramble to wrap my arms around the spine, suddenly unsure I should let her have it.

"You don't trust me, do you?" she asks. "That's good. You shouldn't trust anyone here. It doesn't matter anyway. Just open the book and get the codes. We'll use those to open the outer gates."

I push myself to sitting and grab the outside flap. Just as I'm about to open the book, a blast explodes through the room, sending chunks of the wall flying through the air. Agent Carol and I duck as debris rains over us, pounding our bodies with plaster.-

Dust and wallpaper bits billow about the library. Coughing and blinking against the gray, I clutch the book tighter as three guards wearing yellow masks and coal-black suits stride into the room, holding Joe and Jake at gunpoint.

"Jake!" I leap to my feet in horror. "What's going on?"

"The guards found us," Jake says. "Whatever you do, don't give them what they want."

Joe glowers at me. "I told you not to go this way."

"Hand over the book," one of the guards says. "And I won't shoot your friends."

I hold my breath, unsure what to do. Even though this

is my dream, if Jake thinks this was real, his brain could tell his body he's dead. I can't risk him getting hurt.

Carol drags herself off the floor. She's coated in dust and grime, but her wide, frantic eyes find mine and she says, "Hurry! Open the book."

I glance back over at Jake for confirmation. He nods. "Open it, Aria."

Except his voice sounds weird, stilted. Or maybe it's just that my ears are still ringing from the explosion.

The guard points his gun at me. "Don't do it."

The ground at my feet shakes, and I wobble in place. The crystals on the chandelier above tinkle and a few books tumble off their shelves.

Suddenly, Operative Joe calls out, "Now!"

Both he and Jake turn on their captors. Joe does a series of karate-type moves. Within a few moments, his captor is on the ground and he's kicked the third guard's gun free. It skitters out of reach across the floor. The guard goes to fetch it, but Joe punches him in the jaw, jerking the man's head sideways. Blood spews from the man's mouth.

Meanwhile, Jake has managed to grab his guard's gun and is twisting it so it's pointing at the guy's head. "You're safe to open the book now, Aria," Jake says.

"Wow." I gape at him. "Where did you learn those moves?"

There's something odd about him. Maybe it's his eyes that don't look blue anymore, but dark black.

Before he can answer, the far bookshelf transforms

into a long snow-white wall lined with red doors. They burst open and a stream of men wearing body armor and holding guns burst into the room. Gunfire thunders across the library. Bullets hit the couch cushions, ripping them open. White feathers explode into the air. Books fall off the shelves and lamps shatter under the gunfire.

"Hurry, Aria!" Jake yells.

Heart slamming into my chest, I yank back the cover and open the book.

THIRTY-THREE
THE SECRET CODE

The silence is knife-sharp and disorientating after the firework-popping sounds of the gunshots. My vision clears and I find myself standing beside Agent Carol whose hand is clutching my arm. She must have grabbed onto me at the last minute.

We're in a large white room, and when I say white, I mean snow-white. White walls, shiny white floor, and white ceiling dotted with can lights.

The strangest part about this place is the three long silvery tubes floating in the center of the room. They're as long as my bed and at least five times thicker than a telephone pole.

"What is this place?" I whisper.

"The secret place," Carol says. "These are the cartridges that I put the codes in. Some terrible people were interrogating me for this information, but I wouldn't let them have it."

I frown. "Wait. I thought this book held the code to escape this messed up place."

Suddenly, the room tilts slightly as if responding to my confusion. Carol slides across the floor, unable to stand like I am.

"What's going on?" she cries. "Why aren't you moving? Are you doing this?"

Then it hits me all over again. This is a dream! It has all the strange elements of a dream, but I'd forgotten. I rub my head and suddenly the room straightens once again returning to the way it was before.

Except for the green plant that suddenly pops in front of me. I bend down and inspect the plant. "This pot looks just like the kind my mom uses for her greenhouse."

"Why would that be here?" Carol asks from where she's sitting on the floor.

"Unless this isn't just any dream," I muse. "I've never seen those cylinder things, but you have. Yet, I'm the only person, other than my mom, who knows what her plants and pots look like. Which means this Dreamscape might be running more than one person's dream at the same time and somehow merging them together."

"I'm so confused." Carol twists her hands together.

"Don't worry." I help her to her feet. "The important thing is to find that code and get out of here."

"Yes." Carol nods, her face as pale as the room. "I need to get out of this place. I think I'm losing my mind."

She scurries to one of the silver tubes and gingerly touches it with her palm. A rectangular portion of the tube slides back, revealing a panel with numbers. I slide in next to her, studying everything. The numbers are blurry at first, but one by one, they crystalize into well-defined red numbers.

"3, 4, 9," I start to read the first three from the book. "After all the numbers appear, what do we do?"

"We memorize them and then run back out to the gate outside the complex, punch them in, and then escape!" She takes my hand and squeezes it. "Thank you so much for coming and finding me. I've been so scared I'd never escape this place."

My stomach dips. I don't have the heart to tell her that I don't think we're able to get back to that complex we were at. That segment of the dream has faded away.

I refocus. "So you're saying we have to memorize all three of the codes on all three tubes."

"Well." She scratches her head. "I don't know. Maybe?"

"You work on this code, and I'll work on the next one."

I hurry to the next tube and press my palm to the tube. But instead of just one small section pulling back, the entire top part slides away, revealing...

I scream, jumping backward, horrified.

"What's the matter?"

"There's a...a man inside." I point to the silvery tube, hands shaking.

"A man?"

We creep closer and peek inside. Sure enough, a man with dark hair and light olive skin, wearing what looks like a very expensive gray suit, is sleeping.

"His hands are handcuffed in front of him," I whisper, pointing to the cuffs. "Maybe he's a prisoner."

The man's eyes blink open. We scream again, leaping backward. Suddenly, he sits up and frantically scans the room until his eyes land on us. "Are you here to rescue me?" he asks.

"Um..." Carol glances my way with wide eyes as if asking me what to say.

"Yes." I clear my throat and try to stand a little taller and look confident. "Yes, we are Mr..."

"Lau," he supplies. "Heng Lau."

"Mr. Lau," I say. That name is so familiar. It hits me like a sledgehammer, and I suck in a shocking breath. "You wouldn't happen to know a Zhang Lau would you?"

"She's my wife." He begins to awkwardly climb out of his silver tube. "But aren't you a little young to be my rescuer?"

"That's what I told your wife," I grumble. "In fact, I wouldn't be in this mess if it wasn't for her kidnapping me and taking me to Peru."

"A little help here would be nice." He indicates his handcuffed hands and inability to climb out of the tube.

Carol goes to assist him, but I hold her back. "We don't know if we can trust him yet. Let's just see how things go."

But wow, I think, shaking my head. He's her husband! This is the guy Zhang Lau wanted me to find. Unless this is just part of my dream and he's not real. I groan. Honestly, I don't even know what's real anymore, which is very bad.

Rule number one is to never lose yourself in the Dreamscape.

"I need to touch a wall," I mutter, and hurry over to the closest wall.

"I think something's not right with her," Mr. Lau tells Carol.

"You know you're in a dream if you touch a wall and it bends," I explain. "I just need to get my head wrapped around everything."

"I have been faithful to my wife for ten years," Lau mutters and points to me. "And this is the wacko she sends to rescue me? Is this some sort of joke?"

I ignore him and instead press my hand against the wall. Sure enough, it bends to my push, stretching like a rubber ball.

"Yep," I say. "We're still in a dream. Which means Mr. Lau here could either be Mr. Lau hooked into the Dreamscape, a figment of my imagination, or planted by whoever is running this Dreamscape."

"Or maybe I'm the one who has lost his mind." Mr. Lau frowns, scratching his head.

"I wish we knew who was keeping us in here," Carol says.

"Yeah." I bite my lip, feeling like I had known but somehow forgot because the name oddly has slipped my mind. "Me, too."

Frustration builds inside me. I feel so out of control.

A boom rocks the room, tossing Carol and me to the floor and sending Mr. Lau falling back into this tube. Red cracks splinter across the white walls. An alarm blares across the room.

"What's going on?" I scream over the alarm.

"I think they've realized we're here," Carol says. "And they're trying to get the codes or stop us from using them."

I stagger to the third tube and open it. A silvery circular disc lies flat inside. Numbers swirl across its surface, dancing about as if trying to find their order. If this Dreamscape is anything like the one we had a MaxLife, there's a recording being done of what the dreamer and Dream Walkers can see.

So it only makes sense that whoever is watching, wants to see these numbers. Everything I've done in this dream has pushed me to get to this room, I realize. Carol telling me the codes are her escape, the guy on the cliff shooting at us, and the tunnels leading us back to Carol when we got off track. Even Jake encouraging me to open the book.

If I'm right, this Dreamscape pulls in numerous people's dreams to create one massive Dreamscape. It makes sense that Carol, Mr. Lau, and my dreams are all merged to create this space.

Then a terrible, horrifying realization slams into me as I remember Operative Joe and how he had said his agents were being interrogated.

"These codes aren't our escape," I say. "They're the codes from your mind, Carol, and the owners of the Dreamscape want those codes."

This is just like when they stole the Swift codes from Jake's mind using his dreams.

"I'd never give away sensitive codes," Carol says.

Operative Joe warned us the agents held valuable information that if stolen could have catastrophic implications for the American people.

Which is why my kidnappers brought me here.

I have to assume that just as Reasner knew, whoever owns this Dreamscape knows that my mind can manipulate the Dreamscape. If anyone can get the codes and get Carol to trust her, it's me.

Crap. I fell right into their trap like a bug swarming to a light.

The rumbling sound shudders the room once again, and the floor shifts like there's an earthquake. The cracks in the walls widen and thick red lava oozes out and slides down the walls. A burning scent fills my nostrils, sharp and strong.

But that's weird. I've never experienced the scent of smell before in the Dreamscape. Based on our studies at

MaxLife, we thought it was only a theory. One of the scientists on Dad's team, Dr. Kelli, believed it could be possible for the sense of smell to be triggered if a mind was so immersed in the Dreamscape that it would stimulate all the senses.

This means things are worse than I first thought. I'm deep in a dream. It might be a very long time before Carol, Mr. Lau, and myself escape.

If ever.

"The important thing is we can't let this code get into the wrong hands," I say. "No matter what."

Carol nods. "No matter what. So how do we escape then?"

"I have a plan, but you'll have to trust me."

She stares at me skeptically but then nods.

"Okay. Here goes." I press my lips together and without looking at the numbers, I will them to go into a different pattern. A wrong combination.

Sweat drips down the sides of my face and my body quivers from the effort. I've never actually been a dreamer in a Dreamscape, much less tried to manipulate it. But I did it with the spider webs, right? If I did it with those, I think I can do it again with these numbers.

Subconsciously, I feel the numbers shift and move. They resist against my mind, wanting to be in their correct order, but mentally, I hold them in place for one, two, three seconds.

Then I look at the numbers purposely so the Dreamscape records the wrong set of numbers, and then reach down and snatch the disc up.

Another boom explodes across the room, sending me sprawling to the ground. Red lava-like liquid snakes across the floor, bubbling with steam rising from it.

"Hurry!" I yell. "We need to leave."

Carol and I help Mr. Lau out of his tube, but then the three of us stand there, unsure what to do.

"How do we get out of this place?" Carol asks.

"Great," Mr. Lau mutters. "If you are telling me the truth, I'm going to die having a nightmare."

BOOM! The wall in front of us explodes. We cry out and duck for cover as white tile, red lava-like liquid, and concrete spew around us. Uniformed men with guns swarm the room. And there in the center of the group stands Jake, sticking out like a sore thumb in his jeans and T-shirt.

"Hello, Aria." Jake smiles widely, but it's a stilted, wide smile like that of a clown's. Nothing like that easy-going, slightly crooked one of Jake's. And the eyes are dark spheres. Lifeless. Empty. "Tell me what the real codes are and you can leave. Otherwise, these men are going to shoot you. Which would be too unfortunate for you."

I back away, grabbing Carol's arm and pushing Mr. Lau back with me. My mind swirls with panic, trying to figure out a way of this situation.

"Jake!" I say brightly and plaster on my own fake smile as I continue backing up. "So great to see you again. I agree with you one hundred percent. Being shot at would definitely be bad."

My eyes flick around the room, but all I see are white walls webbed with red liquid. It's like some horror freak house. My pulse ticks against my skin.

Except freak houses have exits for the workers, right? I just need to find that exit—or better yet—create the exit with my mind.

Closing my eyes, I try to create a door that would take us away. But when I open my eyes again, nothing has changed other than Mr. Lau hopping beside me, dancing between rivulets of bubbling lava.

"Ouch!" he cries. "Hot!"

"It's about to get a whole lot hotter," Jake drones, the smile now flat as his lips press together, clearly not pleased.

The burning scent intensifies, and I hate the fact that I'm going to die here in this dream, and I'll never get to tell Dr. Kelli she was right.

Unless the problem is I'm not following through with my theory of this being a Dreamscape that holds all three of our dreams together is correct.

I turn to my two companions. "I need you to imagine that wall over there has a door." I point to the wall on my right. "Can you do that?"

"A door?" Mr. Lau's face scrunches up. "My feet are burning, and you want to play imagination games?"

"If you want to escape," Carol yells. "Do it!"

"Okay, okay!" Mr. Lau says.

Together, we focus hard on the wall. A door shimmers into existence.

"Hey!" Mr. Lau exclaims. "It worked."

"You have three seconds to give me the code," Jake orders. "Or you all die."

"Now imagine the door opening," I say, my heart now hammering hard against my ribcage.

"One."

The door pops open, revealing darkness. I drag the two closer to the door, trying to figure out what to imagine next.

"Two."

"Next, imagine a staircase," I continue. "This staircase will take us outside the Dreamscape. And we'll all wake up."

"They're about to shoot!" Mr. Lau cries.

"Imagine it!" Carol screams.

"Three!"

Bullets burst around the three of us and Carol's body buckles from one hitting her in the side. Mr. Lau screams, covering his head with his hands while something hits my leg. I cry out as searing pain rushes through me. Blood darkens my pants. I've been shot.

Is this real? Or is it like what happened in Reasner's Dreamscape, and it was all in my mind?

There isn't time to debate because a staircase has appeared.

I shove Mr. Lau through the doorway and onto the staircase while Carol manages to stagger in next. Then I stumble inside and slam the door shut behind us.

We start to climb, one step after the next. Blood coats the ground, making it slick and hard to walk. Carol groans with each step she takes. Mr. Lau continues to bawl. My injured leg crumbles beneath me, forcing me to crawl my way up. Tears of pain stream down my face. My whole body starts shaking.

I'm not sure how much longer I can go before I collapse.

A shuddering white light bursts through the stairwell, washing over the three of us and swallows us whole.

THIRTY-FOUR

FASTEN YOUR SEAT BELTS

One moment I'm walking up a stairwell.

The next, I'm lying on a gurney, rolling down a white-walled hallway, full speed.

Confusion sweeps over me as I stare at the ceiling above, light after light whizzing past. I cast my gaze about. Shouting and gunfire echoes through the corridor, coming from somewhere in the distance.

Am I still dreaming? I don't think so. Everything feels real.

Two men are on either side of my gurney, running along as they push me. Sweat beads down their faces while someone yells at them in what sounds like Russian.

"What's happening?" I ask and try to move. I'm strapped onto the side rails with safety restraints. "Let me go! Where are you taking me?"

The two men on either side of me don't answer, but my words seem to inspire them to double down and run faster. That's when I realize I'm awake and remember I'm a captive in Sadir's facility.

I lift up my head, desperately searching for someone to help me, but there's no one at the other end of the hall. Hope springs inside me when I see the men glancing worriedly behind them. Since there was gunfire, maybe someone is attacking the facility and can rescue me.

I cry out, "Help! Someone, please help me!"

Doors swoosh open. The moment we leave the corridor, the air shifts, warmer and thicker. They rush me out into a large space where people are running about, yelling, and gathering equipment. A grinding sound rumbles above. It's the roof slowly splitting in half, revealing fading stars and streaks of sunlight purpling the dark sky.

Equipment and a few bookshelves litter the concrete walls, but I'm shocked to find, looming in the center of the concrete floor, a helicopter. This place must be a secret helicopter pad, hidden beneath the jungle floor.

The chopper is large in size, black as night with the nose cupped in glass. Six small windows run along its side.

Sadir is striding across the tarmac toward the chopper, barking out orders in Russian. Men frantically toss equipment into the back like the place is about to blow up. My heart seizes. Unless it *is* about to blow up. Along with Jake and all those other captives still inside.

Except as my gurney flies closer and closer to the helicopter another revelation hits me, making my pulse throb.

They're taking me with them.

My gurney races toward the chopper. I renew my efforts in freeing myself from the straps. The strap to my right is looser so I twist myself enough that it allows my hand to start working at the buckle, holding me in place.

But then a bump and a jarring stop slams my body against the side rail. Pain shoots along my arm, and I grunt from the impact. Tears threaten the corners of my eyes, and my heart starts racing. I'm so scared. I don't know how to get out of this situation.

"What's happening?" I ask. "Where are you taking me?"

Sadir appears at my side, his face grim, but there's a strange gleam of hope—or perhaps insanity?—in his eyes. "Your people showed up before we could finish our work. My facility might be dispensable, but unfortunately, you are not. So you will come with us."

"Wait! What?" My head spins as men undo my straps.

"We need your mind for the Dreamscape to work properly," he explains. "We tried to link one, and even two minds, incorporating them as the main dreamers. But their minds didn't believe the dream until we brought you in as the third dreamer. That's when I knew you were indispensable. Reasner was right. You are the key."

The men haul me off the gurney. My arm gets caught in the side rail. I cry out in pain.

"Be careful with her!" Sadir yells, slapping one of my guards across the face, sending him stumbling back. "She must not be harmed."

Then he steps in closer to me. "You may have found a way to escape my Dreamscape," he says with a smirk, "but with a little tweaking, I know we can make this work. You will become my Little Torturer and never even realize it."

He chuckles at this as I'm dragged roughly toward the chopper, despite Sadir's warning to be careful.

"Where are you taking me?" I yell, tears streaming down my face.

"Back to my homeland until our work is finished," Sadir says.

"Russia?" I gape at him. "Can this chopper even go that far?"

"Siberia. Not to worry. We will make a transfer."

"Siberia?" I choke, my heart plummeting into the pit of my stomach.

I can't...I can't go to Siberia. My family will never be able to find me there. They'll hook me into their Dream-scape, and I'll never escape. I'll just be running through dream after dream until my mind is completely deranged.

Sadir turns away to bark more orders at his men. Meanwhile, my guard tosses me onto a seat inside the chopper. He turns for a half-second, reaching for a strap to tie me up with.

I seize that moment to twist around and leap over the

seat into the one behind it. The guard growls angrily, reaching for me when an explosion rocks the building.

The door we had exited the facility from bursts into flaming shrapnel that spews across the loading dock.

The chopper shudders and rocks back and forth. Through the cockpit's glass window, I watch as fire flares across the area and men duck and cry out from the heat.

Since my guard is also watching the carnage. I seize the distraction and scramble further toward the back of the chopper, searching for another escape.

Shouts and gunfire ripple through the air. Men wearing camo and holding guns burst across the pavement. Sadir's men start dropping left and right. The pilot leaps into his seat and the whirl of the helicopter blades cut through the chaos.

Meanwhile, Sadir and some of his other men hop into the chopper.

"Fly!" Sadir yells at the pilot who must be an English speaker. "Get us out of here!"

I don't have much time. I dart to the back of the chopper and find the loading door is still gaping open from where they were loading equipment.

Excitement bursts inside of me. I could escape from there!

But my guard rushes after me with a growl. I manage to squeeze through the netting between the seating area and the cargo hold section. I'm about to race off the ramp when my eye catches a glimpse of a logo on a sleek silver case. The word Dreamscape is printed on it along with a digital moon and stars.

This has to be Sadir's version of the Dreamscape! I glance back to find my guard is fighting with the netting. Do I escape and save myself or try to take his Dreamscape?

I can't let him get away with it. Otherwise, this madness will never end.

I climb over containers and crates, shaking so hard from terror that I stumble along the way. My fingers slip around the handle of the case just as the guard seizes my other arm, squeezing it hard and yanking me back.

Adrenaline rushes through my veins and I react. I heave the case through the air and smash it against the side of his head. His grip loosens as he staggers backward, blinking.

Quickly, I dart away, racing toward the edge of the ramp. The chopper lifts off the ground, and my heart seizes in despair.

One thing I do know, the Dreamscape can't stay here in this chopper with Sadir. So as I run to the edge and fling the case overboard. Before I can jump out with it, fingers scrape along my back, keeping me from escaping. The chopper rises higher. Wind rushes over my face

I don't want to go to Siberia.

I don't want to become his Little Torturer.

I won't.

With a burst of power, I rip myself free and leap off the edge of the chopper. I fall through the air, the ground rushing at me.

For once I wish I were in the Dreamscape.

Because this fall sure is going to hurt.

I land on the hard pavement. My knees buckle beneath me. Something snaps in my left ankle and shooting pain rears up along my right leg.

I cry out from the impact, stars swirling in my vision. Buzzing fills my ears. Vaguely, I'm aware that people are surrounding me, shouting, while gunfire ripples through the air in the midst of it all. But I'm in too much pain to even think straight. Moaning, I try to get up, but dizziness washes over me and I crumble to the pavement.

"Don't move," a guy tells me. "You had a hard fall."

"The case," I mumble, trying to think straight. "We need to get that case."

"Don't you worry," he says. "You did good. I'm a medic. We're going to take care of you."

I grimace and blink away the fuzziness of my vision.

Soldiers in camo uniforms swarm the premises, racing about with quick precision.

"We've gotta get out of here," one of the men says, who I think is their commander. "The place is going to blow. We've got minutes at best."

"Copy that," my medic says. "I'm going to need a stretcher for her."

I don't like the sound of that. I want to get up on my own but pain sears down my leg and across my ankle ankle.

My attention is suddenly pulled to across the tarmac where Jake is racing out of the tunnel, helping Operative Joe and four others straggle out. Two of the strangers look familiar. Lau's husband and Agent Carol that I met in the Dreamscape.

Then Jake's eyes land on me and he breaks into a run toward me, worry clouding his face.

"Aria!" he shouts as he comes to join me. He kneels at my side. "You're here. I was so worried when I saw them running away with you. I was terrified they'd taken you. But what happened? Are you okay? Can you move?"

"Pretty sure she broke her leg, maybe both of them," the medic says. "I don't want to risk her moving unless she has to."

"I jumped from the helicopter," I explain with a grimace.

"You what?" Jake's eyes bug out.

"I didn't want to go to Siberia," I say.

Tears edge the corners of his eyes, and he kisses my forehead. "Of course. Of course. Why am I not surprised?"

Suddenly the sound of a chopper fills the air again. My heart seizes in panic, and I squeeze Jake's hand. "They're back! Sadir is back."

"Just stay calm," the medic says. "That's your ride."

"Hurry up people," the commander calls out. "We've got no time left."

A large military-sized helicopter sinks into the pit that we're in. Wind rushes around me and snaps at my braid. Soldiers hurry those who were prisoners into the chopper while others are yelling for us to move.

"Just grab her and let's get out of here," the commander orders my medic. "This place is about to blow."

Hands lift me up. In a daze, I realize the medic and Jake are carrying me into the helicopter while Operative Joe yells, "Quick! Get her inside!"

"Wait!" I scream. "Someone grab that silver case."

I point to Sadir's Dreamscape. Joe nods and rushes over toward it, but before I can make sure he's gotten it, searing pain overwhelms me and my vision blurs.

I grit my teeth, sweat dripping down my face, as they settle me against the far wall. Then I grip the straps hanging from the chopper's wall for support, trying not to throw up or pass out. Jake joins me, one hand on my arm and the other holding a strap of his own. The other prisoners are already inside the chopper, their expressions a little dazed and confused. Meanwhile, soldiers are diving inside the chopper even as it's lifting back up off the ground.

"This is for the pain," my medic explains, and then plunges some sort of pain relief into my thigh.

I gaze out the open door as we rise higher and higher. It's dawn in the jungle, the sun slicing across the endless line of mossy-green trees and glistening on the river curling through the forest.

Suddenly, a massive boom shudders through the air erupting from below. A burst of angry-red flames balloons up from the helicopter pad we had just left. Our chopper trembles from the impact. Hot wind rushes through the open door.

Some of the soldiers cheer, "We did it!" while others give each other high-fives.

I take in everyone. "We were their rescue mission," I say.

"Look like it," Jake says in relief. His face is pale and his usual tone body now looks like he could use a few burgers.

The door slams shut, and the helicopter swoops off, away from Monkey Island and the horrors of Sadir's facility.

But I can't rest yet, not until I know my friends are safe and we have Sadir's Dreamscape.

"Joe," I say. "What about the others? Sun, Tony, and Javier?"

"Oh, no!" Jake's eyes widen in horror. "Don't tell me that—"

His words choke off as if he can't even say them.

Joe moves over to us and kneels down by my side. "Don't worry. My men found them first and we extracted them right away."

"Thank God." I sigh and lean back in relief. "I was so worried."

"They're already at the airport," he explains. "We'll be joining them shortly and then we'll all fly back to the U.S."

"What exactly happened?" I lick my lip and taste the bitterness of blood. "How did all these soldiers get here?"

"You have your dad to thank for that," Joe says. "He was already in talks with the U.S. intelligence about his work and pushed to get me the backup we needed for this mission and just in time. When I went through that hatch, Sadir's people used sleeping gas to incapacitate me and my partner. Next thing I remember was being in that strange Dreamscape with you. That was messed-up stuff."

"No kidding." Then my muscles tighten. "The codes. Oh no. Don't tell me we gave Sadir those secret codes."

"Apparently not," Jake pipes up. "When you kicked me out of that dream, I woke up to see Sadir stalking back and forth by the equipment. He was furious because you kept outsmarting him in the dream. That's when he sent my double into the dream to convince you to give him the codes. But somehow you managed to not only give him the wrong codes, but you also extracted yourself and the other two hostages from the Dreamscape all on your own."

"It took the three of us, Carol, Mr. Lau, and myself, working together to unlock things," I muse. "I think that was the key. Using all three of our minds is what made the difference. Which reminds me. Where is Sadir's Dreamscape case? Did you get it?"

"Don't worry." Joe points to the large silver case across the chopper. "I grabbed it and threw it onboard. But are you sure you don't want that thing destroyed?"

"Yeah," Jake mutters. "Maybe we should've left it at Sadir's facility to get blown up with everything else."

"No." And despite the pain and everything I've been through, hope surges through me. "I think that saving that Dreamscape might be the answer we've been seeking."

The helicopter begins to descend and lands with a thud on the ground. The soldiers throw open the door and everyone streams out. Two soldiers gently carry me out of the chopper. Hot, moist air drenches my skin once again.

We're back at the airport in Puerto de Maldonado, the same airport that Danny flew us in. It feels like a lifetime though since that moment.

The soldiers carefully lay me onto a gurney that has been brought out for me. It brings back bad memories of when I found myself strapped to the one after I woke up from Sadir's Dreamscape. But considering there's no way I can walk, I can't complain.

Pain continues to radiate down my leg, but thanks to whatever painkillers that medic gave me, it's bearable. Suddenly, I hear Sun scream out my name.

"Aria!"

I look over to find Sun, Tony, Javier, and Danny running across the tarmac toward me. Within seconds they've surrounded my gurney, huddling around me.

"What happened?" Sun shrieks, grabbing my hand. "I've been sick, so worried."

"Are you okay?" Tony asks. "You don't look okay."

"Of course she isn't okay." Javier frowns at Tony, but his gaze softens when he looks down at me. "Don't you worry, little hermanita. We're going to get you home real soon."

"Aria?" a voice that sounds just like my dad's cuts through everything. "Is that my baby girl?"

Suddenly, pushing through my friends, is my dad. His white hair looks even whiter than I remembered, and his face is furrowed, showing off deep worry lines. But just seeing him once again, sends tears streaming down my face.

"Dad!" I exclaim. "You're here!"

He takes my hand and squeezes it, tears filling his eyes. "You're safe. I was so worried. After I got your message, I finally got some people to listen to me and hear how serious this situation was. I finally got the support to get you back home."

He pulls me into a gentle hug.

"I'm sorry I missed your calls," he continues. "I was in the air at the time. But the moment I landed in Lima, I got your message and we came here as soon as we could. I'm just so thankful you're okay."

A commotion behind Dad draws our attention. It's Zhang Lau clipping at a startling fast pace despite her heels across the tarmac, a red scarf wrapped around her neck flying behind her like a kite. She rushes into the arms of her husband who I vaguely remember from the Dreamscape.

"Looks like Zhang Lau found her husband," Jake says, grimly joining up with us.

Sun scowls. "This is all her fault that she brought you into this mess."

"I guess love makes you do things you aren't always proud of," Dad says.

To my surprise, Zhang Lau and her husband come over to where our group is huddled around me.

"Aria." Zhang Lau lifts her chin and pulls back her shoulders as if she's having a hard time keeping herself cool and collected. "I know you did not want to be involved in rescuing my husband. But I was right. If you had not come, I would never have found him."

"Thank you, Aria." Her husband nods to me. "If it were not for you, I believe my mind would never have been able to be unlocked from that computer system Sadir had me in. You not only rescued me, but you rescued my mind."

"We are deeply grateful," Zhang Lau says and from her tone, I can tell she means it.

"I'm glad I was able to help in the end," I say. "But please don't ask me to do any more rescue missions for you. I'm retired."

I try to laugh it off, but no one else around me joins in. Instead, they seem to draw closer to my gurney as if to protect me.

"Those are kind words," Dad tells her. "But stay far away from us. We don't want to ever see you again."

"You shall have your wish," Zhang Lau says. "But you, Aria. You need to know that you're an extraordinary woman. I have a feeling your greatness has only just begun to shine."

"Thank you," I say, letting out a long breath, just glad this is all behind me now.

When they turn and head over to a private plane, a wave of relief that she's gone washes over me.

"I really don't like that woman," Dad grumbles.

"Same," everyone else chimes in.

"Excuse me, sir." It's Joe, poking his head into our huddle. "Here's that Dreamscape case. You said this was stolen from you?"

Dad's face darkens when his eyes land on it. "The trouble that has brought our family. It should be destroyed."

"No, Dad." I take his hand again. "We need it."

"What do you mean?" he asks.

"I think I've found some good in the middle of this nightmare," I say.

"Really?" Dad asks.

"We set out to help dementia patients reclaim their memories, right?" I say. "I think I've finally found a way to make that happen."

THIRTY-SIX
A DREAM COME TRUE

Florida, U.S.A.

Grams' hand is warm in mine as I stand by her side in the MaxLife lab. Lines worry her face as she settles into the sleep pod. I need to ease her fears so I grab a soft gray blanket and tuck it around her while Sun coordinates her vitals to the sleep pod.

"Don't worry, Grams." I squeeze her hand. "This whole procedure will all happen while you're sleeping. When you enter a dream, we're going to see if we can help recover your lost memories."

"You're a nice nurse," she says, her voice shaking a little. My heart tightens. She doesn't remember me. "But I'm not so sure about all this fancy tech."

"It is pretty fancy." I smile and pass her a sleep mask. "There are some people who'd—" Steal? Lie? Kill?

Kidnap? Check on all of those, I think morbidly. If she knew half the things that Dad and I had to go through so we could have this moment, she'd never have allowed it.

"Some people who would do a lot to get a hold of this fancy tech," I finish. "But I'm excited you'll finally get to see it all unfold."

"What a lovely ring you've got there." She points to the emerald ring on my hand. "It looks just like one I used to have."

"That's right." I brighten that she recognized it. "You gave me this ring, Grams, during our Fourth of July party." I stare at its shiny sparkles, the memory still sharp in my mind. "You said it was your mom's and you wanted me to have it, too."

I don't tell her she gave it to me when she realized her mind wasn't what it once was, knowing she didn't have much longer before she'd forget what made it so special.

"Well." Grams frowns and her eyes move back and forth between the ring and my face as if she can't quite put the pieces together.

"Hello, Mother," Dad greets her as he strides into the sleep zone. He's wearing his lab coat. The beard he started to grow the day we left Peru is starting to look pretty bushy now. "I see you're having a nice chat with Aria, your granddaughter. Are you ready to enter the Dreamscape now?"

Grams takes his hand in hers and stares at him intently. "You look familiar."

"That's because I gave you such a hard time when I was a kid." He chuckles, rubbing his beard and shaking his head.

"Did you now?" Grams leans against the soft padding of the sleep pod. "Are you a good doctor?"

"According to you, the best. Now, listen carefully. Aria's going to meet up with you in your dream." He points to me and I smooth the wrinkles on my scrubs, trying to calm the butterflies in my stomach. "When you see her in the dream, I want you to talk to her, okay?"

Grams fiddles with her sleep mask, hands shaking. "Okay."

"We're going to have fun." I help slide the sleep mask over her eyes. "What do you want to dream about?"

"A nice dream," she says. "A time when I was happy."

"Perfect," I say. "You're going to hear a lady give a countdown in your pod. As she is counting down, I want you to focus on that memory as you go to sleep."

"I can do that," Grams says.

"I'll get her onboard." Sun steps to my side wearing her usual red cashmere slippers. "You go ahead and get into your pod."

"Thanks." Then I kiss Grams on the forehead. "Sweet dreams."

Eagerly, I head to my own sleep pod. Once I enter my employee code, I slip into its curved lines, the soft padding a far superior surface than lying on the hard floor in that hut in the jungle. A thrill of eagerness mixed with nervousness shoots through me as I strap on my pulse tracker and put on my heart monitor patches.

Last night, Dad warned me to not get my hopes up too much for this to work. But if it does, it could completely revolutionize the way we operate our Dreamscape sessions to unlock memories. After my Neuro-Read sleep mask is in place, I wait for Dad and his techs to commence the Dreamscape.

"Sleep induction enacted, Ms. Hale," the melodic voice says in my pod. "Sweet dreams."

The Sound Oasis of seagulls and the crash of waves fill my ears along with the faint hum of the noise, stimulating my brain waves into sleep mode. Just like always, I count down with the voice.

10, 9, 8, 7…

THE FIRST THING I notice when I enter the Dreamscape is the sound of cheers and laughter filling the air. That familiar sick churning in my stomach I get when I first enter the Dreamscape is back, and I lean against a wall, waiting for my body to orientate itself.

The room swims into focus. I take in the balloons floating through the room and streamers hanging from the ceiling. Right away, I recognize this place.

It's my house.

Hope springs in my chest. Grams is dreaming! It

worked. I really entered her dream! Quickly, I look for my team. I spy Javier in the corner, leaning against the wall being as inconspicuous as possible. He smiles and nods when he sees I've spotted him.

Tony should be here somewhere. Finally, he stumbles into the dream near the front door. He runs into it and then shakes his head.

"Tony!" I whisper-yell. "What are you doing?"

He swivels at the sound of my voice, rubbing his head. "Sorry. Got a little confused there. Oh, wow. This is your house. How cool is that?"

"Don't do anything stupid, Tony," Javier warns him.

"Why do you always assume I'm going to do something stupid?" Tony huffs. "Which reminds me, I got a scholarship for MIT! I just got the acceptance letter yesterday."

"That's amazing!" I hug him. "I'm so happy for you."

Javier gives him a fist bump. "Congrats. You earned that."

"It will be a big adjustment from community college," he admits. "But totally worth it."

Movement by the kitchen pulls my attention from the guys. It's Grams and she's putting candles on my cake. My pulse kicks up at seeing her in the Dreamscape, and I hurry to join her. I'm not exactly sure how this will all play out, but I'm eager to test my theory if using my mind to help piece together fragments and missing parts of her memories will work.

"Hey," I greet her. Usually, we don't interact with the dreamers, but after all my recent experiences, I think actively guiding a dreamer has been more effective.

Except she doesn't even glance my way. Instead, she keeps putting candles on the cake. A quick count tells me there are twelve candles. No matter how many more she puts on there, there still are always twelve.

"Twelfth birthday, huh," I continue, realizing the significance of this memory. I swallow down my eagerness to tell her everything instead of letting her mind fill in the blanks. "Whose birthday is it?"

"My granddaughters," Grams says. "It's her twelfth birthday."

"Yes, it is." I want to jump up and down, knowing she still has that memory, but manage to remain calm and collected. "So that's her birthday cake. You made that, didn't you?"

Grams stares at the cake in confusion. "Well, I don't—"

I close my eyes and pull up the memory of eating that cake. The moist chocolate flavor and rich creamy vanilla frosting.

"You make the best chocolate cake," I continue.

"Yes..." she finally says. "I do. It's Aria's favorite, too."

Kids cheering in the other room disturb the silence and she suddenly drops the candles and vanish. She abandons the cake and steps through the doorway into the sunroom. A magician is standing in front of a group of kids sitting on the floor. He's got a cute white rabbit in one hand and a black hat in the other.

"Can I pet the bunny?" a kid is asking.

"I love magic!" another kid says.

I blink at the scene before me. This must have happened when I snuck off to take a peek at my presents. My mom had been so upset I'd missed it. And she was right. I really did miss some cool stuff.

"Oh, dear," Grams says to me. "Aria isn't here. She's missing the whole show."

Grams takes off down the hall and I scurry after her. The walls start stretching out further and further so the hall looks like it will never end. We pass by door after door until soon Grams is running, her breath coming out in heavy gasps.

"Grams." I reach out, touching her lightly on the arm. "You okay?"

She startles at my touch and the hallway shudders, shifting back and forth like it's not sure of itself.

"Be careful," Javier whispers behind me. "You nearly woke her up, startling her like that."

I glance over my shoulder to find Javier and Tony have followed me. A sense of comfort washes over me, knowing my teammates are here. After what happened in Sadir's Dreamscape, I now realize how much I relied on them in the past for support and confidence. But then my eyes focus on Tony, holding a plate with a huge piece of cake and fork.

"Are you eating my birthday cake?" I ask. "Before I've blown out my candles?"

"It's delicious." Tony takes a large bite. "Your grams really does make the best chocolate cake. Besides, your Dream-you isn't going to care."

"It's a dream, dude," Javier mutters. "You've no idea what that really tastes like."

"But I can imagine." Tony's eyebrows waggle.

Grams moves to the wall and starts running her hands along it, her brow furrowed. "It must be somewhere here."

I step to her side, saying, "What are you looking for? Maybe I can help you find it."

"My granddaughter...I have to find her. She's missing her magic show."

My heart aches. So this is what it must feel like to hunt and search for memories, and yet never find them. Frustrating and confusing.

But I know what will happen next at my party because I was there. Hiding in the living room, secretly peeking under the wrapping paper of my presents.

"I think I know where your granddaughter is," I say.

Then just like I did in Sadir's Dreamscape, I focus hard on the wall, imagining a doorway that opens up to the living room. The wall shivers as if resisting my mind. But I push my memory of Grams stepping through the doorway, catching me opening the presents.

Suddenly the doorway focuses and there in front of us is twelve-year-old me, sitting in the center of a pile of presents, face reddening like I've been caught being very naughty.

"Oh!" twelve-year-old me exclaims. "I was um ... just checking out the presents."

Grams steps into the room, frowning. Before she can ask who I am like my memory tells me she's going to stay, I interject, "There's your granddaughter. I think she's sneaking a peek at her presents."

Twelve-year-old-me giggles. "I know." She sighs, flushing even more. "I'll head back outside with the others."

The dream version of my dad strolls into the room. "What's going on here?" he asks Grams.

"This girl..." Grams pauses.

And I wait to see what she'll say next. Will my memory unlock hers and make the connection? Or will she tell him some girl is trying to open Aria's presents?

"Aria was opening her presents," Grams finally says. "She's missing out on her magic show."

The moment she says this, it's like the room becomes sharper, clearer. Deep inside, I know my memory has connected and bonded with hers.

Every inch of me wants to throw my arms around Grams and dance around the room, but at the same time, I don't want to disrupt the memory healing that's happening right now. Instead, I just smile over at my twelve-year-old self.

And suddenly, I have so much I wish I could tell her.

I want to tell her things are going to be hard. So hard that at times it will feel impossible. But she's going to overcome those tough times, and it's all going to be worth it.

Because this is the moment she's been working for. And that wish she's almost about to make, blowing out those twelve candles, just came true.

"Come along, Aria," Grams tells twelve-year-old me. "Hurry now. You don't want to miss your magic show."

"Where are we going?" I grumble at Jake as I hear the car's engine turn off. I'm still not happy he made me wear this blindfold for the drive. "And when can I take off this blindfold?"

"One more second." I hear his car door open and shut, telling me he just left. Before I know it, a wave of warm Florida air washes over me as my door opens.

Jake's hands touch mine and he helps me out of the car. We shuffle along for a bit until a sharp coolness replaces the muggy air.

"This is really weird," I complain. "Are there people where we're at and are they looking at me? If I trip, you're going to leap in front of me so I land on you and not break my nose, right?"

He laughs. "Yes, of course."

Then suddenly, he stops me from moving forward, squares my body, and unwraps the blindfold.

I blink against the light and take in my surroundings. We're standing in a circular atrium with a giant dinosaur in the center and aquariums full of fish along the side walls.

"We're inside the Orlando Science Center," I realize.

"That's right! I thought it would be a fun place for a date."

"I love it! But why all the cloak and dagger secrecy?"

Then he points to a sign that's over a doorway right in front of us. Somehow I missed that. It reads, *Aria, no matter where you are in the world, you'll always be my shining light.*

My heart melts as I read those words. I turn to him and cup my hands around his face, kissing him. "It's beautiful. I love it."

He grins, eyes twinkling. "That's just the beginning."

Then he takes my hand and tugs me along to follow him through the doorway. As we step inside the room, I realize it's not just any room but a planetarium.

"I reserved this place for just the two of us," he explains, leading me further inside to where two seats are set up beside a small round table with drinks, popcorn, and candy.

"How did you afford to rent out this place?" I ask, sitting in one of the chairs. "It's not like you haven't been busy running from people who want to kill you or recovering from gun wounds to find time to work a job."

He grins, settling down beside me. "While I was gone taking bullets and getting kidnapped for the girl I love, the game I've got on the app store was selling like crazy."

"Wow." I tilt my head. "Really? That's freaking awesome."

"The money is good."

"Not about the money," I correct him. "That you would take a bullet and get kidnapped for your girlfriend."

He leans in closer and kisses my lips. "She's worth that and more."

I suck in a deep breath, overwhelmed by this boy that I've fallen in love with. The lights dim around us and soft soothing music begins playing. Above, stars blink into existence and the world is finally calm and peaceful.

"I brought you here specifically because I wanted to show you something special," Jake says.

Suddenly, in one section of the planetarium's night sky, a single star grows brighter and brighter as if we're zooming in closer to it.

"See that star?" Jake asks. "I bought it and named it after you."

I gasp in shock. "You named a star after me?"

"It's just like the sign says out there, you'll always be my shining light. When we were huddled in the catacombs in Lima, coated in bone dust and spider webs while being hunted down by Sadir's men, I knew it was all going to be okay. Because you were there with me. You've been my light through all these tough times."

"A lot of guys wouldn't have stood through all of that with me. But you never left my side."

He kisses my hand. "I'm here for you always. And now every time I look at the stars, I'll be reminded of what we've gone through and what we have."

"Thank you," I whisper. "For everything. I love you so much. I'd say you're better than my wildest dreams, but then, we did first meet in a dream. So maybe you are my dream guy."

"I think that's a winning description."

And he kisses me once again.

A NOTE FROM CHRISTINA

THANK YOU FOR READING! If you loved this story, I invite you along another reading adventure with Estrella in THE IMMORTAL SECRET. Cast out from her immortal people, Estrella is sent to live with mortals without her memories. As she uncovers her past, she meets two rivals for her heart. But soon she discovers her secret is more dangerous than she could ever imagine.

A sizzling romance of supernatural thrills, impossible choices, and heart-stopping adventure.

FROM ME TO YOU

This was such a fun story to write! If you follow me on social media or read my newsletter, you may have recognized the places I visited in Peru, which inspired *The Dream Hunt*. Our family trip might not have been as thrilling as Aria's, but we had many fantastic adventures along the way in this incredibly beautiful country.

If you enjoyed this story, I'd appreciate your time and effort if you'd leave a review or even drop me a note at Christina@ChristinaFarley.com. I love hearing from readers. Reviews are a powerful tool and can help a book be more visible.

I hope you'll stay in touch by joining my newsletter so we can take more adventures together. If you sign up, you'll receive a free book as my way of saying you're awesome.

Christina's Newsletter: Reader news, writing tips, giveaways, and book updates: https://tinyurl.com/ypb9pm9a

Christina's VIP Reader Club: Weekly update with insider news, exclusive content, and giveaways: https://tinyurl.com/mryncvmf

ACKNOWLEDGMENTS

Writing a book is like taking a part of your soul and sharing it for all to see. If you've made it this far and are reading these acknowledgments, thank you so much for coming along with me on this Peruvian adventure!

First of all, I'm so grateful to all my readers who have supported my books. You mean so much to me and without you, I couldn't keep writing these stories. So thank you!

A special thanks goes out to my VIP Reader Group for their support of this story when it was a serial on Kindle Vella:

Christy S, Laura P, Mila C, Beth G, Andrea M, Ava M, Kendra P, Laziz T, Ana B, Amanda F, Jennifer A, Aziza E, Marisela Z, Eva M, Jenny H, Christina V, Amber J, Shana D, Kelli J, Bert B, Dianna B, Tez M, Bri L, Candi M, Julianne J, Amy P, Kris D, Sheree W, Jamie G, Jan W, Stephanie B, Ells, Heath W, Willa Z, Jerry N, Kate H, Joyce K, Tiffany L, Vivi B, Alison R, Callie T, Sunny B, Finely T, Margaret T, Billy F, Jocelyn M, and Merry M.You all are the best!

To my writing friends at the Cabin on Slack. I appreciate all of your support as I drafted and revised this novel.

To my writing friends who supported me in so many ways as I wrote this serial, which became a novel: Amy Christine Parker, Vivi Barnes, Janice Hardy, Sarah McGuire, Fred Koehler, Andrea Mack, Debbie Ridpath Ohi, Carmella VanVleet, Beth Revis, Megan Shepherd, Brooke Hatchett, and Mindy McGinnis. You all are amazing!

To Jessica Khoury for this jaw-dropping cover. You are so talented and knew exactly how to create the perfect cover for this book.

A huge thanks to my mom, dad, sister, brother, and nieces! You have been there for me through every step of this writing journey—the highs and lows. Having your support means everything to me.

This book wouldn't be possible without Doug, Caleb, and Luke. We took a trip together to Peru and had so many adventures that found their way into this story. Whether it was being terrified in the catacombs, zip-lining through the rainforest canopy, fishing for piranhas, sleeping in a hut in the Amazon rainforest, searching for monkeys on Monkey Island (the only wildlife we found were mosquitos—or perhaps they found us?), or strolling through the ancient city of Machu Picchu, we always had so much fun together. I love you three so much! Where should we go next?

Finally, as always, I'm so thankful to God for giving me another story to tell. Writing is never easy, and without Him and His strength, I'd have given up long ago.

Photo by Abby Liga

CHRISTINA FARLEY the bestselling author of numerous novels. She also worked as an international teacher and at a top-secret job for Disney where she was known to scatter pixie dust before the sun rose. When not traveling the world or creating imaginary ones, she spends time with her family in Clermont, Florida where they are busy preparing for the next World Cup, baking cheesecakes, and raising a pet dragon in disguise as a cockatiel. ChristinaFarley.com.

Instagram: @ChristinaLFarley
Facebook: @ChristinaFarleyAuthor

YouTube: @ChocolateInspired
TikTok: @ChristinaFarleyAuthor